Wicked Dirty

"*Wanted* by J. Kenner is the whole package! A toe-curling smokin' hot read, full of incredible characters and a brilliant storyline that you won't be able to get enough of. I can't wait for the next book in this series . . . I'm hooked!"

—*Flirty & Dirty Book Blog*

"J. Kenner's evocative writing thrillingly captures the power of physical attraction, the pull of longing, the universe-altering effect one person can have on another. . . . *Claim Me* has the emotional depth to back up the sex . . . Every scene is infused with both erotic tension, and the tension of wondering what lies beneath Damien's veneer – and how and when it will be revealed."

—*Heroes and Heartbreakers*

"*Claim Me* by J. Kenner is an erotic, sexy and exciting ride. The story between Damien and Nikki is amazing and written beautifully. The intimate and detailed sex scenes will leave you fanning yourself to cool down. With the writing style of Ms. Kenner you almost feel like you are there in the story riding along the emotional rollercoaster with Damien and Nikki."

—*Fresh Fiction*

"PERFECT for fans of *Fifty Shades of Grey* and *Bared to You*. *Release Me* is a powerful and erotic romance novel that is sure to make adult romance readers sweat, sigh and swoon."

—*Reading, Eating & Dreaming Blog*

"I will admit, I am in the 'I loved *Fifty Shades*' camp, but after reading *Release Me*, Mr. Grey only scratches the surface compared to Damien Stark."

—*Cocktails and Books Blog*

"It is not often when a book is so amazingly well-written that I find it hard to even begin to accurately describe it . . . I recommend this book to everyone who is interested in a passionate love story."

—*Romancebookworm's Reviews*

"The story is one that will rank up with the *Fifty Shades* and Cross Fire trilogies."

—*Incubus Publishing Blog*

"The plot is complex, the characters engaging, and J. Kenner's passionate writing brings it all perfectly together."

—*Harlequin Junkie*

Wicked
DIRTY

J. KENNER

DEDICATION

For Don, who was in the trenches.
And for Laura and Natasha, who had my back.

PROLOGUE

*I*T SEEMED LIKE *the perfect plan. Let a guy into my bed. Let him touch me. Let him fuck me.*

Why not?

I was desperate, after all. And you know what they say about desperate times.

Besides, it's not as if I was going to fall for one of my clients. I'm not one of those prissy girls who loses her heart at a kind word or a soft touch.

I'm not a woman who falls at all. Not for a man. Not for anybody.

I've been screwed far too many times. And if I'm going to get screwed anyway, I might as well get something out of it.

That's what I thought, anyway.

Then he opened the door, with his beautiful face and his haunted eyes. Eyes that hinted at secrets at least as painful as my own.

He touched me—and despite all my defenses, I fell.

And now…

Well, now I can only hope that when I hit the ground, I won't shatter into a million pieces. And that maybe—just maybe—he'll be there to catch me.

CHAPTER 1

THE SETTING SUN cast a warm glow over the Hollywood Hills as nearly naked waitresses glided through the crowd with a rainbow-like array of test tube shots. Or, for the more traditional guests, highball glasses of premium vodka and bourbon.

The liquor flowed, the guests laughed and gossiped, the hottest new band in Los Angeles shook the roof, and entertainment reporters took photographs and videos, all of which they shared on social media.

In other words, the lavish party at Reach, the hip, new rooftop hotspot, was a dead-on perfect publicity event.

The purpose, of course, was to officially announce that Lyle Tarpin, one of Hollywood's fastest rising stars, had joined the cast of *M. Sterious,* next year's installment in the wildly popular Blue Zenith movie franchise.

The script was solid, the action pulse-pounding, and Lyle still couldn't believe that he'd been cast, much less that he was set to play the eponymous M, an emotionally wounded antihero.

It was a role that could catapult him from the A-list to over-the-moon, transforming him into a Hollywood megastar with his choice of meaty roles and the kind of multimillion dollar paydays that had only been a glimmer of a dream when he'd started this Hollywood journey.

In other words, this was an opportunity he didn't intend to fuck up.

Which was why he forced himself not to wince and turn away when Frannie caught his eye and smiled. She tossed her head, making her auburn locks bounce as she walked toward him, her sequined cocktail dress revealing a mile of toned legs ending in a pair of strappy sandals that showed off a perfect pedicure.

One of Hollywood's most bankable stars, Francesca Muratti was set to play Lyle's love interest—the Blue Zenith agent who turns M from his dark ways and recruits him to the side of justice—both saving him and, hopefully, adding another long-running hero to the franchise.

"Hello, lover," she said, sliding her arms around his neck and pressing her body against his. Frannie had a reputation for being a wild child who made it a point to sleep with almost every one of her male co-stars, and she'd made no secret that she wanted Lyle to join that little fraternity.

Honestly, Lyle didn't know if she was insecure, overly horny, or simply into method acting. All he knew was that he wasn't interested. Which, considering the damage a pissed-off Francesca could do to his career, was ten kinds of inconvenient.

"Kiss me like you mean it," she murmured, then leaned in, preparing to make the demand a reality, but he angled back, taking her chin in his hand and holding her steady as her eyes flashed with irritation.

"Anticipation, Frannie." He bent close so that she shivered from the feel of his breath on her ear. "If we give them what they want now, why would they come to the movie?"

"Fuck the fans," she whispered back, her hand sliding down to grab his crotch. "This is what I want."

And goddamn him all to hell, he felt himself start to grow hard. Not from desire for her, but in response to a familiar, baser need. A dark room. A willing woman. Just once—hard enough and hot enough that it wore him out. Soothed his guilt and his pain. Quieted the ghosts of his past, the horror of his mistakes.

Enough to tide him over until the next time. The next woman.

And to maybe, if he was lucky, chip away at the wall he'd built around his heart.

His thoughts churned wildly, and he imagined the feel of a woman's soft skin under his fingers. A woman who wouldn't look at him with Jennifer's eyes. Who wouldn't remind him of where he'd run from or what he'd done. A woman who'd give herself to him. Who wouldn't care about his flaws as he let himself just go, hard and hot and desperate, into the wild, dark bliss of anonymity.

"Mmm, I don't know, Lyle," Frannie murmured, her hand pressed firmly against his now rock-hard erection. "Here's evidence that suggests our onscreen chemistry is real. Give me a chance and I bet we can really raise that flag."

"I like you fine, Frannie," he said, taking a step back

and cursing himself for giving into fantasy. "But I'm not fucking you."

From the glint in her eye, he was certain her famous temper was about to flare, but an editor he recognized from *Variety* walked up, and Frannie downshifted to charming.

Lyle hung around long enough to greet the guy and answer a few questions about the role, then made his escape when the conversation shifted to Frannie's new endorsement deal.

He grabbed a bourbon from a passing waiter and sipped it as he crossed to the edge of the roof. He didn't like heights, which was why he sought them out. Hell, it was why his apartment was on the thirtieth floor of a Century City high rise, and the reason he'd spent count-less hours getting his pilot's license. When something bothered him, he conquered it; he didn't succumb to it.

And that's part of why this bullshit with Frannie irri-tated him so much.

"You never struck me as the stupid type."

Lyle recognized the throaty, feminine voice and turned to face his agent, Evelyn Dodge. An attractive woman in her mid-fifties, Evelyn had been in the industry for ages, knew everyone worth knowing, and was as tough as nails. She also never took shit from anybody.

Lyle studied her face, trying to get a bead on what she was thinking. No luck. His agent was a blank slate. Good when negotiating deals. Not so good when he was trying to gauge a reaction.

"That girl's got more power than you think," she

continued when he stayed silent. "You want the quick and dirty route to Career-in-the-Toilet Town? Because that path runs straight through your pretty co-star. You piss Frannie off and suddenly Garreth Todd will be playing M and you'll be lucky if you can get a walk-on in a local commercial for a used car lot."

"Thanks for giving it to me straight," he said dryly.

"You think I'm exaggerating? I thought you knew your ass from a hole in the wall. Or have I been misreading you all this time?"

"Christ, Evelyn. I'm not naive. But I'm not sleeping with Frannie just to make things nice on the set. Are you honestly saying I should?"

"Hell no, Iowa," she said, using his home state as a nickname. "I'm telling you that you need to be smart. As long as you're single, she's not going to let it drop." She sighed. "You've worked damn hard to get where you are, and you're flying high. But let me remind you in case you think that makes you invincible—the higher you are, the more painful it is when you crash back down to earth."

"I'm not going to screw anything up, Evelyn."

"You don't know Frannie the way I do. She's destroyed careers more established than yours—and that was before she had a hefty gold statue on her mantle."

Fuck. He ran his fingers through his hair.

"How long have we worked together?" she asked, obviously not expecting an answer. "Two, three years? And never during all that time have I seen you date. A few women on your arm at a party, but you go stag more often than you go with a woman."

"What the hell, Evelyn?" He knew he sounded defensive, but she was coming dangerously close to pushing buttons he didn't want pushed, and to peering into dark corners that were better left in the shadows.

"You told me once you weren't gay, and that's fine. Thousands of teenage girls across the country sleep easier knowing you're on the market."

"Is there a point to this?" He tried—and failed—to keep the irritation out of his voice.

She cast a sharp glance at his face. "I'm just saying that if you have a girlfriend tucked away in an attic somewhere, now's the time to pull her out and dust her off. Because our girl Frannie is like a dog with a bone. A very pampered, well-groomed dog, who has one hell of a bite when she doesn't get her own way. But she doesn't mess with married men."

"So, what? I'm supposed to trot off to Vegas and make a showgirl my bride?"

"Just be smart. And if you do have a girlfriend hidden away, then bring her to a party or two. And if you don't, then get one."

"It's bullshit," he said mildly. "But I'll take it under advisement."

"Good. Now let's go mingle."

With a sigh, he glanced around the set-up. At the free-flowing alcohol and never-ending stream of finger foods offered by waitresses in outfits that were just a little too skimpy to be decent, but which covered a little too much to be obscene. At the napkins and stemware that displayed the series' logo, and at the band in the corner that was playing a never-ending stream of music from the franchise, while on the opposite side of the roof, clips from the previous movies played in a continuous loop on a giant screen.

It was opulent, ridiculous, and completely over the top.

Jennifer would have loved it.

She would have swept into Hollywood and conquered it, making Francesca Muratti look like an amateur in the process.

Go big or go home. Wasn't that what she'd always told him? Jennifer? With her innocent eyes and her not-so-innocent mouth?

But she'd never gotten the chance.

And now here he was, thirteen years to the day since that goddamned hellish night. And Jenny was dead, and he was standing in a spotlight wearing Armani and living her dream.

How fucked up was that?

"I lost you somewhere," Evelyn said. "Let's head to the bar. I think you could use another drink."

Damn right he could, but he shook his head. "I was just thinking." He gestured with his hand, indicating the whole area, including the city beyond the rooftop. "This really is where dreams come true."

But only an unlucky few—like Lyle—knew how many nightmares hid inside those bright, shiny dreams.

He forced a smile for Evelyn's sake. "It's past seven. I've been here for almost two hours. I've been effusive and charming and a team player. I've done everything they've asked. Officially, anyway," he added, thinking of Frannie's overtures. "That should at least earn me a cookie, don't you think?"

She crossed her arms, shifting her weight as she looked at him. "Depends on what kind of cookie you're looking for."

"I'm leaving—"

"Dammit, Lyle."

"Do I ever cause you problems? Do you have to run interference for me? Do I not live up to my damned golden boy reputation?"

She said nothing.

"Make an excuse for me. Anything. I don't care." For just a moment, he let his mask down. The innocent Iowa boy who'd been discovered at seventeen, plucked out of obscurity to ride to fame on his Midwestern good looks and piercing blue eyes. He'd thrown himself into the work, scrambling up through television and indie films to where he was today. A genuinely nice guy, untarnished by Hollywood's bullshit.

Except that was all just a part, too. And for a flicker of a moment, he let Evelyn see the pain underneath. The loss. The darkness. And all the goddamn guilt.

Then he was the movie star again, and she was looking at him, her brows knit with an almost maternal concern.

"Please," he added, his voice low and a little hoarse. "It's not a good day. I need—"

What? A drink? A fuck? Magic powers so he could change the past?

"—to go. I just need to go."

"Do you want company?"

Hell, yes.

He shook his head. "No. I'm fine. But thanks."

9

But he did want company. Just not the kind that Evelyn was offering. He wanted the kind of company that was raw. That was dirty and fast and anonymous. With complete discretion. And absolutely no fucking strings.

Wanted? No, he didn't want it. Not really.

But he damn sure needed it.

Needed to open the valve and release the pressure. To erase the guilt, even if only for a few glorious minutes. To escape the ghosts and the memories and all the shit that he tried so hard to keep buried. That he never let anyone see.

That's what he needed, because without that release, his mask really would start to crack, and the whole world would learn that the clean-cut Lyle Tarpin was nothing more than a goddamn fraud.

CHAPTER 2

"**Y**OU COULD PULL an extra shift," my best friend Joy says, looking up from my spiral notebook filled with columns of unpleasant, uncooperative numbers. "I mean, it would suck, but if you need the money, then you need the money."

And I *do* need the money. That sad reality is laid out right there in my notebook, in gallons of glorious red and a few small scratches of black. But unless I want to give up sleeping, I'm all out of hours in the day.

"You're here now," she replies, when I tell her as much.

I stick out my tongue. Not the classiest retort on the planet, but it sums up my feelings nicely.

Here is Totally Tattoo, the Venice Beach tattoo and piercing parlor where Joy works as the piercer-in-residence. Or the Needle Queen. Or whatever other title she happens to have grabbed onto that day. We met when I wandered into the shop almost five years ago, feeling lost and alone and desperate for a change. Somehow, I'd gotten into my head that if I could just change my look, then everything would be better. I'd be reborn, all the bad stuff washed away.

And all I needed was a shiny stud on the curve of my ear.

Unfortunately, that theory wasn't ever put to the test, primarily because I passed out when Joy came at me with the needle.

So instead of body art, I got a best friend.

All in all, I figure that was a fair trade. Even if she does still tease me about the fainting.

Now, I'm perched on the stool behind the reception counter and Joy's standing on the other side, her fingers tap-tapping on my dastardly little numbers. It's still an hour until closing, but the place is empty. So we're using the counter as ground zero for the recap of my financial woes.

"You know I was just kidding," she says. "But honestly, Laine, I don't have a better idea. Unless you want to rob a bank. Or, you know, win the lottery or something."

I thwap my temple with the heel of my hand. "You're brilliant," I say, slamming the notebook shut. "Problem solved."

Joy rolls her eyes and shakes her head, making the colored gemstones that line the curve of her left ear sparkle.

I lean forward and prop my chin on my fist. "Honestly, you're right. I should figure out a way to grab a few more hours. But I just don't know how. I'm already pulling shifts at Blacklist and Maudie's," I say, naming off our favorite bar as well as a local diner.

"Plus, Mrs. Donahue's letting me come in once a week to deep clean sections of her house. And Jacob is paying me to walk Lancelot most mornings." My neighbor, Mrs. Donahue, is perfectly capable of scouring her own house, despite having just celebrated her eighty-first birthday. But she's a sweetheart who takes in stray pets and people, and she offered me the cleaning gig the minute she learned about my financial woes. Jacob, the UCLA business major who lives in Mrs. Donahue's garage apartment, is less of a sweetheart, but I'm not about to turn down the extra cash.

"Jacob just wants to get in your pants."

I grimace.

"What? What's wrong with Jacob?"

"You mean other than the fact that ever since he learned my first name he won't stop asking if I taste like candy?"

Joy snorts. "Like you've never heard that one before."

My name is Sugar Laine. Which, as names go, is about as bad as it gets. Couple that with blonde hair, huge brown eyes, and tits that I consider unfortunately large, and I probably should have chucked it all years ago and signed up to be a stripper or a hooker.

Then again, maybe I got off lucky. I mean, my last name could have been Buns.

That's me. Always looking on the bright side.

Despite having saddled me with an utterly ridiculous name, I'm certain my parents loved me. Or, at least, I'm certain my mom did. And she always swore that my dad loved me, too, and that his sudden and unexpected departure when I was nine had nothing whatsoever to do with the way he felt about me or my little brother Andy, who lucked out with a completely normal name.

Maybe Mom was right. But I'm still operating under the assumption that my father is a soulless, charmless prick who feels nothing for nobody.

I figure if I'm wrong, he can damn well crawl out of the woodwork, track me down, and then bust his tail to prove it.

My mom, though…

Well, despite her unfortunate choice of names, she did love me. And when I once asked—after having been teased in fourth grade—what she could possibly have been thinking, she said that when the nurse put me in her arms, she thought I was the sweetest thing she'd ever seen. And what was sweeter than sugar?

How could I get upset about that?

I couldn't. So I didn't.

But I did start calling myself Laine.

An uncomfortable tightness grips my chest as I think about my mom. How we'd settle on the couch with Andy between us to read or watch TV. How she let me make Christmas cookies in July because every day should be like Christmas. How she used to listen to classic country music and cry, because she said it cleared her soul and refilled her well.

Oh, God. I try to draw in a breath, and realize my throat is clogged with tears.

"Hey?" Joy's moved around the counter, so now she's pretty much nose to nose with me. She takes my hand and squeezes, the pressure bringing me back to myself. "Hey, you okay?"

"Sorry. Sorry. I just—I started thinking about my

name, and that made me think about my mom and Andy and—"

I break off, tears threatening.

"It's okay. Come on, girl. Deep breaths."

I sniffle and manage a wobbly smile. "I don't know what set me off," I say when I can talk again. I swipe the edge of my forefingers under each eye, drying my tears. "It's not like thinking about them is an unusual occurrence. Hell, I think about them every time I walk through my front door."

My breath hitches and tears fill my eyes again. "Dammit," I murmur as I grab a tissue. "It's the house. I just can't cope with losing the house. It's all I have left of them."

My mom and thirteen-year-old brother were killed when a drunk driver plowed his SUV into their car five years ago. I was finishing my first semester at UCLA, and they were on their way to pick me up so that we could celebrate by driving to Anaheim and going to Disneyland.

They both died at the scene. The officer who found me in my dorm told me that it had been fast. That they wouldn't have suffered. I don't know if that's true or not, but I believe it because I have to.

My mother had scrambled her entire life, waitressing, working temp jobs, manning the checkout stand at grocery stores. Her only asset was the house, which my dad had paid off before he bailed. But it hadn't been kept up well, and at the end of her life, my mom had a mountain of debt, a house in desperate need of repairs, and no money in the bank.

Which means that I inherited the house, and pretty much nothing else. But if I don't come up with thirty-one thousand and change in the next two weeks to pay off a short-term equity loan, the bank's going to foreclose and I'm going to lose that last connection to my family.

And I have no freaking idea how I can get that much money.

"I'm so screwed," I whisper to Joy, feeling fragile and lost and alone. I'm only twenty-three. I should have finished college instead of dropping out so that I could work to buy food and pay taxes and fix the house. Hell, I should be applying to grad schools.

I should be bringing my laundry home and begging my mom to do it for me while I harass my little brother. I should be going out to bars with friends at night, not actually serving the drinks.

I shouldn't have the weight of the world on my shoulders.

But I do. And I've accepted that. I'm dealing—I am. But any more pressure and I swear I'll shatter into a million pieces.

"I can't lose the house." My voice cracks, and I hate that my weakness is showing, even to my best friend. "I can't. But they're gonna take it anyway."

"The hell they are." She taps my notebook authoritatively. She's only three years older than me, but Joy is the maternal type. Originally, I'd thought she was the bossy type, but she'd assured me that I was wrong. "Leave this depressing pile of shit and come with me."

"Where?"

"You need a drink."

"I can't afford a drink."

"Ha ha. I'm buying. Come on. Let's go."

"Joy … you're supposed to be working."

"So? You need me."

I hear the back door snick open, and realize that Cass—the owner of the shop and one of the best tattoo artists I've ever met—must be back.

"I don't have any more appointments," Joy continues. "My instruments area all sterilized. My area is clean. And my boss," she adds in a much louder voice, "is not a raging bitch."

"I heard that!" Cass calls. "And you're wrong. I'm a stone cold bitch, and you know it."

Joy snorts, then calls out to Class. "You had a walk-in a few minutes ago. I told him you were gone for the day, but would be in by ten tomorrow. And I can stay if you really, really want me to, but poor Laine is having a shitty day, and she really needs a drink."

"Joy! Don't you dare blame me for cutting out early."

"It's Friday," Joy says. "I'll take whatever excuse I can get."

"Careful, or I *will* turn into a raging bitch." Cass rounds the corner, coming toward us. She's wearing black leather slacks and a silver tank top that shows off the plumage of the amazing bird tattoo that starts at her shoulder blade and trails down her arm. Today, her hair is coal-black with red at the tips, so she almost looks like she's on fire. A tiny diamond stud decorates her nose— the piercing courtesy of my bestie, Joy.

She's stunningly beautiful and always outrageous, and

she's one of my favorite people. Now, she aims a wide smile at me. "Hey, Laine, how are you?"

"Fine," I say, lying.

"Broke," Joy says.

I sigh. "An open book," I tell Cass as I glare at Joy. "Apparently, I'm an open book."

Joy holds up her hands. "Hey, I can't lie to my boss. Who looks amazing, by the way. You went home and changed. Big plans tonight?"

"Siobhan and I are having dinner with a few of the folks from her job," Cass says, referring to her girlfriend. "Tomorrow is opening night for her first big exhibit since she started working at the Stark Center. So she's nervous. I'm the designated hand-holder."

"Me, too," Joy says, looking meaningfully at me.

"I'm not nervous," I tell her. "I'm freaking out. There's a difference."

"You're that bad off?" Genuine concern colors Cass's expression, and I immediately regret saying anything. I hate the idea of the whole world knowing the width and breadth of my problems.

"It's fine," I lie. "Really. Things are just tight right now, and I'm looking for another job to add to the mix."

"Hmm. Well, I can't afford to bring anyone on full time right now, but I could hire you for a couple of weeks. Answer phones. Clean. Help me organize all the paperwork."

"Could you? That would be—"

"Really nice," Joy puts in. "But probably not necessary."

I turn to gape at her. "Um, yeah. Necessary."

"You're awesome, Cass," she says, completely ignoring me. "But let's put a pin in it. I just thought of something that's a perfect fit for Laine. And the pay's stellar, too."

"Yeah?" Cass looks between the two of us. "Well, if it doesn't work out, the offer stands."

"What?" I demand. "What's perfect?"

"Let's go get that drink, and I'll tell you." She aims puppy dog eyes at Cass. "Just this one time. Laine needs me."

Cass shakes her head in mock exasperation. "Go. I'll close up. But you open tomorrow," she says.

"Deal. We'll go to Blacklist," she adds, turning her attention back to me. She winks. "Since you work there, maybe they'll give us drinks for free."

I grimace. "I'd rather David let me pick up a shift."

Like my house, Totally Tattoo is located on some prime real estate. The street runs perpendicular to the beach, just a few blocks from the boardwalk. As soon as we step out the door, we turn right, so we're walking away from the Pacific. The sun is low over the ocean behind us, and our shadows stretch out on the sidewalk, as if racing us to the bar.

Blacklist is just a few doors down, with glass and wood exterior walls that open like an accordion, so that patrons can sit at tables that are both in the bar and also on the sidewalk. It's a Venice Beach icon that's been around since the Thirties, though it's now considerably more upscale than the dive it used to be.

A couple is just leaving, and as we snag their table, Joy waves at Nessie, who hurries over with two glasses of water.

"Hey, Joy. Hey, Laine. You're not working today?"

I shake my head. "David said the schedule was full." I make a face. "Too bad. I could use the bucks."

"I hear you there. I'm *dying* for this insane pair of Christian Louboutins I saw last week. And with tips and the allowance my dad sends me, I'll have enough to get them. I mean, I would seriously die if I had to wait another week."

"I know exactly what you mean," I say, as Joy looks at the tabletop, obviously trying not to laugh.

I order wine for both of us, and when Nessie is gone, Joy finally looks up. "Ya gotta love her cluelessness."

I shrug. "Home foreclosure, fancy shoes. It's all about perspective." And, yeah, there are times when I wish that *my* perspective included a dad who bought me a convertible, set me up in a beach condo, and sent me a weekly allowance. But it is what it is, and I learned a long time ago that the only thing that matters is doing. As far as I'm concerned, wishing is for birthday candles, and that's about it.

"What is it you want to tell me?" I ask. "What perfect scheme are you concocting that's going to keep the bank from ripping my house out from under me?"

"Wait for the wine." Her forehead scrunches up as if in thought. "Actually, we'll wait until you're onto the second glass of wine."

I lean back and cross my arms. "This isn't some multi-level marketing thing, is it? Because, *no*."

"Oh, please. You know me better than that. No, this is solid—and lucrative. But you need an open mind."

I add narrowed eyes to my already crossed arms. "Is it legal?"

"Yes, of course. Technically, it's totally legal."

"Technically? What does that mean?"

She's saved from answering by Nessie's return with two glasses of Cabernet.

"David said these are on the house. It's a bottle he got from a new distributor. Give him a thumbs-up or down and he'll call it payment."

"What did I tell you?" Joy says, clinking our glasses even though mine's still on the table. "Here's to good friends and free drinks."

"He also said that Carla can't come in tomorrow. If you ask him, maybe he'll let you—"

"On it." I'm out of my seat before she even gets to the end of the sentence, and I wave to the regulars as I hurry toward the back.

The inside of the bar is jam-packed with an eclectic mix of bikers, cops, locals, and buttoned-up business types. Venice Beach is colorful, and Blacklist is pretty much a mirror of the community.

David's not behind the bar like he usually is on a Friday night, but Jerry, the bartender, tells me that he went to his office to take a call. I don't want to interrupt, but I also don't want to blow this chance, so I push through the swinging doors into the kitchen, then hover in the doorway of David's cramped office.

He looks up, sees me, and gestures to the black metal folding chair that sits across from his battered wooden desk.

I plunk myself down, and although I don't want to

eavesdrop, I can't help but tune in when he starts talking about plumbing and wood rot. Those two are the main culprits in my current loan fiasco. About four years ago, not long after I met Joy, I had to deal with some serious repairs on the house or risk the city condemning it. Now I have to pay back the loan I took out to pay for the repairs to save my house … or risk the bank foreclosing on it.

"Bad news?" I ask when David hangs up. He's a former cop who looks like he stepped out of Central Casting. A burly, bear of a man with a shaved head and the kind of eyes that belie his take-no-prisoners attitude.

"Damn restroom is a shit hole, no pun intended." He shakes his head. "I love this place, but it's held together with spit, Band-Aids, and chewing gum."

He leans back in his chair, then kicks his feet up on his desk. "But you're not here to listen to me gripe. I'm guessing Nessie told you about Carla?"

"I was hoping I could pick up her shift. I need it. The Band-Aids and chewing gum that are holding my place together were expensive."

"I am sorry for that, Lainey. Damn banks. And yeah. She's only on the schedule from ten to two, but if you want it, you got it."

I stand, relieved. "You are absolutely the best."

He shakes his head. "Saturday night, and me short one waitress? Trust me, you're doing me a favor, too."

"Either way, I owe you one." I almost put my arms around him—David acts gruff, but he's all Teddy bear—but I fight the urge. Instead, I say *thank you* about a half dozen more times, then practically skip back to Joy.

"He said yes," she guesses.

"Four hours on the clock on a Saturday night. That's prime tip time. It won't get me there—but it's something."

"Won't get you there? It won't even get you close."

"Thanks so much for the reminder." I scowl at her. "You know, if you're going to pop my happy bubble, at least tell me your idea. That's why you dragged me here, right?"

Her eyes dip to my wine, and I sigh, then swallow the rest in two big gulps.

"There," I say. "And I don't want a second glass, so tell me now."

She hesitates, but then speaks. "Okay, you remember the foot guy?"

"That blind date from a couple of weekends ago? The one your cousin hooked you up with?"

"Right." She leans forward, lowering her voice. "Well, it wasn't exactly a blind date."

"What was it?"

"An easy grand, actually."

"Okay, you're going to have to run that by me again, because you can't mean what I think you mean." Except, maybe she can. Because right now, she's looking more than a little abashed, and Joy's not the kind of girl who gets embarrassed about, well, anything.

I do a mental rewind and regroup. "You're telling me you got paid a thousand dollars for him to do ... *stuff* to your feet?"

"Pretty much."

"How—I mean, well, I'm not sure what I mean." I

try again. "How did you meet him?"

"My cousin. I told you."

"Did she know when she introduced you that—"

She lays her hand over mine. "You, my friend, are way too innocent. Marjorie arranged it, just like I said." She leans in closer, then whispers. "She runs an escort service."

I gape at her. "Seriously?"

Joy nods. "But keep it to yourself, okay. It's high end, and very discrete."

"Yeah. Sure. But what's this got to do with me?"

And that's when it hits me. Honestly, I can't believe it took me so long. I blame the wine. And the fact that never in a million years would I think that my best friend is trying to whore me out through an escort service.

"Are you crazy?" I blurt.

"Oh, come on. It's just sex."

Just sex.

Is there such a thing?

That, of course, is a rhetorical question.

Because no, there isn't any such beast. There are always strings. Always consequences.

My first time, sex was like a weapon, and even though I'd been the one wielding it, I was also the one who got hurt. And the scars ran deep enough that I've avoided a repeat performance for almost five years now.

Not that I've been a pure little flower during that time. I've dated. I've fooled around. There've been fingers and tongues and a couple of really nice orgasms. But I drew a line after that first, horrible night, and I haven't let anybody cross it since.

And maybe that's silly, but it's important to me.

So, no.

Sex isn't *just sex*. It's big and it's confusing and it's messy and it's complicated.

And I can't.

"Yes, you can," Joy says firmly when I tell her as much. "It's not like you're dating anyone."

"*That's* your main consideration?"

She rolls her eyes. "Actually, my main consideration is the ten grand you're about to give up."

I freeze. "What did you say?"

"You heard me." She puts a five on the table as a tip for Nessie before getting out of her chair on the sidewalk side. That's when I notice the double-parked Fiat with a ride share placard in the side window.

"Is that for us?"

"I called Marjorie while you were talking to David," Joy admits.

"*What?*"

"I figured she'd be able get you a gig or two, but it's even better than I expected. She's scrambling to find someone last minute for tonight—and this guy pays a premium even without the rush job."

"But—"

She holds up a hand. "You know what? I don't even want to hear it. For days you've been telling me that you're desperate to keep your house. And I've seen the numbers, Laine. You should be desperate, because unless you know different math rules than I do, you could work shifts at Blacklist twenty-four seven for a full month and still not earn enough to pay off that note."

She heads for the car, tossing her words back over her shoulder. "Make up your mind, okay?"

Ten grand. *Ten. Freaking. Grand.*

Ten thousand dollars of debt knocked out in one fell swoop. Maybe even more.

I stand beside my chair, my hand clutched tight on the backrest as I think about it. That, plus what I've saved so far, plus another two in cash advances from my credit cards will get me kissing close to fifteen thousand.

That leaves sixteen thousand to earn in two weeks.

And even though that's still a scary number, it's ten thousand less scary than it would be without this job.

I think about my house and all the weekends I spent refinishing the wood floors and kitchen cabinets. I think about the claw-foot tub I spent weeks searching for. And the pipes that better not burst again in my lifetime, considering the time and money it cost to fix them.

I think about my mother and the hours she spent landscaping the backyard. The way we laughed the day we painted the shutters.

I think about everything I've lost over the last few years, and I know that there is no way I'll survive losing the house, too.

And that's when I know that I have to do this thing.

Just sex.

Once again, Joy's words fill my head. And once again, I know that she's wrong. So very wrong.

Sex is a tool, and it can either build or destroy.

My first time, it was a wrecking ball that broke me into a million pieces.

But this time…

This time sex is a lever.

This time, it's going to save me.

CHAPTER 3

"Wow," I say as we step off the private elevator and into the foyer of Marjorie's high-rise condo. It's all marble and shine, sparkle and polish. "I mean, seriously, *wow*."

"I'm glad you like it."

The speaker's voice is low and melodious, and is accompanied by the click of high heels. I turn toward the sound and find myself staring at one of the most elegant women I've ever seen. Tall and model-thin with platinum blonde hair upswept into a chignon, perfectly lined red lips, and wide gray eyes with just a hint of gold.

"I'm Marjorie." She extends her hand, her smile revealing brilliant white teeth that must have cost a fortune. "And you must be Sugar."

"Laine," I correct as we shake hands, her grip firm and confident. "Please."

She laughs. The slight crinkle at the corners of her eyes makes her seem more approachable, and I relax just a little. "You're right," she says to Joy. "She's charming. And as for your name," she continues, her focus returning to me, "all things considered, I think we'll call you Sugar."

All things considered.

"Right," I say, forcing a smile. "Of course."

I've often thought my mom saddled me with a hooker's name. Considering the job I'm about to take, I guess I wasn't far off the mark.

"Joy's explained to you what I do, I'm sure," Marjorie says as I follow her out of the foyer and into an equally elegant living room. This space, however, is designed as much for comfort as for appearance, with overstuffed couches and chairs, along with an area rug, a coffee table topped with water and wine, and the soft strains of classical music emanating from hidden speakers.

All in all, much less intimidating, and I start to relax. Just a little, anyway.

"So, um." I'm not sure if I'm supposed to sit or talk, so I do both. I take a seat on a silk upholstered armchair and tell Marjorie, "I *think* I know what you do. But maybe you should tell me anyway. Because I'm going to be really embarrassed if I'm wrong."

She doesn't laugh, but I see a smile tugging at the corner of her mouth. And somehow that small gesture relaxes me. Because her expression isn't mocking, but maternal. No matter what it is that's in store for me, Marjorie has my back.

Or, at least, she's good at pretending she does.

"It's quite simple, really." She takes a seat on the sofa, then gestures for Joy to do the same. Joy does, then kicks her feet up on the coffee table, her funky, paint-splattered sneakers in stark contrast to the ornamental glass vase and fresh roses.

Marjorie, however, takes it in stride, merely lifting an eyebrow in approbation.

Joy frowns, then tugs her feet to the ground. She looks at me and crosses her eyes, and I fight a laugh, immediately more at ease.

"I act as a liaison. Nothing more. Nothing less." As Marjorie speaks, a tall, thin man with graying temples enters the room and sets down a tray with three flutes and a clear pitcher filled with something orange. "Thank you, Daniel. I can pour. Mimosa?" she continues, as Daniel leaves the room. "I know they're traditionally a breakfast drink, but they're my current guilty pleasure."

"Sure. That would be great." Joy was right. I should have had that second glass of wine. "A liaison," I prompt as she passes me my glass. I take a quick sip. "So, men come to you, and you find a girl who—I don't know— matches some set of qualifications?"

"Essentially. Yes."

"And my job?"

"Is simply to be a companion."

I have a feeling it's not as simple as that, but I'm also not sure I'm ready for the nitty-gritty to be said aloud yet. So I dodge. "And you have a job for me already planned for tonight. How did you know I'd fit the bill?"

"I didn't, of course." She leans back and crosses her legs. "But Joy told me a bit about you. You seem like a strong woman, which this particular client finds attractive. She sent me a picture, and you're certainly lovely enough to be on my roster."

"Thanks," I mumble automatically. At the moment, I'm dressed in an oversized T-shirt and jeans, so I'm not exactly showing off my assets. And the truth is I don't show them off very often. I'm not prudish about sex—but I am discriminating. And it can be both overwhelming and frustrating to be constantly hit on.

"Of course, looks aren't everything. But now that I've met you, I agree with Joy's assessment that you're charming and bright. Frankly, you're a perfect fit for Mr. Z."

"Mr. Z," I repeat thoughtfully. "So, is he a regular customer?"

"He's on my client roster, obviously. But I wouldn't call him a regular. He's not weekly. For that matter, he's not even monthly. And when he does call, it's always unplanned, like tonight, and I have to scramble to find him a suitable companion." Again, she flashes an elegant smile. "Of course, that's one of the reasons he's willing to pay such a premium over the usual rate for both your fee and mine."

"The ten's all yours," Joy says. "Marjorie's fee is handled separately."

"Oh." I feel strangely better knowing that not all her clients pay five figures to get a date.

That sense of relief fades almost immediately, though, and I frown. "What's wrong with him?"

"Not a single thing," she says.

"Well, then why doesn't he just go to a bar and pick up a girl?"

"He's a man who values his reputation and his privacy. A bar hook-up wouldn't suit his image at all."

And sleeping with a call girl does?

I don't say that out loud, of course, but Marjorie obviously understands what I'm thinking, because she says simply, "He's paying for discretion, of course. That's not something that tends to come with a more traditional one-night stand."

I nod. Despite the oddity of this whole thing, I really do understand what she means.

"So, who is he?"

"I told you. Mr. Z."

"Wait. I don't get to know his name?"

"Not until you arrive at his suite. As I said, he's extremely protective of his privacy. Some of my girls report that he never formally introduced himself. They, however, knew who he was."

"Oh." I'm not sure if that makes me more or less confused. "You're saying that basically he's a last minute, famous guy. Which explains why he pays so well." I lick my lips. "That, and for the, um, service. Because it's not just about being a companion, is it?" I glance toward Joy. "I mean, he's going to want more than just to play with my feet, isn't he?"

"Laine…" Joy scowls at me, her eyes wide in an expression that is obviously supposed to be a signal for me to just shut the hell up.

But, come on. If I can't say it, I can't do it. And so I take a deep breath, and say, "The bottom line is sex, right? I mean, I'd really like to be absolutely certain I know what I'm getting into."

"Oh, my God." Joy looks like she'd give anything to sink into her couch cushion.

I glance at Marjorie, afraid she's going to look perturbed as well. But to my surprise, she laughs, the sound musical. "Joy, don't you dare be frustrated with Laine. Of course, she's going to ask questions. I'd be more concerned if she didn't."

"And yes," she adds, turning her attention fully to me. "It's likely he'll want sex. I'd go so far as to say it's probable. But I wasn't being coy earlier. I really am a go-between. He's paying me to find a date. I'm paying you to be his companion. And if you and the gentleman do choose to do what consenting adults sometimes do, that's between the two of you."

"Oh." I consider that. "Does he—I mean, it's just sex-sex, right? Or does he like—"

"Kink?" Joy chimes in, and this time, both Marjorie and I turn to glare at her.

"I don't know specifics," Marjorie says, focusing again on me. "But I can tell you that all my girls have hard limits. He's never crossed that line—and under the terms of the NDA, they're not only authorized, but required to tell me if he asks them to engage in any dangerous activity."

"NDA?"

"Non-disclosure agreement." She leans forward and opens a drawer in the coffee table, then pulls out a thin folder, which she passes to me, along with a pen. "Part of my role is to also ensure complete discretion."

I open the folder, then frown at the document, written in fluent legalese. "I'm not allowed to say anything to anyone?"

"That about sums it up," she says as I skim the document. "But, then again, neither is he. As I said, if you have safety concerns, you can share those with me. Of course, we wouldn't consider things like spanking and light bondage to put you at risk."

I look up, startled.

"Oh, dear," she says, looking at my face. "Is that something you have a problem with?"

"I—" I glance at Joy, then back at Marjorie. "Honestly, I don't know."

I'm not completely naive, but my knowledge of anything other than vanilla with, maybe, the tiniest drizzle of chocolate sauce, comes exclusively from books.

My head is spinning, and I take a long, deep breath as I hold onto the pen like a lifeline. "The thing is, this is all pretty unexpected and incredibly fast, and—"

"I'm afraid fast is part of the job description, at least for tonight. You're expected by eleven. We still need to do wardrobe and make-up, not to mention taking care of some, shall we say, administrative loose ends. Which means you're out of time, Sugar. I need to text the client a confirmation in exactly five minutes." She glances at her watch, then eyes me. "What do you want me to tell him?"

"I—"

I cut myself off, not sure what I intended to say. Or, rather, I know exactly what I intended to say—*yes*. I'm just not sure I want to be that kind of woman.

Even though we're getting down to the wire, Marjorie's smile is patient. "You won't believe me, of course," she says, "but I do understand. I've been there. Broke and uncertain and scared that if I make the wrong choice my entire world will come crashing down around me. No, don't be mad at Joy," she adds, when I glare at my friend. "She only told me that you needed cash—who doesn't? I guessed the rest. I've met a lot of young women, and I recognize the scent of desperation."

"Being desperate doesn't make it right."

"But it doesn't make it wrong, either. For that matter, who's to say what's wrong or right? I provide a service. He pays for that service. It's a free market transaction. What's cleaner than that?"

I say nothing.

"Nobody's telling a lie in a bar. Nobody's sitting by the phone wondering if he's going to call again. There's no worrying about whether he likes you or if he's married or about anything at all. Because that's not what's happening here. This isn't romance. It's a commercial transaction. It's no more emotional than buying a box of paperclips. But it just might be a little more fun.

"And," she adds with a wink, "depending on how much fun you two consenting adults have, I would expect him to treat you very, very nicely."

I frown, confused.

Joy leans forward. "She means that if you get naked with him, then you can pretty much expect a tip."

"Seriously?" As I look between the two of them, a stocky man with thick, curly hair enters the room. He looks about thirty, and has laugh lines around his eyes. There's really nothing remarkable about him. Nothing, that is, except the fact that he's wearing scrubs and carrying a tray with a syringe on it.

"Ben, this is Sugar. Sugar, if you'd be so kind as to let Ben take a small blood sample…"

I gape at her.

"My clients are very safety conscious. Just another service I provide. Ben can have the results back to us before you're out of wardrobe. And as I mentioned, we're on a bit of a time crunch."

I hesitate, then I glance at Joy, who nods and mouths, *Do it.*

"Um, okay." I hold out my arm for Ben. "And Mr. Z? I mean, do you have this kind of information on him, too?"

"Of course. To be honest, that requirement has cost me a few clients. But I'm not interested in putting my girls at risk. By the way, I assume you're on birth control?"

"What?" I look away as Ben draws blood, his work swift and almost painless. He bandages the site, gives me a single nod of acknowledgement, then walks off. "Oh, yeah. I'm fine in that department."

"Excellent," Marjorie says. "And now I'm afraid we're out of time. I need you to either sign that NDA or tell me you're not interested so that I can let Mr. Z know that he's out of luck this evening."

I draw in a breath to buy a few more seconds, a little irritated with myself because I went through this whole thought process once already while we were sitting at Blacklist. But that was when the idea was vague and amorphous. Now it's real and dark and full of sharp edges.

Honestly, it's not the moral ambiguity of having sex for money that's eating at me. It's the thought of being with a stranger. I did that once—only once—and I've been beating myself up ever since.

But I'd been vulnerable then. And tonight, I'll be the one with the power. Because I can say no if I want to—and if I choose to say yes, it's because of the payday. A payday that can go a hell of a long way toward digging me out of my current financial hole. Especially if what Joy said about a tip is true.

After my first and only time, I promised myself I was going to hold out for the right guy. A good guy.

I don't know if Mr. Z is good or not. But if sleeping with him can save my house, then I guess that makes him the right guy. At the very least, he's the guy I need.

"All right," I say, meeting Marjorie's eyes, and then exhaling loudly. "I'm in."

"Lovely," she says, then taps out a quick text. "My dear, he's going to adore you." She stands. "Now, to get you ready."

I follow her down a carpeted hallway to what would normally be the master bedroom. Here, however, it's filled with racks of outfits, a giant make-up station, and at least half a dozen trifold mirrors.

"I adore this condo," Marjorie says, noticing my confusion. "But I use it as an office, not as my home."

"Oh."

"This is cool," Joy says, pulling a shocking red dress from one of the racks. There's probably less than a yard of material, and even if I did manage to wriggle into it, I doubt I could walk.

"Uh, I'm not sure—"

But I don't have the chance to finish before Marjorie interrupts. "That would be darling on her, I'm sure. But it screams sex. And while that may be in the cards, Mr. Z prefers a more elegant look. But set it aside, and I'll tag it in the database as one of Sugar's possible outfits."

"Why—"

"Tonight won't solve your financial problems," Marjorie says with a small smile. "And after the initial awkwardness, I think you'll appreciate being on my roster. Even when you're past this crunch, a girl can always use some pocket money."

"Right, but if Mr. Z doesn't like that kind of—"

She cuts me off with a sharp shake of her head. "He never sees the same girl twice. If you end up on my roster, you'll be introduced to other men, and most prefer to see a girl at least a few times. But," she adds in a lighter tone, "we're getting ahead of ourselves. Right now, you simply need a dress. How about this one?"

She's moved to the rack opposite Joy, and she tugs out a pale pink dress with a low-cut bodice that buttons up, a fitted waist, and a flared skirt. It's simple, managing to be both classy and elegant.

She passes it to me, and I realize it's exactly the kind of dress I might pick out for myself. "I like it," I say, and immediately feel better. No matter what I'm about to set out to do, at least I won't be decked out in leather and hooker heels.

And, as an added plus, Marjorie tells me that I get to keep the clothes. Considering what I'm about to do, I figure I'm earning them. But still, the unexpected bonus makes me happy.

Before I know it, I'm standing in the doorway practicing deep breathing techniques. I have a fresh pedicure and am wearing heeled sandals that show off my feet.

The dress fits as well as I'd expected, and the skirt swishes when I walk. My underwear—also courtesy of Marjorie—is La Perla, and very sexy, adding a bit of contrast to my more conservative dress.

Marjorie did my make-up herself, and I look better than I ever have. Made-up, but still natural.

Everything about me is ready. Everything, except that niggling fear. And that, I'm just going to have to deal with.

"Remember the house," Joy says. "Keep your house in mind, and everything will be easy."

I nod. "Easy."

"Want me to wait at your place?"

"That's okay," I say. I love Joy, but considering what I'm about to do, I think I'm going to want to be alone. "But can you swing by and feed Skittles?" I rescued the now-fat tabby cat from a sack in a Dumpster when he was only few days old. His siblings didn't make it, but I nursed him to health, bottle-feeding him and keeping him safe and warm in a little bed I made out of a crate and a heating pad. It was two weeks after Andy and Mom died, and Skittles saved me as much as I'd saved him.

"Will do," Joy says.

"Your driver is downstairs," Marjorie tells me, glancing up from her phone where she's obviously just received a text. "Any last minute questions?"

"No," I say, though I'll probably have a million the moment I get in the car. "Now that I've decided to do this thing, I just want to get started, you know?"

"Then good luck, Sugar." She hands me a small envelope. "Open this when you get to the hotel. Your driver's name is Lionel, and Joy can walk down with you. I'll contact you tomorrow about transferring payment. And Mr. Z will take care of any tip he might offer you on-site. Okay?"

I draw a deep breath, then nod.

Holy crap, I'm really doing this.

As Marjorie promised, there's a black sedan waiting under the porte-cochère, and a well-dressed man with silver hair is holding the back passenger door open for me. "Miss Sugar," he says, as I hug Joy and promise to call her in the morning to tell her absolutely everything.

Then I slide into the car, Lionel shuts the door, and it all feels suddenly very, very real.

I'm actually going to have sex with a stranger.

I let the words hang in my head for a while, as I decide if I'm truly okay with that basic truism. And you know what? I am. I have a good reason. A purpose. And that's more than most women who meet a guy at a bar and go home with him can say.

Of course, those women have the benefit of being attracted to the guy. And, probably, of being at least a little tipsy, if not downright drunk.

What if he's all *wham, bam?* What if he doesn't have lube or doesn't even care if it hurts?

What if I'm too nervous to get turned on even if he's freaking Casanova?

What if I'm a complete and total idiot for doing this?

Shit.

Shit, shit, shit.

There's a screen between me and the driver, and a

control panel on the seat back. I can't find the button for the screen, but I do find an intercom, and I ask Lionel to swing by a drugstore before we go to meet Mr. Z.

"I understood you were on a schedule."

"Trust me. This is important."

Lucky for me, Lionel's a nice guy, and when he pulls into a Rite Aid, I practically sprint inside—despite the impractical four-inch shoes—and head straight for the sex aisle, where I'm faced with a remarkable amount of lubricant variety. I choose a small box with a familiar brand name, then hurry toward the cashier, pausing only long enough to grab a spritzer of minty breath spray and one of those disposable glasses pre-filled with red wine. The top peels off, and I assume Lionel won't mind if I have a quick drink in the back of the car.

As for the breath spray, it's easier to be confident with a little minty goodness.

Once I'm all paid and back in the car, I tuck the lube and breath spray into my purse, then carefully peel the lid off the wine. I want the drink, but I don't want to stain my dress.

I drink it fast, then close my eyes and let a warm buzz wash over me.

Just in the nick of time, too, because Mr. Z is apparently tucked away at the Stark Century Hotel, one of the ritziest hotels in the city. Lionel pulls in front of the valet stand, and a uniformed bellman opens the door for me and I step out of the car. I'm not entirely sure what I'm supposed to do now, but then I remember the envelope and slide a finger under the flap. I pull out a small notecard, on which is written: Z – 2848.

And absolutely nothing else.

I use my amazing powers of deduction and conclude that 2848 is Mr. Z's suite number. I use the revolving door to enter, then pause in the tastefully elegant lobby. There's a concierge desk nearby, and a woman glances at me, her smile clearly offering help. I just smile back and head toward the elevator bank, as if I'm just one of the regular guests. *Nothing to see here. Nothing at all.*

The elevator is fast. Too fast. I was hoping for a slow crawl as I gathered my wits, but that's not what I get. Instead, when the doors open on twenty-eight, I'm still trying to calm my crazy-rapid pulse, which kicked into overdrive the moment I stepped out of the car.

I pause in the elevator bank to collect myself. There are four elevators, two on one side of the rectangular area, and two on the other. The hallway is to my left. A floor to ceiling window is to my right, an upholstered bench sitting right in front of it. A man with curly blond hair and a goatee sits on the bench, scowling at his phone and tapping at the keypad. He's wearing jeans, a sports jacket, and a baseball cap, and I'm guessing that his date is either late or has stood him up.

He lifts his head to glance at me, and I immediately fumble in my purse for the breath spray so that I won't look like a terrified little girl off to meet the big, bad wolf. Instead, I'll look like a girl primping for a hot date.

After I spritz, I redo my lipstick. And then, of course, I'm all out of excuses. With a sigh, I move toward the hall, check the placard so I know which way to turn, and head for Mr. Z's suite.

It's to the right at the end of the hall, and I'm guessing it's one of the larger suites. Probably the kind with a kitchen, a living room, and at least one bedroom. In other words, the kind I've only seen in the movies.

So, that's another perk, right? Cold, hard cash *and* a really cool hotel room.

Way to keep up the optimism. Because, really, tonight is all about the room.

I close my eyes, trying to shut down the conversation running through my head, then knock firmly on the door. Although why I bother, I don't know. My heart is pounding so hard, I'm sure he can hear it on the other side.

Then the door opens, and my heart picks up tempo again. This time not out of fear but out of—what?

Lust? Surprise? Anticipation?

Because I know this guy. Hell, *everyone* knows this guy. He's plastered on the side of a freaking building on Sunset Boulevard. He's on the cover of at least two different entertainment magazines. And I saw him this morning on a local talk show.

He's Lyle Tarpin, and he's reaching for me.

He's taking my hand and pulling me inside.

He's pressing me against the foyer wall, one hand at my waist, the other tangled in my hair.

His mouth is closing over mine, hard and hot and wild and desperate, and I'm melting.

I'm just freaking melting.

And the only thing I can think when he finally pulls back, his mouth quirked up in his trademark lazy grin, is that I really, really, *really* won't need that lube.

CHAPTER 4

M Y BLOOD POUNDS through my body, my heart beating so hard that I can feel the pressure not only against my ribs, but against the wall behind me. My lips are parted, my breath coming in shaky gasps.

He's only inches away, so close I could reach out and touch that famous, gorgeous face. His eyes, as deep and blue as the summer sky, roam over me. He eases closer, moving slowly, his face reflecting a hunger that sends shivers through me.

Once again, my mind conjures the image of a hungry wolf. Only now I'm thinking that maybe getting eaten wouldn't be so bad after all.

Besides, I'm here. Might as well enjoy it.

Then, of course, I remember exactly what *it* is.

Oh, God.

His fingertip brushes my forehead, and I almost jump out of my skin. I meet his eyes, see something that looks like irritation, and want to kick myself. I need to focus, dammit.

"You were somewhere else." He speaks flatly, as if he's working to keep all emotion out.

I shake my head, conjuring a lie. "I'm right here."

And then, because I've seen movies with call girls, I put my hand flat on his chest, trying to seem seductive. He's wearing a gray T-shirt, and I can feel his heart beating beneath the planes of his muscled chest.

I read somewhere that he was getting in shape to play a superhero in an upcoming movie. And kudos to whoever's orchestrating that transformation, because this guy is rock solid.

He's still looking at me, and I fist my hand in the material of his shirt, needing an anchor against the storm of emotion I see playing out on his face. Desire. Hunger. Longing. Regret.

And pain. I see so much damn pain that I have to fight the urge to cup my palm against his cheek and tell him that whatever it is, it's going to be okay.

Instead, I simply whisper, "Lyle?"

I'm not sure if it was the wrong thing or the right thing to say, but I know that it was unexpected. And before I can apologize or cover or say anything else at all, he is on me. One hand at my throat, the other hard on my breast. I'm pinned against the wall, helpless, as he claims my mouth again. Wildly. Brutally.

I try to think what I'm supposed to do—try to respond. But I'm trapped. I'm not Sugar. I'm not Laine. I'm not anyone. This isn't about sex. It's about pain and need and that storm of horrors I saw on his face. I might as well not even be here. And as his hand squeezes tight on my breast—as his mouth clashes so hard against mine that he draws blood—my only thought is that I shouldn't have come at all. That this was stupid. Foolish. And that this night is going to leave me scarred.

I squeeze my eyes shut, trying to be what he wants. A warm body. An anonymous female.

But I can't do it. I can't do it at all.

All I can be is *me*. A woman desperate enough to have sex for money. A girl trying anything and everything to save her house. To protect her family's memory.

I can be that girl.

But I can't be nothing. I can't be no one.

And as his hand tightens in my hair—as he kisses me violently—as his body presses hard against mine and I feel the steel of his erection—I know that I've made a terrible, horrible, awful mistake.

Stop!

The word rips through me, but it's only in my head. He doesn't hear it, and he presses harder against me. His hand on my dress, yanking it up. His fingers closing on the band of the pretty La Perla panties. He starts to tug them down, and suddenly I can't stand it anymore. Being trapped. Being crushed.

One palm is on his chest, the other hand hanging limp at my side. I bring that hand up now, hard and fast, so that I knock away his hand that is clutching my breast.

I feel him flinch. The pressure of his mouth lessens against mine, and his grip on my neck relaxes as well.

I take advantage, shoving my free hand hard against his chest, then using both hands to push him away.

He stumbles back, obviously startled. His eyes go wide and his lips part as he stands in front of me. I'm still against the wall, and I cross my arms over my chest, holding tight to my shoulders.

"Oh, God," I say. "I'm sorry." I'm not sure if I'm

apologizing for breaking free or for not knowing how to ease his pain. "I'm so, so sorry." I draw in a breath. "I have to go. I shouldn't have—I just have to go."

We're still in the foyer, and so I turn, then launch myself toward the door. It's happened so fast, and he hasn't really moved at all. But even when I turn away, I can feel his eyes on my back. Can feel the shock and surprise, now thick in the air between us.

I reach for the door, and that's when his hand closes over my shoulder.

I spin around, my arm now behind me and my hand clutching tight to the knob.

He steps back, as if instinctively knowing that I need space. "You're leaving?"

I can't tell if he's surprised or angry, but I nod. "I'm sorry," I say for about the billionth time. Hollow words. Useless words.

I know that I *should* stay. I need the money. But I feel so twisted up inside. Like I can feel his pain—and there's so damn much of it.

I swallow, my mouth suddenly dry. "I just—you just—"

I snap my mouth shut, knowing I sound like an idiot. Knowing I'm making it worse. But then I open my mouth again, and the words just spill out. "Why are you doing this? Me? The other girls? Anybody? You don't want a date. You don't want a woman. You don't even want sex." I feel tears on my cheeks, taste the salt. "You just want a witness. Or not even that. You want a wall. Something you can rail against. Someone who'll take it because they have to. And I—I'm sorry," I say again lamely. "I'm sorry, but I just can't."

"A wall," he repeats. His voice is low, his expression hard. I'm certain that he's angry, but I'm not sure if that anger is directed at me or himself or someone else entirely.

I'm not going to hang around to find out.

I turn back toward the door.

"*Sugar,*" he calls, and I freeze. It's the first time he's spoken my name, and I'm shocked at how much I like the sound of it.

I swallow, then grapple for the handle again, because clearly I need to get away from this man who's messing with my head.

"Please," he says more gently. "Wait."

I hesitate. I know I shouldn't, but I do. I stand there with my hand tight around the cool steel of the handle, tears clinging to my lashes. I'm not even sure why I'm crying. For my house? For my stupidity? For this man's pain? A man who projects such kindness and innocent charm to the world, but here in this room is so obviously, painfully tortured?

He says nothing else, and I think he's afraid that if he speaks, I'm going to bolt. As if I'm a small, cornered rabbit, and if he moves too quickly I'll somehow manage to hop away.

"Tell me what you're talking about." His voice is firm. Demanding. But I can't answer.

Besides, he already knows. He's the one trying to work something out, after all.

Finally, I face him again. "Don't take this out on Marjorie, okay? I get that you need … something. But this is my first time doing anything like this, and I messed it all up. She thought I'd be okay, but she was wrong. Please don't blame her. I feel terrible enough already. If I thought she lost a client, then I'd really—"

"I won't," he says. "I don't."

"And I'm sure she'll give you a refund." A fat tear rolls down my cheek, and I wince at the thought of what I'm sacrificing by walking away. "Fuck," I whisper as I wipe the tear with the back of my hand.

I manage to stop myself before I say that I'm sorry one more time. Instead, I turn toward the door again, this time pulling it open a few inches before a single word stops me.

"*Why?*"

I pause, my eyes down so that I'm focusing on the pattern of the carpet in the hallway just outside this door.

I hear the rustle of clothes and feel the shift in the air. He's stepped closer to me, and this time when he speaks I feel him gently lay a hand on my shoulder. "You said it was your first time. Why were you doing it?"

I twist out from under his touch. "Does it matter?"

"It matters to me." He reaches over me to push the door shut. As he does, his entire body brushes mine. I stiffen, hyperaware of his touch, of the ripples of electricity that zing through my body. And I breathe only when he eases back, once again giving me space.

I close my eyes tight, hating that I reacted so viscerally to this man. But something about him—his pain, his loneliness—has settled inside me. And even though I want to ignore the question and run out that door, I already know that even if I leave, I won't really be escaping him at all.

And so I stay. I draw in a deep breath. And then I turn to face him. "The money." I say the words simply. Flatly. As if there's no emotion attached to them at all. As if I don't understand how much I'm giving up by walking out this door.

"That much I assumed. What do you need the money for?"

I tilt my head as I look at him. "Is this *your* first time?"

The corner of his mouth twitches. "No."

I nod, as if considering that. "Why were you doing it?"

The twitch turns into a full-blown smile. "Does it matter?"

I meet his gaze. "It matters to me."

Our eyes lock, the words hanging in the air between us. There's heat and humor and something else I don't recognize but makes me feel safe. Comfortable. I like this guy. Despite the weird circumstances, there's something about him that I really like.

The moment seems to last for an eternity, though I know it's really only the space of one breath. Then he takes a step back. "Touché," he says, breaking the spell.

I shift my weight from one foot to the other. "So, anyway. I should go."

He takes my hand, and suddenly the only thing in the whole world that I'm aware of is that connection between us. His firm grip. His warm skin.

His hand is just a little rough, not soft and prissy like some manicured, pampered actor. He feels like he's struggled. Like he's earned what he's achieved. But as I remember the pain I saw in his eyes, I can't help but wonder what price he's paid along the way.

I glance down at our joined hands. "I really—"

"What were you expecting?" he demands.

"Expecting?"

"When you came here tonight. This first time, for money. What did you think was going to happen?"

"I—I'm not sure." I tug my hand free, then rub my suddenly sweaty palms down the skirt of my dress.

"You must have had some idea. Didn't Marjorie say anything?"

I look up at his face. "I get the impression she doesn't know that much about you."

"Not many do."

For some reason, those three little words make me incredibly sad. "Why?"

But he just shakes his head. "You still haven't answered my question."

I exhale loudly, coming to terms with the fact that the only way I'll avoid the question is if I yank the door open and take off running down the hall. And if I do that in these shoes, there's no doubt that he'd catch me.

"I don't know," I say, punctuating the words with an exasperated sigh. "Sex, of course. But I guess I thought it would be capping off a seduction."

"Really?"

He's obviously holding back laughter, and I scowl at him. "It's not *that* far out of the realm of possibility. I mean, I've seen *Pretty Woman*. Richard Gere bought her strawberries."

"Are you saying you're hungry? I think there's a selection of cheeses in the fridge, along with some wine."

"Ha, ha. And no, I'm not—" I take a deep breath, because what the hell. "Actually, wine would probably be a really good idea."

"All right, then. After you." He gestures toward the living room that opens up just past the foyer in which we've been standing. I pause when I reach the room, uncertain where to go. But he indicates a stool on one side of a freestanding wet bar.

I take a seat, and he goes behind the bar, then bends down. Apparently, he's opening a refrigerator, because when he stands again, he has a bottle of white wine and a plate with cheese and grapes.

He takes the plastic wrap off the plate, then sets it on the bar between us. Then he holds up the wine for approval. When I nod, he pours a glass and hands it to me.

"You're not having any?" I ask when he puts the bottle back in the fridge.

"Honestly, I haven't decided if I need to keep a clear head around you or have something stronger."

I narrow my eyes in a mock glare, and he laughs. The sound startles both of us, I think. And I realize that despite the overall awkwardness of the situation, this moment is actually okay.

"I have to debate your seduction theory," he says, pouring a shot of Jack Daniels into a highball glass.

"It wasn't a theory," I correct. "Just an expectation. Apparently, a lame one."

"I'll say. Under the circumstances, a seduction is the

last thing you should have expected."

"The circumstances?"

He's lifted the glass to take a sip. Now he raises his other hand and rubs his fingers together, indicating money. "Isn't the whole point of paying so that I don't have to put on the show? Don't have to seduce or entice or play games of any type at all?"

"I guess." I frown as I trace my fingertip over the rim of my wine glass. "But isn't that ... I don't know ... anticlimactic?"

"Interesting choice of words." The smile he flashes is wide and genuine and full of the confident charm that has fueled his ride to stardom. "But I assure you that no one has ever accused me of being anticlimactic."

"Oh." I clear my throat, then take another sip of wine. "I just mean that sex is like a dance. Or a symphony. You can't jump straight to the climax. You need the rise. The crescendo."

"I think you're confusing sex and romance." He's looking down at his drink, his hands clutching the side of the counter so tightly that his knuckles are white. After a moment, though, he looks up, his blue eyes dark with a pain I don't understand, but can't deny. "What I want— what I'm paying for—is the cymbal crash at the end. That release. That moment when everything shatters. I'm not paying for pretty words and flowers."

I start to protest, but keep my mouth shut. Because you know what? He's right. That *is* what he's paying for.

And it's not like I really came here to be seduced. I'm not delusional. I just didn't expect things to move quite so fast. But if he wants the whole wham-bam-thank-youma'am experience, then who am I to argue? As they say, the customer is always right. And tonight, that would be him.

As for me...

I'd already stepped out of my comfort zone by coming here. So absent Lyle pushing for anything truly scary, I need to remember that I came with a goal. And walking away now isn't going to help save my house.

I finish off the last of my wine in one very large gulp, then slide off my stool. I stand for a second, a little lightheaded and wobbly on the heels. At the same time, he comes around the bar, walking toward me.

"I'll stay," I say.

He stops walking. "What?"

"I said I'll stay." I draw in a breath, then exhale slowly as I meet his eyes. "That's why I'm here. Because you're paying, right? And that means you're calling the shots. So just tell me what to do."

My fingers go to the line of vertical buttons on the bodice. "Do you want me to just take it off? Should I get undressed and into bed? Do you want to rip the damn dress off me?" I meet his eyes defiantly, daring him to suggest that I don't have the moxie to be the wall he needs to wail against.

"I'm sorry I got out of sorts earlier," I continue, my fingers fumbling at the buttons. "But I'm good now. So let's rewind and start over. Tell me what you want and we'll go from there."

His hand closes over mine, stilling my nervous fingers. "Stop." His voice is gentle, and he says nothing else.

"What? Why?" I try to keep the frustration out of my voice, but I can't. I'm quivering from nerves and adrenaline and determination. I've decided to do this, and now I just want to get on with it. "Dammit, please. Just tell me what you want from me."

"What I want?" He traces his fingertip along the neckline of the bodice, making me shiver. "Isn't that a loaded question?" His touch dips into the small, open V made by the two unfastened buttons, and his finger barely strokes the curve of my breast.

I actually whimper.

"So much," he murmurs, the words so soft I can barely even hear them. Then he draws in a deep breath, lifts his head, and looks me in the eyes. "But I can't have any of it."

"But—"

He backs away, breaking contact, and leaving me feeling cold and hollow. "You were right the first time," he says. "You need to go."

I open my mouth to protest, then shut it again. My skin feels hot, and I know my face is burning with the deep red flush of mortification.

And then, before I can stop myself, I lash out and slap his face.

I gasp, my hand flying to my mouth as tears stream down my face. *I'm sorry*, I say. Or I try to. The words don't come. Instead, I'm fleeing to the door, trying not to trip in the stupid shoes.

I yank the door open and race into the hall, then pause only long enough to slip out of the shoes. I bend and grab them, then take off again, sprinting for the elevator bank. There's someone else in the hallway, but I keep my head down, not wanting anyone to see my mortification.

When I reach the elevator, I jam my finger against the button, willing it to come faster. What the hell was I thinking? Did I really believe this was a way to make money?

But that's not the worst of it. I actually let myself *feel.* I trembled under his touch.

And, damn me, I wanted more.

Fuck.

I jab my finger against the button again. Then again and again, because where is the elevator? Where's my goddamned escape route?

It feels like an eternity passes before I hear the chime, though I know it's only seconds. The light above the middle set of doors flashes, and I step closer, eager to get on the moment those metal doors slide open.

They do, a couple gets off, and I'm about to enter when I hear him call, "Wait. Please, wait."

I know I should ignore him, but I can't help myself. I pause, and then he's at my side, and then I've missed my chance.

The elevator doors snick closed, and I'm standing there, my face tear-stained, my feet bare, and this gorgeous, tortured man holding tight to my upper arm.

"Just let me go." In my head, the words are a harsh demand. In actuality, they're a defeated whisper.

"Take this," he says, shoving a book into my hands.

I frown at it, struck dumb by the incongruity of the moment. "What—?"

"Please. Just take it." His voice is a gentle whisper. Low. Apologetic. "And I'll text Marjorie. She'll transfer your money tonight."

I shake my head. "No. No way. I didn't—I mean, we didn't—"

I suck in a breath. "I didn't earn it," I say firmly.

He's looking at me hard. Then—without another word—he cups my head, pulls me toward him, and kisses me so hard and so deep that my knees go week, and it's only his other arm that has snaked around my waist that holds me up.

When he steps back, breaking the kiss, I have to reach out and steady myself against the wall. "There," he says. "You've earned it."

Then he turns and walks away, leaving me standing on shaky legs, my heart pounding as I clutch the book in my free hand and wonder what in the hell just happened.

CHAPTER 5

IT'S ALMOST THREE in the morning when the taxi turns onto my street. I know I could have saved the cab fare by paging Marjorie's driver, but I wasn't sure how long I'd have to wait, and I really wanted out of there.

Although now that I'm away, I'm not sure I feel better. I'm still confused. Twisted up. My emotions bouncing all over the place. Irritation. Apprehension. Arousal.

And complete and total mortification.

He'd wanted me to stay—I was sure of it. But then he turned on a dime and sent me away, and I don't understand why. Was I not sexy enough? Did I talk too much? Did I piss him off?

Of course I pissed him off. *Dammit.* All my talk about seduction when he'd gone and hired an escort? What kind of an idiot am I?

Apparently, I'm the kind of idiot who insults her meal ticket—because even before I rattled off at the mouth about seduction, I was accusing him of banging call girls because he needed to work out his issues.

Holy crap, what the hell was I thinking?

The answer? I wasn't thinking at all. I was nervous.

And stupid. And it cost me that job.

Except it didn't. I'm still getting the money, after all. And I didn't have to sleep with him.

So I guess I should be grateful.

Except I'm not grateful. I'm perplexed. And, damn me, I'm just a little unsatisfied. Because I liked talking to him. I liked the way he looked at me. The way his mouth curved when he was fighting a smile, and the way his eyes crinkled when he laughed.

Crap. What the hell am I thinking? I was on a job, not a date. And it's over. Doesn't matter how wow that final kiss was, or how much the feel of his lips still lingers. One time—wasn't that what Marjorie said? One time, and I'm done, and I won't ever see him again.

It's over, and despite my mistakes, I survived.

I should be celebrating, not wallowing in melancholia.

That's what I tell myself, anyway. Too bad I'm not following my own advice.

With a sigh, I slip my hand into my purse and run my finger along the edge of the little book. I'd glanced at it in the elevator, but it's just a slim, hardcover volume with a plain brown dust jacket. I'd opened it on the elevator, but the title page simply said *Collected Poems,* and before I could flip through it more, the express elevator had reached the lobby, and the doors had opened to reveal a very drunk couple stumbling toward me. So I'd tucked the book in my purse and hoofed it to the taxi stand.

Now, of course, it's too dark to see, anyway. But I brush my fingertip over the spine, and decide I'll tell

Marjorie about the book in the morning. Maybe it's like his trademark. Hire an escort, share some literature.

I roll my eyes at my crazy, meandering thoughts. But crazy and meandering make sense under the circumstances. After all, a book of poetry with no explanation falls squarely into the realm of *what the fuck?*

"Which house, Miss?"

"Almost to the end of the next block," I say. "Next to the blue two-story."

I love my street. The houses are all charming, and they range from smallish—like mine, with only eleven hundred square feet—to huge and fantastic. Most are older and fixed up to pristine condition. But there are a few that need a facelift, and every time I pass one, I want to grab a bucket of paint or a toolbox.

That's why I'd taken out the equity loan that is the current monkey on my back—I'd needed the cash to fund massive renovations on my house after a series of pipes had burst, decimating the kitchen and bathroom. I hadn't done the plumbing work myself, of course, but I'd spent countless hours refinishing cabinets, searching out new fixtures, and refurbishing the floors. Not to mention sanding and painting and a whole bunch of other details.

I'd started the project in order to save the house I'd grown up in. But as I'd gotten deeper into the work, my motives had changed. I wanted to save the house, sure. But I also wanted to transform it.

I love my mother and my brother—and I miss them so damn much. But living here—coming home from work every day to the memories that filled each and every room—it was too much. I spent two years balancing on a precipice, and the smallest thing could send me tumbling over into tears and depression. I was lost and alone and scared. And the only thing I had was the house and my memories, and I let myself be entombed with them.

But as the house changed, so did my feelings. It still held memories, sure, but coming home stopped feeling like torture. I started looking forward to walking through the door. And the house started feeling like a home instead of a tomb.

The renovations had given me peace, and that could have been enough. But in the process, I'd discovered a love for that kind of work—and a talent, too. And as soon as I dig my way out of the financial hole I've sunk into, I'm going into the business of buying ramshackle houses, fixing them up, and selling them. Not original, I know. Half the television shows these days seem to be about folks flipping houses. But that's okay. It's what I want. And I fully intend to make it happen.

Right now, though, I just need to focus on my own little house on my own little street in my own little corner of the world.

As soon as the driver brings the car to a stop, I pay him, then step out of the taxi and head to the wooden gate that stands sentry in the middle of the stucco fence that fronts my property and keeps pedestrians and tourists off my lawn. A necessity since this close to the beach the street is often noisy and crowded.

But it's also close to local hangouts like Blacklist, not to mention a decent market, an ATM, and most of my friends. I rarely use my persnickety car, instead choosing to walk or bike most everywhere.

Now, of course, the street is dark and quiet, illuminated only by the dim glow of the few street lamps that line the block like soldiers.

I have a keypad lock on both the gate and my front door, and I enter the six digits of Andy's birthday to unlock the gate, then step into the sanctuary of my little front yard. The walk is paved in flagstones that I laid and mortared myself, and the lawn is green and lush, thanks to the wonderful California weather.

My tall lemon tree provides both shade and a bumper crop of lemons that Mrs. Donahue next door turns into lemonade, chocolate-dipped candied lemon peels, and a limoncello that's perfect for sipping on the back porch on a lazy Saturday afternoon.

Unfortunately, lately I've been working so many hours that I haven't had a lazy Saturday afternoon. But drinking, reading, and relaxing are tops of my To Do list the second I get this damn loan paid off.

My motion sensor porch light comes on as I approach the front door, and I quickly key in Mom's birthday, then step inside. Now that I'm here, exhaustion is catching up to me, and I can't stop fantasizing about falling facedown onto my bed and passing out for three glorious hours.

I'd prefer eight glorious hours, but I have the eight to eleven shift at Maudie's in the morning, and if I want tips, I should probably shower, too.

As I move from the tiny entrance hall to the tiny combination living and dining area, I hear a squeaky *meow.*

"Hey, you," I say, sitting on the couch next to Skittles, who's curled up on the side he's claimed as his own. He raises his head, his eyes narrowed as he yawns. I shrug. "Sorry, big guy. I had to work. And don't give me that look. I know Joy came by to feed you."

Joy, however, wouldn't have stayed. And that means Skittles didn't have his usual evening ritual of eating while I sit at the kitchen table with a glass of wine and a book. I read until he finishes, then he gets on the bed while I take off my makeup. Then I join him, read for a while, and finally drift off to sleep.

It's ridiculously domestic, but it's our routine, and so even though it's past three, I stand with a nod to the kitchen. "Come on, then," I say. "Late night snack."

At the word *snack*, he leaps off the couch and does figure eights through my legs all the way to the pantry. I grab a can, make him a plate, then put it on the placemat I keep on the floor for him.

And since I can hardly break tradition, while he attacks the salmon in savory sauce, I sit at the table with a glass of red wine and the book that Lyle gave me.

It's a narrow volume, its plain dust jacket a bit stained, as if someone put a drink on it more than once. The pages are brown, the paper cheap, and the title page says simply, Collected Poems.

But when I turn to the next page, I see that the book is a collection of poems by William Ernest Henley, and I feel a little chill creep up my spine. Because Henley wrote the poem *Invictus,* and it was the memory of that verse that I'd learned in high school that later helped me survive those first days after Mom and Andy died. That reminded me I *could* survive. That I had, like Henley said, an unconquerable soul.

Did Lyle know that?

How could he have known that?

With my pulse pounding, I start to flip the pages, because I know that poem has to be in here. It's by far his most famous work. That's when I realize that the backside of the dust jacket is being used as a bookmark. I open the book to the page and gasp.

Because not only is it marking the page with *Invictus*, but tucked in beneath the dust jacket flap is a one thousand dollar bill in a little plastic sheath on which has been written in Sharpie, *Sell, don't spend.*

I stare at it, not comprehending. *Sell?* What does that mean? Is it art? A joke?

Do they even make one thousand dollar bills?

I do a quick search on my phone and, apparently, they used to. And though they aren't in circulation any more, they're still legal tender.

But the note is right; I'd be stupid to spend it. Because from what I can tell in my five seconds on the net, that single bill is worth almost three thousand dollars.

So why the hell did he give it to me?

JOY TAKES A sip of coffee from one of my Mickey Mouse mugs, then sighs with such deep emotion that I think I should abandon my kitchen and give her some privacy.

"This is like liquid heaven," she says. "Very essential liquid heaven."

"Traditionally it's called coffee." I take a seat opposite her, sipping from my own mug. "But on a morning like this, I think we can call it ambrosia."

Joy's waggles her eyebrows. "A morning like this, eh? Does that mean that last night was both late and energetic?"

"Um, hello? Last night was a job, remember? Not a first date."

"Sorry," she says, looking immediately contrite. "I'm an idiot. Was it okay, though?"

"Odd," I say.

"Really? Why?"

I just shrug. "Doesn't matter. But at the end he gave me this." I pass her the book.

She frowns at the volume. "You sleep with the guy, and this is what he gives you as a tip?"

"Actually, there wasn't sex—"

"Wasn't sex?" Her voice rises with incredulity.

"—and I'm not supposed to be talking about any of this to you, am I?"

"The NDA, you mean? You can tell me whatever you want."

I must look dubious, because she crosses her heart and holds a hand up like a Boy Scout. "No, really. And not just BFF rules. I'm totally, legally allowed to hear."

I peer at her over the rim of my mug. "How?"

She makes a face, then lifts a shoulder. "Because Marjorie hired me about two months ago to do administrative stuff, so I'm part of the formal staff, and formal staff is outside the NDA. I'm her only employee who sees the whole picture. She needed someone to help because, honestly, she runs a pretty big operation. And I got tagged since I'm family and I could handle working some extra hours."

"The whole picture? You know who Mr. Z is?"

She shakes her head. "Nope. That's the only part Marjorie keeps locked up tight. In her head and in her safe."

"I can't believe you didn't tell me that you work for her."

"That would violate the whole secret part of the gig. At least until you'd officially taken the job, and by then you were out the door. Speaking of secrecy, you're not required to tell Marjorie anything that goes on unless it's dangerous, but you're not forbidden, either. Marjorie discourages it because she doesn't want a flood of girls giving her the down and dirty, but it's all in your contract. Marjorie sent you a copy last night. Check your email and read it if you don't believe me."

"I believe you," I say. "And the book wasn't the tip. This was." My purse is on the kitchen table where I left it last night. I'd put the bill in there for safe keeping until I figured out what to do with it, and now I pass it to Joy. "It's worth more than two grand."

Her eyes go wide. "That is seriously cool." She passes it back to me, and I tuck it safely away in my wallet. "Of course, I was hoping he'd just pay off your house, but an extra two K is pretty cool. Especially if he didn't fuck you. There really wasn't sex? You're serious?"

"There was kissing," I admit. "And then we talked. It

was—wait. Pay off my house?" I frown as her words finally worm their way into my sleep-deprived brain. "You're joking, right?"

"Slight exaggeration," she admits as Skittles leaps into her lap. "But I was holding out hope."

"Holding out hope," I repeat. "Okay, but why?"

"I told you there might be a tip. I just didn't tell you how generous he sometimes is. Marjorie told me about one girl a year or so ago—he bought her a car."

"Seriously?" I was about to get more coffee, but now I sit down again.

"Okay, not entirely. But her car was broken, and he got it fixed, and it was a major engine thing. Like serious-ly pricey, and she never could have afforded it. Pretty nice of him, right?"

I agree that it was.

"And there was another girl who was doing the es-cort thing to earn tuition money. He paid all her tuition and fees for that semester and the next. Swear to God."

"Why?" I ask. "I mean he's already paying a ton of money just for the date. And then to top that off…"

"Dunno. Maybe he's a genuinely nice guy."

I nod thoughtfully, thinking about the man I met in the hotel last night. A man who'd aroused me. Who'd intrigued me. A man who'd run after me so that he could give me one hell of an amazing tip even though I hadn't done anything to earn it.

"Yeah," I say. "He's nice. An enigma," I add, be-cause I still don't get why he's hiring escorts in the first place. "But nice."

I glance at the clock—almost seven. "I need to get

moving," I say. "I have to walk Lancelot and then get to Maudie's for the breakfast shift. And I need to hit the bank right when I get off, because it closes at noon today."

Her eyes go wide. "You can't deposit that. You have to sell it to a collector."

"I'm not depositing it. I'm using the ten grand to make a payment on the loan. And as for that old bill, if you really think I can keep it, I'm going to put it in my safe deposit box."

"Keep it? Of course you can." She winces as Skittles starts to knead her lap. "Why wouldn't you? You're keeping the ten."

She has a point, although I feel guilty about that as well. I'd gone to the hotel because Lyle was hiring a girl for sex, and all I ended up doing was freaking out and drinking with him. But I still walked away with cold, hard cash.

"I don't have to open the shop until nine," Joy says. "Want company? I'll walk the dog with you, and then you can serve me breakfast burritos before I have to split."

Since that sounds like a fine plan, I finish getting ready, then we go next door together to fetch Lancelot from Jacob's apartment over the garage.

"Hey, Sugar," Jacob says as he passes me the leash. "You look good enough to eat."

"Have I mentioned how not funny that joke is?"

"Only a couple of dozen times," he says cheerfully. "I'm late for my Saturday study group. You'll put him back in the apartment?"

"No problem." I bend down and nuzzle Lancelot's golden brown coat. He's an eight month old lab, which means he's already huge and about as cheerful as a dog can be. Right now, his tail is banging out a rhythm against the door so loud I'm surprised Mrs. Donahue hasn't stepped outside to see what's the racket.

Lancelot pretty much calls the shots on our walks, and now he leads the way to the boardwalk, his favorite place to wander. He'd prefer the beach, I'm sure, but that's verboten, and he's learned that he has to keep off the sand.

"So you're walking Lancelot," Joy says, as if there'd been no break in our conversation at all. "Then waiting tables. What's after that today?"

"Mrs. Donahue," I say. "I'm deep cleaning her kitchen. I blocked out two hours. And after that," I add, because obviously she's determined to account for my every minute today, "I'm going to Greg's."

"Yeah? He finally convinced you to say yes?"

I roll my eyes. "He's not trying to convince me. We're just friends. We've only ever just been friends."

"He wants more," she says.

"Yeah, he does. He wants to start a business."

"More," she repeats, and I groan.

"You said the same thing about Jacob yesterday. Now Greg? I'm seeing a pattern here."

She sighs. "Just living vicariously."

"Well, stop," I say. "You too can have a life if you'd just jump back in."

"Right. So. How is Greg's place these days, anyway?"

I consider calling her out on the change of subject,

but decide to let it slide. Joy's last boyfriend experience was about as shitty as they come, and she's taking a self-imposed sabbatical. Personally, I think it's time she tested those waters again, but if she's not ready, I'm not going to push.

Instead, I tell her that Greg's house is coming along. "All the structural stuff is done. Everything now is cosmetic. Floors, countertops, walls."

"Can't wait to see it," she says, and I nod.

The truth is, neither can I. I've known Greg since high school, though we really didn't become friends until a couple of years ago when he took a part-time job bartending at Blacklist. He's an aspiring screenwriter who's living rent-free in his seven hundred square foot house in exchange for doing the renovations for his landlord, something he has the skills to do since he grew up working in his family's construction company.

He'd helped me with the work on my house, and we got along so well doing it, that he asked if I'd help with his house project. We've been working on and off for five months now, documenting every step of the project with pictures. When it's done, we'll both have a nice portfolio. And, with any luck, one day we intend to go into business together—investing, renovating, and selling houses. He doesn't plan on giving up the writing, but flipping houses is the kind of job that lets him write on the side. Plus, Greg is realistic enough to know that even with talent, he might not make it as a writer.

As for me, I never had a dream job when I was growing up. And it wasn't until after I dove into renovations on my own house that I discovered how much I love doing it. With my house, it was cathartic—a way to not only save my home, but to work through the pain of my memories. With flips, it's about the plan and the execution. About envisioning something and seeing it through.

So, yeah. I want the business, too. And I'm grateful to have a partner like Greg in my corner.

Of course, at this point it's still all baby steps. But we'll get there. Our plan is solid.

"Want to watch a movie or something after?" Joy asks. "Movie and martini night?"

"I would," I tell her. "But I'll probably watch something with Greg if we finish in time." Lately, our routine has been to work, then relax with whatever movie he's currently analyzing. "Besides, you forget that I've got my own martini night planned."

She stares blankly for a minute, then her face clears. "Oh, right. You've got a ten o'clock shift at Blacklist. Damn."

"Not damn for me," I say. "House. Money. Remember all of that?"

"Like four hours at Blacklist is going to make a difference."

I tug on Lancelot's leash to turn him around as I shoot Joy a scowl. "Hello, Miss Negative Energy. The tips will be good, and you know it."

But as we head back toward Jacob's apartment, I can't deny that good isn't good enough. Not even close.

"Do you want me to call Marjorie? Get you another gig soon?"

I draw a deep breath as I think about my house. And

about how much money I'll still owe on the loan, even after I make a huge lump sum payment today. Then I think about Lyle, and for a minute, I'm actually excited about getting another gig from Marjorie.

But then I remember that he won't be the client. That if I do this thing, it's going to be some other man kissing me. Touching me.

I'll save my house, yeah. But the price will be more than just dollars.

"Laine?" Joy prods.

"Yeah," I say quickly, before I can change my mind. "Make the call."

Why not? Lyle Tarpin is a fantasy, after all.

But the debt on my house is about as cold and hard as reality can get.

CHAPTER 6

"**G**OOD," RILEY SAID as Lyle pivoted and kicked the sandbag for what felt like the thousandth time that afternoon. "Next time get your body and leg completely parallel with the ground. Form's important, Tarpin."

"Fuck you," Lyle retorted amiably, wiping sweat off his upper lip. "We've been at this for six hours. You do remember I'm going to have a stunt double, right?"

"Nice try. You're the one who said you didn't just want to be in shape. I think your exact words were, 'I need more than muscle and strength. Even if I'm only walking, I need to move like someone who knows his way around a fight.'"

Lyle groaned. "How was I supposed to know you'd break from pattern and actually listen to me?"

"Come on. Just do it one more time, and then we'll switch back to upper body work."

"Oh, joy."

Riley laughed. "You're the one who's going to go shirtless in a movie that's gonna be seen by millions. But if you want slack muscle tone when you're on the big screen…"

"You know you're a prick, right?"

"It's one of my most endearing qualities. Okay, go."

Lyle did, managing to bend and pivot a full ten reps without falling on his ass. And, as a plus, he kicked the shit out of that damned sandbag each and every time.

"Not bad," Riley said, when Lyle was upright again and mopping his face with the towel Riley tossed him. "Especially impressive considering you've been off your game all afternoon."

Lyle lowered the towel. "I have, and I'm sorry. It's not the workout—if anything having you ride my ass is helping me to not think."

Riley took a long pull from his water bottle, then lowered it slowly. "Oh, fuck. It was yesterday, wasn't it? Thirteen years since the accident. Since Jenny died. Christ, Lyle, I'm an ass for not remembering sooner."

"You're not," Lyle assured him. He hung the towel over his shoulder, then went to sit on the wooden bench on the far side of the shabby gym space that Riley had lined up for their sessions. "And I'll be fine."

"Fine?" Riley repeated, frowning slightly. "Yeah, sure. You'll get by—you always do. But if you need to talk we can ditch the session, go grab a beer."

Lyle forced a smile. "I'm almost tempted just because my muscles are screaming, but I really am okay. Jenny's death twisted me up some yesterday—I figure it always will—but she's not the reason I'm off my game today."

"Is that a fact?" Riley crossed his arms over his broad chest, his feet hip distance apart. With his dark hair, rugged features, and seriously honed muscles, he looked more like a superhero than Lyle ever would. Then again, considering what Riley did for a living, he pretty much *was* a walking, talking action hero.

"You gonna clue me in?" Riley pressed.

"I wouldn't lay odds on it."

Riley Blade was Lyle's oldest friend. They'd met in Iowa when they were kids, and despite a three-year age difference and all the other shit that should have kept them from clicking, they'd become fast friends. Lyle might not have any blood relatives left, but as far as he was concerned, Riley was his brother.

But even brothers didn't need to know everything.

Still, he'd told Riley part of the truth—he *was* distracted. But not by Jenny's memory. Not by flashbacks of that horrible night.

No, his thoughts were on a gorgeous blonde with a sharp tongue, soft lips, and wide, beguiling eyes that had seen at least some of his secrets.

For the first time in a long time, it wasn't Jenny on his mind. And Lyle wasn't sure if that meant he was healing—or if he was about to climb the ladder to a whole new level of guilt.

Riley still stood there, as if debating whether to press. Finally, he shrugged. "Suit yourself, man. But distraction or not, you better get your shit together sooner rather than later if you want me to be the one getting you camera ready on fight techniques and weapons."

"I know," Lyle assured him. "And I'm focused. Hell, I'm just glad you could squeeze a couple of weeks into your schedule for me." A former FBI SWAT team member, Riley was an expert in hand-to-hand and weapons-based fighting. Not to mention firearms and ordnance, though the latter two had no relevance to Lyle's prep work for *M. Sterious*.

Riley was also dead serious about fitness, and Lyle knew that every day he trained with Riley would make him that much more authentic in the role. Superpowers or not, Lyle had to project strength, confidence, and skill, all of which were qualities that Riley's methods of training honed. And since Riley had worked as a consultant on several films, including *The Price of Ransom,* Lyle knew that his friend understood how to train and prep an actor.

"You never told me where you're heading after we finish here," Lyle said. "Back to Texas?"

Riley had left law enforcement for the private sector several years ago, and he hadn't looked back. Now he was working as a consultant with McKay/Taggart, a Dallas-based a private security firm that Riley swore was top notch.

"I wish," Riley said. "No, the assignment's for a short term security detail. I meet the client in Illinois. Then we have two weeks traveling around the country in a tricked out bus."

"Rock star?"

"Politician."

"Sounds like hell," Lyle said.

"Better than LA." Riley took another long drink from his water bottle. "I swear, I must love you, man, to come back to this hell hole."

Lyle flashed the trademark smile that had made his face famous back in his sitcom days. "What can I say?

I'm lovable." He tossed the towel aside. "We still have another hour. Might as well let you get back to tormenting me."

They were just about to get back into it when the door opened and Evelyn marched in, accompanied by Lyle's assistant, Natasha, who looked efficient as always in black slacks, a white sleeveless shirt, and a red leather portfolio held tight in her hands.

"Sorry to interrupt, Lyle," Natasha said, without acknowledging Riley. "Evelyn needed to see you right away, and I thought it would be easier to drive her here than to explain where this shithole of a gym is hidden. Especially since it's a shithole without any decent WiFi or cell service."

"Not a problem," Lyle said at the same time Riley said, "Good to see you again, Natasha."

She only gave him a half nod, then stepped back as Evelyn moved in to fill the gap. She clutched the portfolio to her chest with one arm, her attention still locked on Lyle. If anything, it looked as if she was avoiding even turning in Riley's direction. And, Lyle noticed, she was twisting a strand of long dark hair around her finger. She'd worked for him for going on four years now, and he recognized the nervous habit.

All of which, he thought, was pretty damn interesting.

Whatever was—or wasn't—going on between his assistant and his friend, however, was pushed out of his mind when Evelyn took another step closer. "I'm going to assume you haven't seen this," she said as she thrust her phone at him. "But I damn sure hope you have an explanation."

He looked down at the image—and as he did, he felt his guts twist inside him. It was him, no doubt about that. And the picture showed him in a passionate lip lock with Sugar. At least, *he* knew it was Sugar. About all anyone else could tell was that she was blonde and a head shorter than him.

"I think it's pretty self-explanatory," he said, giving the phone back to Evelyn.

"Who is she? Someone you've been seeing? Someone you met in a bar?"

"Something like that."

Evelyn scoffed. "Dammit, Iowa. I may not be able to tell who that girl is, but I do know she's not Frannie. Who, by the way, has called me twice. Which is nine times fewer than the studio calls I've fielded—every department from publicity all the way up to Ronald himself," she added, referring to the head of the studio backing the film.

"You're lucky you chose today to work out, or you would have gotten an earful, too," she continued, looking more harried than he could ever remember seeing her. "Ignore all your voicemails, by the way. I'm fielding everything."

"It's that bad." He said it as a statement, not a question. All these years he'd been so damn careful. Then one woman slips in through the cracks in his armor, and suddenly everything he's worked for is on the verge of shattering.

"Hell yes, it's that bad."

"Hold on." Riley's attention had been on Natasha,

who'd moved back to lean against a wall as she tapped on her phone, presumably answering emails. Now, however, he stepped forward. "The studio actually gives a rat's ass about one photo of our boy and a blonde?"

"With the money they've invested in this picture, they care about what brand of toothpaste he uses. You're under a microscope, Iowa. You know that. Hell, we talked about it just a few hours before this photo was taken. So do you want to explain to me how this happened?"

"Not really, no. But I'll fix it."

"Too late. I already fixed it. Or, at least, I put a Band-Aid on it."

Lyle stiffened as trepidation shot through him. "What did you do?"

"What I told you to do yesterday. Congratulations, Iowa, I got you a girlfriend."

Lyle stared at her, uncomprehending. "Hang on. You got me a—how? Who?"

"The woman in the photo, obviously. I told Ronald she was your girlfriend, that you've been seeing her for months, but that she's not in the business and doesn't like the spotlight. And, most important, that you're not going to cheat on her just to make Frannie or the publicity department happy."

He opened his mouth, but no words came out.

"As for Frannie, so long as the relationship seems serious, she'll leave you alone. She screws around, but she's also got a romantic streak. As long as you bring this girl to Wyatt's opening tonight and look madly in love, I think we'll be back on track."

"Tonight?" He was already planning on attending the opening of his friend Wyatt Royce's highly anticipated photography show. But he'd intended on going stag.

She stared him down. "That photo's all over the internet. Right now, it looks like you're cheating on Frannie. Pull the girl into the spotlight—get a few shots of you and her and Frannie having drinks and a few laughs—and everything will be smoothed over."

She pointed a well-manicured finger at him. "Remember Ace, filming hasn't started yet. It's not too late for them to replace you."

"Great," Lyle said. "Just great." He pressed his fingers hard against his temples. "And if the girl doesn't want to join our merry band of players?"

"Then find another blonde," Evelyn said dryly. "At this point, I think any girl will do."

About that, Lyle thought, she was absolutely wrong.

He watched as Evelyn strode away. Nat hesitated, her eyes on Riley. A moment later, she blinked, as if realizing she was staring, and turned her attention to Lyle.

He glanced at her familiar red portfolio. "Anything we need to go over?"

She shook her head. "Nothing that can't wait until tomorrow. Do I, um, I mean, is there anything I need to do about tonight? About the girl?"

Despite his frustration, he almost laughed. Nat was the most efficient assistant he'd ever had, and he could hear in her voice how much it bothered her that she didn't have a clue how to solve this particular problem for her boss. "Don't worry about it," he said. "I've got it covered."

"Good. I'm glad to hear it. In that case, I'll see you in the morning. I'll see you at the opening tonight."

"Thanks."

Riley took a step forward. "Nat—"

Her brow rose as she cut him off curtly with, "Have a good evening, Mr. Blade." Then she turned and walked out without another word.

Lyle turned to Riley. "Something you want to share with the class?"

"Not really."

As far as Lyle knew, there'd never been anything between Riley and his assistant. But maybe that was the problem. "You know, if you're interested, you could ask her out."

Riley tilted his head with what looked like sudden interest. "She's not seeing someone else?"

"Not that I know of. You're free and clear. Ask her." He grinned. "What woman has ever said no to you?"

"Natasha has," Riley said flatly.

"Wow," Lyle said, genuinely surprised. "I didn't realize it was the apocalypse."

That got a smile from Riley. "Yeah, well, my female problems don't hold a candle to yours." He cocked his head toward the door. "Go on and give this girl a ring and get tonight squared away. Then we'll get in the rest of your workout."

"Love to. But I don't have her number."

Riley chuckled. "So Evelyn was right. Who is she? Someone you picked up at a bar?"

"No," Lyle said evenly, watching his friend's face. "I

didn't pick her up at a bar."

"Then where'd you—oh, fuck, Lyle. I thought you told me that was over."

Lyle raked his fingers through his hair. "It is. Mostly. But sometimes I need—"

He cut himself off with a shrug. "Sometimes, it's just hard."

"I get that it's fucked up, man. But you have to find another way to deal all the shit. Jenny's death. The pressure of living under a microscope. Whatever it is, you gotta find another way."

"I know." He paced the gym, back and forth between the bag and the chin up bar. "I know," he repeated. "But it's not just about me burning off steam. It's about the girls, too. You know that."

"The hell I do. Do you think I don't get it?" He caught Lyle on a pass and held him still, getting right in his face. "I was there, remember? I know what your life was like. What you and Jenny ran from."

Riley backed away, pain written on his face as he continued. "You think I don't have my own ghosts to deal with? But you can't screw call girls and think that's a substitute for a relationship.

Lyle winced, but Riley just kept on talking.

"And you can't toss money at them and think you're saving them. You're not. You can't save them any more than you could save Jenny."

"Is that your great wisdom talking?" Lyle snapped, because Riley's words were hitting just a little too close to home. "Because you're so damn good with relationships?"

"Watch yourself, buddy."

Lyle deflated, feeling like a total prick. "Sorry. Shit, you're right. I know you're right, and I don't much care for having reality thrown in my face, especially when it's a mirror for all my fuck ups."

"Lyle—"

"No." He held up a hand. "I don't need to be psychoanalyzed right now."

"Fair enough. What do you need?"

Lyle drew in a breath as he lifted a shoulder. "Haven't you been paying attention? Apparently, I need to get myself a date."

CHAPTER 7

B Y MID-AFTERNOON, I'VE finished my shift at Maudie's and have scoured Mrs. Donahue's kitchen from top to bottom. I feel sticky and gross and I'm pretty sure I smell like grease. And that's really not the way I want to smell during a business meeting.

Not that I expected to even be in a business meeting. I'd come to Greg's house anticipating an afternoon of bathroom renovation followed by two hours of eating popcorn and watching a movie.

But here I am, in all my greasy, stinky glory, sitting at Greg's kitchen table, my T-shirt splattered with paint and my manicure ruined, while Anderson Morton-Gray sits across from us, looking positively dapper in a dark blue suit.

I've met Anderson before, of course. His husband, Steve, is a working screenwriter and a friend of Greg's. So we've met over drinks a couple of times, and I know that he's a real estate broker who lives in West Hollywood. What I didn't know was that he'd asked Greg if he could come over today.

I also didn't know that his company owns the house Greg lives in.

And I definitely didn't know that he's seen pictures of the work I did on my own house, a lot of which was with Greg's help.

I know all of that now, though. And, in fact, my head is spinning a little bit as Anderson wraps up his proposal. "So that's the idea," he says, glancing at Greg and me in turn. "What do you think?"

What I think is that it sounds amazing, and tell him so. He has a client who's buying a rundown bungalow in Santa Monica as a flip. But the client's not interested in doing the work. As for Anderson, he's not only a real estate broker, but like Greg, he grew up in his family's construction business, so he's offered to act as the general contractor for the work. Work that Greg and I will do, with the exception of stuff like plumbing and electrical, which we'll subcontract out. Then, after the sale of the house, we all take an agreed-upon share of the profit.

"And having a buyer as part of the mix is just for this initial job," Anderson says. "Assuming it all goes well, in the future I'll buy the properties through my company. That means more profit for us, because we'll be splitting it with one less party."

I glance at Greg, who looks as giddy as I feel. Anderson has just put on the table the very business that Greg and I have been dreaming of—and with the added value of not having to come up with the money and the credit to buy that first property.

Greg's eyes widen just slightly, but I know him well enough to understand the question. I nod, knowing that he'll understand my answer.

"Yeah," he says to Anderson as I grin. "We're in."

"Excellent." He pushes back from the table. "Well, all right, then. I'll get some pictures and floor plans of the property for you, and arrange a walk through. The buyers close on Tuesday, so we can jump right in next week. He smiles, wide and charming. "I think this is going to be great. Fun and lucrative."

"Can't beat that," I say, and both men laugh.

We walk Anderson to the door. "Tell Steve I'll see him tomorrow morning at the group brunch," Greg says, referring to his screenwriting critique group.

"Will do," Anderson says as he shakes my hand. Then he's out the door, and Greg surprises me by grabbing my waist and swinging me around until I'm laughing and begging him to stop.

He puts me down, and we're both breathing hard.

Can't say I blame him. The opportunity is exciting, and I'm practically giddy.

Then he leans in, and in that moment I know that Joy was right about Greg wanting more. It feels like the world is shifting into slow motion, and I press my hand to his chest and lean back, whispering, "Greg, no. I'm sorry, but no."

I see the mortification color his face as he practically leaps backwards away from me. "Shit. *Fuck*. I overstepped. The moment. I didn't—"

"It's okay," I say. "It's just that I—"

I pause, because how do I tell a guy that there's no *zing* with him? Especially when I'm measuring that zing factor against a guy I'm never going to see again, and probably shouldn't even think about. A guy who's obviously broken, and yet who keeps popping into my thoughts at all the most inconvenient times.

A guy who's now set the standard for *zing*, and it's a bar that Greg just doesn't reach.

"You just want to be friends," he says, saving me from finishing.

"Is that so bad?"

For a moment, he simply looks at me, and I wish that I could read his thoughts. Then he shakes his head. "Honestly, it's probably better. I've got too many ex-girlfriends who aren't even in my life anymore. That would suck if it were you."

"It would," I agree as relief sweeps through me. "Especially since we're going to take the real estate world by storm."

"True, that." He tilts his head, as if trying to find an answer to some unknown question.

"What?"

"Is there someone else?"

"Greg…"

He holds up a hand, pushing away my words. "Not jealous, I swear. I'm just curious."

"No," I say, because it's true.

But what I don't tell him is that even though there's no man in my life, for the first time in forever, at least there's the idea of one.

"*TERMINATOR* OR *CASABLANCA*?" he asks, holding up two DVDs.

After Anderson left, we'd tried to get back into the groove of painting the bathroom, but we were both too distracted by the possibility of the business. And, to be honest, after Greg's mini-pass, I don't think either one of us wanted the close quarters of his tiny bathroom.

"These are my choices?" I ask, wondering if he's realizes he's picked two doomed romances. "Pass me your list."

Since he keeps his list of movies to study on his phone, he forwards it to me by text. I'm pulling my phone out of my purse to read it when the phone rings in my hand.

I glance at the screen, then almost drop it. *Marjorie.*

Even though I'd told Joy to tell Marjorie I was down for another job, I wasn't expecting to hear from her quite so soon. For a moment, I consider letting it go to voicemail, because maybe I was acting rashly.

Then I think about Lyle. Except, of course, she won't be calling about him. One girl, one time. That's how she said he rolled.

Which means she's calling about a new job. A job with a guy who's not Lyle. A job I don't really want to take even though I need the money. But at the same time, I do want to take it, because I need the money.

It's just that I'm not sure if I can do it, and—

"Aren't you going to answer?"

I yelp, startled, then press the button out of reflex. "Hello," I whisper, then hear Marjorie's relieved voice.

"Oh, good. I was afraid I wouldn't catch you, and this is extremely time sensitive. I have another job."

I lick my lips. "I figured."

"It's a little unorthodox," she says. "I'm quite surprised he called, actually."

"Oh," I say, confused. "Who?"

"Mr. Z," she says. "He wants to hire you again. For tonight, actually."

"Tonight?" I glance at Greg, manage a weak smile, and indicate the back door. Then I scurry outside and shut the door behind me.

"Five thousand dollars for the evening," she continues, as my knees go weak, and I half-fall, half-sit on the concrete step. "He needs you to be his date at an art opening."

Date.

"Oh." I frown, thinking about everything I know about Lyle, including the fact that Marjorie told me he never uses the same girl twice. "Why me?"

"Apparently you two were seen together. Hang on," she says, and a moment later my phone buzzes in my hand, signaling an incoming text message. I put the phone on speaker long enough to look at it, then immediately wince.

"Oh," I say. "Oh, dear."

"Mmmm," she says, the low sound surprisingly thoughtful. "I confess I was surprised. From what I've learned of him over the years, he's usually much more protective of his privacy."

"Yeah, I guess." My words are nonsense, of course. Instead, my mind is going a million miles an hour. *This is my fault.* I refused to sleep with him. I shifted the whole dynamic around. I broke the rules and messed him up. All because I was nervous and scared and didn't want to do exactly what he'd brought me to that hotel room to do. What he'd *paid* me to do.

And because I'd been scared and selfish, now he's at risk of his secret being blown.

"I'll do it," I say quickly. "But I want to do it for free."

"Excuse me?"

"Not you—I mean, whatever he pays you, he should pay. But I'll do the party tonight for free."

"I see," she says slowly, and I don't think she sees at all. "Are you certain?"

I consider the question. Because the truth is, I need the money. But he's already paid me ten thousand dollars plus a rather hefty tip. And for that, what did he get? Not sex, that's for sure. Just a couple of kisses, a girl he barely knows castigating him about his issues, and then a photograph of a private moment that's suddenly gone viral.

Not exactly a great return on his investment.

"I'm sure," I say.

"Very well," Marjorie agrees, though I can tell from her tone that she doesn't understand. "My team will be at your house in half an hour to do make-up, wardrobe, and to get you to the restaurant where you'll meet Mr. Tarpin."

"Not Mr. Z anymore?"

"I think we're past that," she says, and I can imagine her smile. "Good luck," she says before hanging up. "And have fun."

I think about Lyle. About that zing. And even though I'm not entirely sure how tonight is going to go, I can't deny that I'm looking forward to it.

And I'm really not sure if that's a good thing ... or a bad one.

CHAPTER 8

I T WAS FOUR forty-five when I told Greg I'd landed a last minute temp job and had to run.

It was five when I raced through my door, just minutes before Marjorie's team arrived, armed with cases full of make-up and curling irons, shiny rolling racks crammed with dresses, and gigantic suitcases stuffed with shoe boxes.

That's when the whirlwind began. And by five-forty, I'm showered, buffed, dressed, coiffed, painted, and bejeweled. I've never gotten dressed that fast in my entire life, and I feel about as flummoxed as Skittles looks, staring at me through narrowed eyes from his cat tree in the living room, which has become wardrobe central.

Now I'm standing before the trifold mirror the team set up in front of my fireplace, and I have to admit I look pretty good. The cocktail dress is flirty, yet classy, in black and white chiffon with a low-cut bodice that shows off the ruby necklace that's just low enough to draw the eye to my cleavage. And the red gemstone perfectly matches the ruby earrings and tennis-style bracelet.

The shoes are also a deep blood red. And, as an ironic plus, they're Christian Louboutins. Too bad I can't keep them and wear them to Blacklist someday when Nessie's working.

Of course, even though they look amazing, I have to wonder how well I'll survive the night. With so much waitressing on my resume, I tend to live in flats, not heels, and I'm pretty certain I'm going to be wincing by the time I hit Blacklist and can change back into flats for my ten o'clock shift.

As for my hair and make-up, I look like I could be on the cover of Vogue, with my cheekbones contoured, my eyes smoky, and my lips a soft red that complements the jewelry. I look pretty. Glamorous. And the way my blond hair frames my face in bouncing waves only accentuates the look.

"Amazing," Franko the hair guy says. "I'm a genius."

"Only because she's such a stunning canvas," Marianne, the make-up and wardrobe woman, retorts. To me, she says, "You're absolutely lovely."

She glances at her watch, then frowns. "All right, then. We'll be packed up and gone in ten minutes. Lionel will be here in fifteen to drive you downtown. You're expected at six-thirty for a drink and appetizers before the opening."

I nod, wondering if either of them know the nature of Marjorie's business. Probably not. For all these folks know, Marjorie is my manager, and I'm the next big thing, about to make my magnificent public debut.

I bite back a grin, amused by my thoughts, then move to stand by Skittles as Marianne and Franko zip around my living room, packing their things up with expert efficiency. Once they're gone, I have just enough time to grab a quick sip of water and give Skittles a goodbye scratch behind the ears before Lionel rings the bell at my gate.

"It's a pleasure to see you again, Miss Sugar," he says as I slide into the back of the car. Then he shuts the door, and I'm all alone. In theory, it's cool being driven around by a private driver, but with the privacy screen up, it's just me and my nerves and my thoughts about Lyle.

Because the truth is, I don't know what to expect. This is a public event, yes, but is he going to want to escape somewhere private? Will there be public displays of affection? Is he going to kiss me for the cameras?

I haven't got a clue. In fact, all I know for certain is that I want to see him again. And not just because he's gorgeous and kissed me with such intensity it made my toes curl. It's more than that. It's the spark of humor that laced our conversation. And it's the pain I saw hiding behind his eyes, a pain that still calls to me. That for some reason I want to try to soothe.

And all of that is well and good, but I need to re-member that it's not the reason I'm in this car. I'm here because Lyle needs a date with the woman he was caught kissing. Because he's putting on a show for the public.

It's not a date; it's a job.

And as Lionel pulls up in front of Cut 360, a high-end restaurant in downtown Los Angeles, I remind myself to keep that fact very firmly in mind.

But every one of my sternly issued edicts dissolve in a puddle of goo the moment I step into the restaurant.

Because that's when I see him. He's standing at the reception desk checking his phone, but it's as if he feels my eyes on him, because he looks up, then slips his phone into his pocket. He's wearing a dark gray suit with a white shirt and a red tie that matches my jewelry. He has just a hint of five-o'clock shadow on his jaw, and his hair is tousled—but whether from the wind or purposefully styled that way, I don't know.

He has an edgy, devil-may-care attitude, and as I stand there soaking him in, I completely understand why this man has been on the cover of every magazine imaginable.

For a moment, he just looks at me. Then he smiles, slow and sexy, and that's when I start to feel it. A low sizzle in the pit of my stomach. And when he takes a step toward me—when he takes my hand and whispers, "Laine," that's when I feel that *zing* all over my body, a sweet, shocking tingle, as if I've been caught in a lightning storm.

"How do you know my—"

"Marjorie told me." He tilts my chin up. "It's a lovely name," he murmurs, then brushes his lips over mine. "But I think I'm still partial to Sugar."

He takes my hand, then signals to the hostess, who leads us to a secluded booth in the bar area. Several heads turn as we pass, the attention making me uncomfortable. Lyle, however, doesn't even seem to notice.

"I'm sure they'll have a bar and appetizers at the opening," he says once we're seated, "but I wanted the chance to talk before we jumped into the deep end of the pool."

"That's good," I say. "Because from what Marjorie said, we're supposed to act like we've been dating. And right now, all I know about you is what I've learned from Google."

"You researched me?" He looks amused.

"Well, I didn't pull a credit report, if that's what you mean. But I poked around."

"Really." His mouth curves into a frown. "And what did you find out?"

I shrug. "Not much," I admit, then pause as a waitress comes to take our order. I decide on wine, figuring I can have one or two glasses early in the evening and still be fine for my shift at Blacklist later. And since I'm starving, I also order cheese fries, even though this really isn't a cheese fries sort of restaurant.

From Lyle's smile, I'm pretty sure he's thinking the same thing. "I figure there will be tuna carpaccio and barbecued shrimp appetizers at the opening," I tell him. "Besides, I always go for greasy food when I'm nervous."

He nods at the waitress, dismissing her, then reaches across the table to take my hand. "Are you nervous?"

"On a scale of one to ten? I'd say I'm at a thirteen."

"Because of me or the situation?"

"Both," I admit.

His thumb is gently stroking my hand, and it's all I can do not to pull it back and gain some space—both physically and in my head. Because right now, that's about all I can focus on. That touch. That connection. And the fact that I have no idea if touching me is part of the charade, or if it's something he just wants to do.

After a moment, he lets go, then presses both of his palms to the table, as if he's fighting some irresistible urge. "Will you share?" he asks, and for a second, I have no idea what he's talking about.

"What? You mean the cheese fries? Why?" I quip. "Are you nervous, too?"

"Maybe I am."

"Oh," I say. And I'm not sure if he's teasing me or not.

"You still haven't told me what you learned during your research quest."

I shrug. "Not much. You're not exactly an open book."

"I value my privacy."

"It shows. I learned that you moved here with your parents at sixteen, and that they've now retired and live overseas somewhere. I know you were discovered at seventeen—you were working at some fast food place and an agent saw you. Your first role had one line in some teen-centric series that lasted for about four episodes. But you got commercials and then a few more small parts."

"So far, that sounds like me."

"That's about all of you there is, though. Beyond that, I know that your first big deal job was that sitcom with Rip Carrington. And I know you don't date very much, but that the rumor is that you're seeing Francesca Muratti." I shrug. "Other than that, I know your first major film role was *The Price of Ransom*, and that it led to this superhero role, and that you're working out hard to get in shape." I flash a quick smile. "Nice job, by the way."

He laughs, and I really like the sound of it. "Thanks. Sounds like you learned a lot."

"Hardly. It's all pretty thin. Especially when you consider I can find out more than that on the Internet about my eighty-year-old, non-celebrity neighbor."

"Like I said, I value my privacy."

I clear my throat, grateful when the waitress returns with our drinks. "Right," I say, then take a sip of wine. "The thing is, a girlfriend would know more. So, I was thinking that speed dating ought to do the trick."

"Speed dating?"

"Yeah, you know. You get matched up and have about fifteen seconds to ask a question. Then you move on to the next person."

He glances around the bar. "And if I'd rather just stay with you?"

I laugh, but something about the way he says that makes me feel warm and fuzzy inside. "For our purposes, I'm talking the fast questions. Not the changing partners. Although, that could be my first question."

Whatever humor I'd seen in his face disappears, replaced by a completely bland expression. "Go ahead."

"It's just that Marjorie said you don't see the same girl twice." I pause to grab one of the cheese fries from the basket the waitress just slid onto our table.

"Is that a question?"

"No, I'm just wondering why—I mean, why ask me twice?"

His eyes widen, and in this dim light, his blue eyes seem as unfathomable as the ocean. "I thought you knew. There was a picture, and—"

"I saw the picture. That could have been any blonde."

He nods slowly. "True. But maybe the photographer has another picture. One with your face. I show up with some other blonde, and instead of forestalling a media frenzy, I start one."

"That makes sense," I admit. "I thought maybe you just wanted see me again." I say the last lightly, but the deep, dark truth is that I actually mean it.

He takes a sip of his martini, his expression completely bland. "That might have been part of it."

I gape at him, surprised.

"My turn?"

I blink. "What?"

"Speed dating. Is it my turn now?"

"Oh. Yeah. Shoot."

"You never answered my question from yesterday. What do you need the money for?"

"My house," I admit. "I'm having a slight case of foreclosure."

"What happened?"

I shake my head. "Sorry. Your fifteen seconds are up. My turn."

He nods, and I continue. "Tell me about us. How long have we been dating? How'd we meet? What do I say if someone asks?"

"Three months," he says. "And, let's see. We met—"

"—in the ice cream aisle at Ralphs," I say. "You were cheating on your training diet. And I was shaking off the melancholy of an evening spent watching tear-jerkers."

"And there was only one gallon of cookie dough left, which happens to be my favorite."

I nod. "I remember. You looked so shocked when I invited you over to share it with me. And I was even more shocked when you agreed to watch *Love, Actually,* while we ate it."

"Well, you were a good sport. After the sappy romance, we watched the first Blue Zenith movie."

"But only because you were showing off for me," I say. "I'd recognized you from *The Price of Ransom,* but I didn't know a thing about this superhero franchise you've signed on for."

"Is that true?" he asks. "Have you seen *Ransom?*"

I nod. "I actually sort of know one of the screenwriters. Steve Morton-Gray."

"He's a good guy," Lyle says. "He and Jane did a stellar job on the script."

"Everything I read said it was your big break."

"Honestly, *Two Steps Back*, was really the turning point for me. That sitcom ran for five years. Probably could have run a few more."

"But there was that thing with your co-star," I say, remembering something else I'd read. "Rip Something-or-other."

He chuckles. "You don't follow Hollywood too closely, do you?"

"Who has the time?"

"You'd be surprised," he says drolly. "And you're right. What happened between Rip and me was the final nail in the show's coffin."

"What happened?"

He glances at his watch. "We should go," he says. And even though he's right about the time, I can't help but think that he's also avoiding my question.

I don't press, though. After all, we're not really dating. I don't need to know everything. But as I slide out of the booth, I can't help but smile, because I'd enjoyed playing the game with him. He's easy to talk to, and the whole conversation felt comfortable. Familiar. All the way down to the way we finished each other's sentences.

"Thanks for playing," I say. "At least now I feel like I can wing it."

"As long as you stick close to me, it should be easy. And Sugar," he adds with a definite undertone of heat, "I do want you to stay very, very close."

"Right," I whisper. "I will."

He leaves enough cash on the table for the bill and a pretty hefty tip, then slides out of the booth. He holds out his hand to me, then continues to hold it as we walk to the valet stand.

"A Volvo," I say, when the familiar boxy model pulls up, and he opens the passenger door for me. "Nice, but I confess I was expecting something in the two-seater, built-for-speed category."

"Were you? Why's that?"

I have a moment to think about my answer as he circles the car, then enters, and I blush a little when I tell him the truth. "Fast and reckless?" I say, the words coming out as a question.

He pauses, his hand on the gear shift as he looks at me. When he speaks, his words are measured. "Considering how we met, that's fair. But that's not me. It's—"

He breaks off, shaking his head, and once again I have to wonder what kind of wall he's built around himself, and what kind of demon he's trying to keep out.

"At any rate," he continues. "As far as cars go, I'm all about safety."

"Me, too," I say. "But I don't own a Volvo. I just hardly ever drive."

He glances at me. "Why?"

I swallow. I really didn't mean to open that door, but now that it's open, I feel like I have to walk through it. "My mom and brother were killed by a drunk driver five years ago."

I hear him draw in a breath. And then, very softly, he says, "I guess you do understand." He turns his head to meet my eyes. "I'm sorry for your loss." His voice is level. Overly polite. Like a man trying very hard to keep his emotions in check.

It's clear I struck a nerve—and one much more exposed and tender than my own. I want to ask, but I can tell he doesn't want to talk about it. And it's not my place to press. After all, I'm not really his girlfriend, and just because I shared my story, he's not obligated to share his.

At the end of the day, it's none of my business, no matter how much I'd like to help.

So I just sit quietly and clutch my purse in my lap and wish that I hadn't even commented on the car.

After a moment, he clears his throat. "The center's just up the hill, two blocks from Stark Tower," he says, referring to the massive building that dominates the downtown skyline. "We could have walked, but considering your shoes…"

"Thanks." I glance at my feet. "Not my usual style, but it's fun to play dress up. I guess I should thank you for that."

He reaches over and traces his finger over the thin strap of the dress. "Dressing up suits you," he says. "What's your typical look?"

"I'm a jeans and T-shirt girl all the way. Maybe a tank top. And yoga pants are an acceptable alternative. Your basic sundress just to mix things up a bit." I run my hands over the outfit. "Honestly, for what this dress cost, I could fill my entire closet. My favorite shopping destination is Goodwill."

He chuckles. "The one on La Brea was always my favorite. But I found some good stuff at the one on Beverly, too."

I shift in my seat. "And the one on Vine. You shop—"

"My mother was big on thrift shopping," he says, not looking at me. "It was like a family tradition."

I nod, wondering about his pre-Hollywood days. Was his mom just frugal, or had his family struggled before he started working?

I'm about to ask when he abruptly changes the subject. "Marjorie told me you could only stay until nine."

I nod. "I have to cover a shift at Blacklist tonight." I'd forgotten to mention that in the original conversation, but I'd texted her when it struck me just how tight my schedule was going to be today. "I have to be there by ten." I indicate my outfit. "And not in these shoes. Or this dress."

"I'll get you there on time," he promises. "She also told me you're planning to work tonight for free."

"Um, right." I twist the strap of my purse, uncomfortable with the sudden reminder that nothing about this evening is real.

"Unacceptable," he says, and my nervousness vanishes, replaced by irritation.

"Excuse me? I think that's my decision."

"No," he says. "It's not."

"Dammit, Lyle, I—"

"I'm paying you for your time. This isn't a date," he says, his sharp words making me cringe. Because, damn me, I do keep sliding in that direction. "It's a job. For that matter, it's an acting job. You're going to be working this party, Sugar. And you deserve to get paid."

"Maybe. But I didn't deserve to get paid last night. I mean, you didn't get—what you wanted," I finish lamely.

He stops at a red light, then turns to look at me. Very slowly, his gaze skims over me, and my skin heats in the wake of his inspection, as if it were a physical touch. Finally, he settles on my eyes, then reaches out and very gently brushes my lower lip with the pad of his thumb.

"Didn't I?" he asks, as my heart pounds against my ribs, and my mouth goes completely dry.

I open my mouth to speak, but I can't seem to form words.

"I'm serious, Sugar. Tonight you're my girlfriend. You're playing a role. An important one. And I'm going to pay you for it. Understand?"

I nod, my emotions all in a tangle. "Call me Laine in public," I manage to say, my voice little more than a whisper.

He nods, and I settle back in my seat as the light changes, my breath as shaky as my nerves.

He's right. Tonight, I'm an actor. Just like Lyle.

And considering the way I feel right now, I don't think the job's going to be hard to pull off at all.

CHAPTER 9

I'VE NEVER BEEN to an opening at the Stark Center for the Visual Arts, but I've wandered through the permanent exhibits a couple of times. "I like the photographs," I tell Lyle as we wait in line for the Center's valet to take his car, "but the pop art exhibit is my favorite. I love the bold colors and that *zap* and *ka-pow* vibe."

"Lichtenstein?" he asks.

"You like his work?" Pop art icon Roy Lichtenstein's comic-inspired canvases are some of my favorites.

Lyle shrugs. "I lean more toward black and white photography. A friend of mine was obsessed with Lichtenstein, though." I hear the melancholy in his voice and am about to ask him about it when he forces a smile. "Sometimes I think Jenny just wanted to live in a comic book world."

"And you don't?"

He shakes his head. "It's easy to think the world is painted in primary colors when you're young. I guess I grew up and realized there's a lot of gray, too."

"And she never got that?"

His expression closes off so fast, it's as if a shadow

has obscured his features. "No," he says, the word clipped. "She never did."

I frown, certain I've touched a nerve. "I didn't mean—"

But a valet opens my door, cutting off my words. And by the time Lyle gets the ticket and comes around the car to join me, the shadow has disappeared, replaced by a genuine, albeit small, smile. "I didn't mean to get melancholy on you."

"That's okay," I say as he takes my hand and we start walking. "Are you all right?"

"I'll be fine. She was a good friend, and she died."

"I'm so sorry." I pause on the first step leading up to the Center, forcing him to stop behind me. Around us, dozens of people in cocktail attire glide up the twelve concrete stairs toward the angular, modern-style building. "Did she die recently?"

He meets my eyes. "Thirteen years ago yesterday," he says. And then he starts walking again.

I fall in step beside him, and as we make our way up the last few steps, that single word flashes like neon in my mind. *Yesterday.*

I think of the man I met in the hotel last night. A man whose pain was so palpable it hurt my heart. "I'm sorry," I say again, the words seeming small and useless.

"It's okay. It was a long time ago."

Except it's obviously not okay, and I can't help but wonder what happened to her that has haunted him for thirteen long years.

A reflecting pool dominates the plaza, and we walk past it toward the entrance. Now I can see reporters buzzing around. And camera flashes. And microphones.

And, oh God, there's even a red carpet.

"Showtime," Lyle says, and I jerk my head up to look at him, then wish I hadn't moved quite so fast. Because now I'm afraid that I might throw-up the swarm of butterflies that are duking it out in my stomach.

I point dully at the crowd. "I didn't realize—I mean, this is all very—"

"Shhh," he whispers. Then he leans in and brushes a soft kiss over my lips. "You're going to be fine."

He pulls back, his hands on both my shoulders as he studies my face. "Okay?"

I nod, managing a wobbly smile. "Yeah," I say, fighting the urge to lift my hand and brush my finger over my lips where he kissed me. "I just didn't expect all this, well, *stuff*. I've never done a red carpet thing before."

For a second, he looks abashed. "I didn't think. I should have warned you. After so many years, I've gotten used to the hoopla."

"It's a lot of hoopla," I agree.

"I promise it's painless. We'll walk down the red carpet, pause at the step-and-repeat for a photo, and then head on inside."

"No chatting with reporters?"

He shakes his head as we start walking again. "Not today. They'll see you with me and they can draw their own conclusions. Usually, I chat them up so that I can get in a pitch for the Stark Children's Foundation, but considering the erotic nature of this exhibit, we decided that it really wasn't the place."

"Guess that makes sense," I say. I've heard about the SCF, of course. It's a major charity in the LA area that provides help to abused and neglected kids. I also know that Lyle is the current celebrity sponsor. It's hard to miss, since his picture is on donation posters all over town.

"Ready?" he asks, and I realize that the line has gotten shorter as we've talked, and now we're next in line for the picture.

The step-and-repeat is basically an area off to the side with a giant publicity poster behind it. This one for the Stark Center for the Visual Arts. Lyle puts an arm around my shoulder, and I lean in, feeling more comfortable with him than I probably should.

We smile, the photographer snaps, and then we move on.

Lyle was right. Easy-peasy.

At least until we step through the glass doors into the Center's main exhibit space. It's like walking into the annual meeting of the Rich, Powerful, and Well-Dressed Club.

"You okay?"

"What?" I look up at Lyle's face, and see him peering at me with concern. "Why?"

He glances meaningfully at our joined hands, and I realize I'm holding on so tight my knuckles are white. "Oh. Right." I let go, then resist the urge to dry my palms on my skirt.

"This is a little bit out of my comfort zone," I admit. "I mean, the fanciest place I've ever eaten is a place we ate half an hour ago."

This time when he looks at me, I see understanding on his face. "It'll be okay," he promises, then takes my hand again, this time more gently. "I've got your back."

"You didn't grow up attending parties like this either," I say, as he leads me further into the room. It's large and circular, with a few hallways leading off from it. I know from experience that those halls lead to the permanent exhibit areas. Tonight, they're roped off. "Are you comfortable with it now?"

I expect him to say yes. To tell me how easy it is to survive with money and privilege. Instead, he says nothing.

I clear my throat, feeling like a dolt for asking what was obviously a wrong question, and I glance around the room, trying to look like I'm fascinated by the new set-up so that I can hide my embarrassment.

Usually, this room is a large, circular space with four other rooms opening off of it as if at fifteen-minute intervals on a clockface. Today, however, only three of those openings are visible, and each of those three are blocked by velvet ropes that prevent anyone from going into the other exhibit spaces.

The twelve o'clock opening is blocked by a makeshift walkway that comes off that point and extends to the center of the room, like a line partially bisecting a circle in geometry class. The corridor is formed by temporarily erected walls, and some of the show's photographs are displayed on the exterior sides of those walls.

I don't know what's on the inside of the corridor, as the entrance to the walkway—which is right at the center point of the gallery—is currently blocked by a velvet rope, and from what I can see there are no lights inside the corridor itself. I assume that part of the show is in there, and I can't help but wonder what we'll eventually see.

When Lyle clears his throat, I look up at him. I've completely given up on him answering my question, so I'm surprised when he finally says, "Not comfortable," his voice low and steady. "It's familiar now, but I don't know if it will ever be comfortable."

I face him, both surprised and pleased that he's not only answered me, but is also obviously telling me the truth instead of just tossing me a platitude.

"Why not?" I ask as we stroll along the exterior walls and look at the sensual, evocative photographs. The kind that make me want to blush and look away.

The kind that make me think about the man whose hand I'm holding.

"I don't know," he says. "And I didn't mean to bring down the evening. This is supposed to be us out together, having a good time on a date, remember?"

"I know," I say. "But—" I cut myself off, shaking my head.

"What?"

"No. You're right." And he is. This isn't a night of getting to know each other. I'm not going to go home after this and wonder if he's going to call. We came here so that I could be seen on his arm. And once I've been seen enough, that'll be the end of the story.

I know all of that. But clearly, I'm a raging idiot, because the next thing out of my mouth is, "It's just that I'd like to get to know you better."

The words hang between us, all bright and shiny and inappropriate, and I stand there wishing I had a magic wand that I could wave to make them disappear.

I'm sure he's going to ignore the question and keep walking, which is fine by me, since I just want to get past this moment so that I can quietly extract my foot from my mouth.

Once again, though, he surprises me. "It's a very surface life here," he says. "Well, not here in the city. Here in this business. Any business, really, where there's fame and money involved."

"I get that," I say. "It must always feel like people want a piece of you."

He nods. "That's true. And that makes it a lonely profession. Which is fine if you're living your dream— there are always sacrifices. But that doesn't mean that it isn't hard sometimes."

"Is that why—you know. Me. The other girls? Why you do what you do?"

We're standing in front of a line of photographs. Sensual images of women in dim lighting and very little clothing. In the photo right in front of us, the woman's hands are above her head, wrists bound as she stands naked, lit from the side. She's trapped. On display. And yet she's looking out of the canvas with pride and not the least bit of shame.

It's shocking. Disturbing.

And, as I stand with Lyle by my side, a little bit arousing.

Now he moves behind me, then puts his hands on my shoulders, also looking toward that provocative image. I'm hyper aware of his presence. The pressure of his hands. The heat of his body. He's standing close enough that his trousers brush my dress, and with every tiny bit of motion, my pulse flutters in response.

"That's part of it," he says, and I have to struggle to remember my question. "The desire to be with a woman who has no hidden agenda. No secret ploy to use me to try to land a part or get a script read."

"Part of it?"

"I told you," he whispers, leaning in so that his lips brush the back of my ear as he speaks. "It's a pressure release. A controlled explosion."

"Controlled," I repeat.

"Usually," he whispers as his hands glide down my bare arms. "But sometimes it gets completely out of control. Sometimes," he says, "I want it to."

CHAPTER 10

I WANT IT TO.

That's what he said, of course.

But what I heard was *I want you.*

And, damn me, I want him, too.

I know I should look away, but I keep my eyes on the photos, their sensuality only intensified by the feel of the man behind me. And when he eases me back to lean against him, I sigh with pleasure—and then jerk guiltily away the moment Cass calls out, "Laine! I had no idea you were going to be here!"

I raise a hand and wave, and as she hurries toward us, Lyle bends and whispers in my ear. "You don't have to jump away from me, Sugar. You're my girl, remember?"

"Right." I close my eyes, wishing I could will myself not to blush. Because now I feel even more like an idiot. I mean, I was genuinely aroused by his touch—but Lyle's words are a rather dispiriting reminder that for him, tonight is nothing more than another acting job.

Hell.

"You should have told me you were coming," Cass says as she reaches me, then shifts her attention to the man behind me.

"It was a last-minute decision," I say at the same time as Cass says, "Hey, Lyle."

She frowns a little as she looks from Lyle to me and then back to him again, and I wonder if she saw the way I'd been leaning against him, or if our positions had been blocked by the crowd.

Doesn't really matter, though, because even as I'm thinking those thoughts, Lyle puts his hands back on my shoulders.

"So are you two—?"

"Dating?" Lyle says. "Yes."

His fingers tighten on my shoulder. "For about three months now," I blurt.

"Really. Huh. Does Joy know?"

"Um, well, yeah." I swear I want the floor to swallow me whole, and I'm having to force myself not to turn around so that I can see Lyle's face.

"Lyle and I have been keeping it low key," I continue. "I'm not big on all this, um, hoopla. This is the first event he's taken me to."

Cass laughs. "Well, the hoopla tonight is awesome. I should know—Siobhan's been working her ass off. So you picked a good event to bring her to," she tells Lyle. Then she shakes her head, as if baffled. "Honestly, I was beginning to think you only went stag."

"Just waiting for the right woman," he says, then brushes a kiss on my head.

"Well, I'm on a quest to find Siobhan, but Laine, it's great to see you. And you," she adds to Lyle, "don't be a stranger."

She gives us both a little wave, then disappears into the crowd.

I deflate so thoroughly that Lyle has to hook an arm around me to hold me up.

"How do you know Cass?" he asks.

"My best friend Joy works for her." I squint at him. "You probably know Joy. She's the one who introduced me to Marjorie."

"Ah," he says. "And I'm guessing Cass knows none of that."

"Not a bit," I say. "Honestly, I can't believe she bought our little performance just now."

"Why wouldn't she?"

"Because I'm a terrible liar?"

He laughs, guiding me away from the wall and into the crowd. "That's not a bad quality, you know."

"Hey, you're the one who needs this to be believable. I'm just trying to do the job right."

"Method acting."

I pause to glance up at him. "Um?"

He flashes that sexy smile I've seen on so many magazines, only this time, it's meant only for me. "I mean you have to get into the role. It's not only on the surface like playing pretend, it's *being* the role. Truly being my girlfriend."

"But—"

"Here," he says, sliding an arm around my waist as he pulls me closer. And then, before I have time to breathe or think or do anything at all, his body is pressed against mine, and his fingers are twined in my hair. But it's his mouth that is truly making my head spin. The way his lips close over mine, demanding and yet gentle. The way his tongue teases, then takes advantage when I moan with pleasure, sweeping inside my mouth, taking the kiss deeper. Hotter.

I melt against him, letting myself get lost in the pleasure of this moment. Letting everything else fall away, so that I'm nothing more than the sensation of his mouth claiming mine, of his hands clinging to me, of the sparks that rip through my body, firing a deep, hot need that we can't do anything about because we're standing here in the middle of a gallery, and—

With a gasp, I pull away, completely embarrassed and certain that my blush is the brightest thing in the room right now.

Lyle, however, looks perfectly calm. He holds my gaze for a second, then reaches for me, and I shiver from the contact when he sweeps a lock of hair off my face. "You see?" he murmurs. "Method acting. Can you do that?"

I swallow and nod. And all I can think as we continue to walk is that if that's how deep I have to get into this role, I may not survive the night.

We fall in step with the rest of the crowd, moving slowly along the walls of the exhibit, taking in the stunning images, including one of Cass that is so well executed it's impossible to decide if it's dangerously edgy or stunningly beautiful.

When we've seen every erotic image in the main gallery—when I can't deny that my body is tingling from more than just Lyle's kiss—Lyle leads me toward the center of the room where a cluster of cocktail height tables form a small gathering area.

"Wine?" he asks, then snags two glasses from a passing waiter before I can reply. I take it gratefully and sip it as we continue toward a nearby table.

He waves at several people as we walk, all of whom seem genuinely pleased to see him. "That's Bird," he says about one. "He's a director. And the guy beside him is Griffin Blaize," he adds, pointing to an extremely attractive guy whose face is marred on one side with some vicious scars.

"He's an amazing actor. Voice right now, but I wish he'd go ahead and do screen." He shrugs. "I've tried to convince him, but I don't think he'll ever make the jump. Too self-conscious."

We continue like that for a few minutes, him pointing and saying, "That's Anika Segal, one of Hollywood's legends." And, "That's Jackson Steele, the architect. I've gotten to know him pretty well over the last few years. Great guy."

And on and on and on, until I feel like my escort is a walking *Who's Who* of the rich and famous.

When we finally reach the cocktail table, I notice a small placard on it that tells a bit about the show and the artist. "The Stark Center for the Visual Arts presents W. Royce's stunning new show, *A Woman In Mind*," I read. "Featuring a provocative view of sensuality—"

I glance up at Lyle. "Well, *that's* for sure," I say, then continue reading, "the show combines photographic elements with a compelling live performance that will begin at eight. Guests are asked to follow docent instructions when the introductory music begins."

I put the card down and return my attention to Lyle. "I didn't realize part of the show was live. The whole thing is pretty amazing."

"Wyatt's seriously talented."

"You know him?" I've picked up the card again and am tracing the edge, just to give me something to do with my hands other than holding and sipping my wine. Best not to get too tipsy tonight, I think.

"He's a good friend," Lyle says, at the same time I see the photograph on the back of the placard and squeal, "Oh! I know this guy."

"You know Wyatt?"

"Well, sort of. Not personally, but I've seen him around. He comes into Blacklist sometimes."

"Makes sense. He lives in Venice Beach, so that would be his local bar."

"Me, too," I say. "I've probably seen him other places, as well." I glance around. "I really am impressed by the show. Will I get to meet him?"

Lyle skims the room. "I don't see—wait." He lifts a hand to someone behind me, then grins. "Yeah, I think you will."

A few moments later, an attractive man with golden brown hair and a charming smile joins us. He's accompanied by a striking woman who makes her simple wrap dress look like the most haute of couture. "Wyatt, Kelsey, this is my girlfriend, Laine."

"It's a pleasure to meet you," I say, as Kelsey's smile widens and she gives me an enthusiastic hug. Wyatt's reaction is less vibrant. He's polite and pleasant and tells me how glad he is that I've come. But I see the way his eyes cut to Lyle, and I note how they widen just a little, as if in surprise or disbelief.

I glance at Lyle, who doesn't seem bothered, and decide not to worry about it. All I can do is play the role. If Lyle's friends don't get on the girlfriend train, there's nothing I can do about it.

"The show is amazing," I say. "The images—they're all incredible."

"I appreciate that," he says. "We move on to what I call Act Two in just a few minutes. If you like what you've seen so far I think—hope—that you'll be blow away by what comes next."

"I think I will." I tap the placard. "I'm intrigued by the idea of a live part."

"Intrigued is good," Kelsey says. "I'm nervous."

It takes me a minute, and then I understand. "You're the one performing?"

She nods. "I assumed you knew."

"The original plan was for Kelsey to be anonymous," Lyle tells me. "There was a social media leak."

"That happens," Wyatt says, his eyes on Lyle. "You can't control what gets out there."

Lyle says nothing, and I glance at Kelsey, who's frowning slightly, as if she's working out a puzzle. I have a feeling that puzzle is me.

Before I can think of what, if anything, I should say, Wyatt glances at his watch. "Sorry, we need to go do a quick system check. Laine, it's great to meet you." He points to Lyle. "I'll see you Wednesday, right? At Noah's send-off?"

"Seven o'clock. I'm there," he promises, then we finish up the goodbyes, and they hurry away, pausing now and then as they cross the room to speak to other guests.

"Send off?" I ask.

"A friend of ours is moving to Austin."

I nod, thinking, and he tilts his head, his expression amused.

"Okay," he says. "Tell me."

"There's nothing to tell."

"Bullshit."

"You don't know me well enough to read my thoughts."

He reaches across the table and takes my hand. "Nonsense," he says, then lifts my hand to kiss my fingertips. "I'm your boyfriend. I know you better than anyone."

I shiver, more undone by his words than I should be. But I'm starting to realize that I like the way it feels to have a boyfriend. Someone by my side who has my back.

Not Lyle, of course, because I'm not a fool and I know this is just pretend, no matter how much zing there might be between us. But being with him has shined a spotlight through a gaping hole in my life. A hole I'd been carefully ignoring because I have so much else going on.

But now…

Well, now I'm afraid I'm not going to be able to ignore it anymore.

"Laine," he presses. "Tell me."

I sigh. "Nosy much? Fine," I add before he can push again. "I was just thinking how unexpected you are."

His brow furrows. "How so?"

"I guess I'd assumed you were a loner. But here you are, surrounded by friends. And it's just, I don't know…" I trail off with a shrug.

"Because of the girls," he says. "Because I pay for sex, you assumed I was a guy who just lived in his own little world."

I bite back a wince. "Well, yeah. Sorry."

"It's okay. I get it." He takes a sip of wine. "Relationships are hard in this business. And I'm at a point where my career could explode. So I don't … let's just say I'm focusing on work, not dating. Does that make sense?"

"Sure. Like you said, with what you do, it would be extra hard to get close to someone. You never know if they want you for your connections."

"Exactly," he says, and I nod as if I completely understand.

Except I don't.

Oh, I believe that what he says is part of it. But I remember only too well his words that first night. His pressure cooker approach to sex. The realization that he wasn't looking for a companion, but a release.

And maybe that's all it was. But I can't help but think there's more. Because friendships take work, too, and Lyle doesn't seem to be lacking there.

My guess is that it's not about work, but about himself. About denial or punishment or something else. Something I can't see yet because I don't know him well enough.

And even though it's really none of my business, I want to understand. More than that, I want to help.

CHAPTER 11

"I LOST YOU."

I blink, then look up, Lyle's voice pushing through the storm of thoughts in my head.

"Sorry," I say, hitting a mental rewind button. "I'm right here. I was just thinking."

"You do that a lot," he says, his blue eyes teasing. "Should I worry?"

I laugh. "No. I was only wondering why exactly you're playing this game." That's not what I was thinking, of course. But it's still true. "I mean, your friends obviously know you're not big on the dating. So why this sudden performance? Why not just say that you met a woman in a bar and some fan with a camera phone pushed it out on social media. And then that's the end of that?"

He props his chin on his hand and peers at me with just enough intensity that I shift uncomfortably on my stool. "You see a lot," he says.

I shrug. "I'm a waitress. Which pretty much means I deliver food and watch people."

"Can't argue with that," he says. "And it's a good question. There's the reason."

I look in the direction he's pointing and see Francesca Muratti, one of the most famous women in Hollywood, talking to a man I don't recognize. She's tall and absolutely stunning with thick auburn hair and a regal demeanor. And I have absolutely no idea what Lyle means when he says she's the reason.

"Short version?" Lyle says when I ask him. "Frannie has a thing about dating her co-stars, but I'm not inclined to date Frannie, and that frustrates her. A frustrated mega-star isn't good for either the production or my continued employment with the picture."

"Seriously? Your business is crazy."

He nods. "Can't argue with that. But she's also got scruples, and she's hands-off any co-star who's otherwise involved. Involved seriously, at least. Which," he adds, taking my hand again, "we most definitely are."

"Absolutely," I agree. "She makes a move on you, and the bitch goes down."

He'd been about to take another sip of wine, but instead bursts out laughing. "You've definitely got the role down," he says, and I grin, both pleased and amused.

My grin fades, however, when Lyle mutters, "Oh, hell."

I'd turned away from Frannie, but now I shift back and see that the guy she'd been talking to has left, only to be replaced by a short man with a round build and wiry hair. Except for the fact that there's something a little too smarmy about his expression, I'd say he had a Teddy bear quality. Instead, I'm thinking he looks more like the evil marshmallow man at the end of the original *Ghostbusters*.

"Trouble?" I say, as both the marshmallow and Francesca turn toward me and Lyle.

"You can pretty much bet the ranch. That's my former co-star, Rip Carrington. Let's just say we aren't the close buddies that we were in the show."

He looks away, but I keep watching as Rip continues talking to Francesca, who in turn looks our way. After a moment, Rip leaves, and Francesca strides toward us.

"Incoming," I say, just seconds before she arrives.

"Hello, lover," she says, bending down to kiss his cheek. She turns to me. "Only on-screen, of course. From what I hear, that's your real life role. I'm Francesca Muratti, by the way," she adds, extending her hand to me. "Call me Frannie."

"Sugar Laine."

"What a charming name," she says.

"Where'd you hear that?" Lyle asks, his words overlapping hers. "From Rip?"

"What? No." Frannie laughs, but there's something about the sound that makes me think she's lying, and that's exactly what Rip was telling her. "From Ronald, actually."

"The head of the studio," Lyle tells me. Then he looks back at Frannie. "Nice to know our boss takes such a personal interest."

"Mmm."

"Speaking of the studio, we should probably think like publicists." He waves, and one of the photographers wandering the crowd rushes over. "Why don't we get a picture with all three of us?"

"Lovely idea," Frannie says, easing between us and

smiling as the photographer snaps a series of shots, the popping flash making me see spots.

Once the photographer leaves, she starts to pull out one of the two vacant stools. "I understand you two have been dating for a while," she says to me. "Where on earth has he been keeping you?"

"In bed, mostly," I say evenly, then hide my glee as Frannie's eyes go wide, and Lyle almost spits out his drink.

"Oh," Frannie says, then actually laughs. "Well, good for you." She pushes the stool back in, then winks at Lyle. "I like her. I hope she comes with you to the set once we start shooting. Ta."

Then she waggles her fingers, flashes a million dollar smile, and disappears into the throng.

"I'm sorry," I say. "That just came out."

"Are you kidding? You were brilliant."

"I didn't piss her off? I wasn't sure if that was a real or a sarcastic invitation."

"Real," Lyle assures me. "Frannie admires people who can hold their own. I think you just sealed my freedom from being the apple of her eye."

"Good," I say. "After all, as your girlfriend, I want you all to myself."

That just popped out, too, and the moment I say it, I wish I could call it back, especially as I'm pretty sure I see a shadow darken Lyle's gorgeous blue eyes.

I tell myself I'm being overly sensitive. After all, he's the one who wanted method acting. Still, I'm relieved when the silence is broken by the arrival of a tall woman with an athletic build, long dark hair, and a face that looks familiar, but that I can't quite place.

"This is so incredible," she says to Lyle. "Thank you so much for wrangling me an invitation."

"Just one of the many perks of working for me," Lyle says. "Natasha Black, meet Laine."

"Great to meet you," she says, extending her hand. "I would say that I've heard all about you, but we both know that would be a lie. And I'm pretty sure lying is grounds for getting fired, and I actually kind of like my job."

I bite back a smile. Not only because I like her, but because I've remembered where I know her from. And the truth is, I've *always* liked her. "You actually have heard all about me," I say. "We went to high school together. You were two years ahead of me."

Her eyes widen. "Sugar? Holy coincidence, Batman, I haven't seen you in years. How are you?" She tosses her head toward Lyle. "Slumming, huh?"

I bite back a laugh. "Pretty much. But, you know, you take what you can get."

"Nice," Lyle says.

"Whatever happened with you and Harry?" I ask, referring to the boy she dated our junior and senior years.

She makes a face. "That's over," she says, and her voice is so tight that I know better than to press the question.

I'm starting to think I completely screwed up this particular conversation when she shakes her head, as if the thought of Harry is nothing more than an irritating gnat. "Listen, I only have a second. I saw Lyle and I told some friends that I'd be right back. But we should play catch up soon. Lunch, maybe. Or cocktails one night when he's not wining and dining you."

"I'd love to."

"Maybe one night when I'm training with Riley," Lyle says, surprising me, because making fake future plans seems a little unnecessary for a one time gig, even if we are doing the method acting thing. "We could meet up with you two after he tortures me."

He's watching her face as he talks, and so I take his lead and do the same, immediately noticing the way her cheeks stain and her eyes dip to the table.

"Maybe so," she says. "Guess we'll play it by ear." She focuses exclusively on me. "Later, okay?"

"Sure," I say, then watch her back as she hurries away, walking right past Frannie, who's once again chatting with Rip Carrington.

I turn to Lyle. "Was that my imagination, or were you torturing that poor girl?"

"Just satisfying my curiosity. I think there's something going on between her and my trainer. Actually, I think there's *not* something going on."

"But you think they want there to be?"

"More or less."

"So you're teasing her about it? What happened to your nice guy persona?"

He spreads his hands and grins. "What can I say? I'm one hell of an actor."

I shake my head and laugh. And as I do, it hits me. He may be acting, but I'm not. Not that I'm his real girlfriend—that part's as fake as it gets. But the comfortable feeling I have around him is one hundred percent real.

And it's definitely nice.

Unsettling, but nice.

A chime sounds, and Lyle stands up. "I think that's supposed to let us know that the rest of the show will start soon."

I glance at my watch, and since it's almost eight, I assume he's right. He takes my hand, and we start to head for the entrance to the makeshift hall, where other guests are gathering in front of the velvet rope that currently bars the entrance.

"Lyle!"

The speaker is an insanely handsome dark-haired man standing next to an exceptionally pretty blonde woman with girl-next-door good looks.

Lyle detours us into the throng, and as we head toward the couple, I rack my brain trying to figure out why the man looks so familiar. "Laine," Lyle says when we reach them. "I'd like you to meet Nikki and Damien Stark."

"Oh!" I say, sure I sound like an idiot. But it's not every day you meet one of the wealthiest men in the world.

I don't know much about the rich and powerful, but you'd have to be dead not to have heard of Damien Stark, the former professional tennis player turned entrepreneur who now runs a multi-billion dollar enterprise. And whose name is on the door of this gallery.

His wife, Nikki, isn't nearly as famous, but I've heard about her, too. Mostly because of the scandal. Before they were married Damien offered her a million dollars if she'd pose nude for a painting. It was supposed to be an anonymous image with her face turned away, but word got out, and it was all over the tabloids for a while.

My stomach twists as I recall the story, and I feel an uncomfortable kinship. Not that what I'm doing is the same, not really. But it's secret. And a little bit naughty. And for money.

So, yeah, there are parallels.

I shiver, thinking how horrible it would be if the world found out about me.

"Will we see you at the Foundation picnic next Sunday, Laine?"

I jerk my head up, realizing that Damien's speaking to me. "I'm sorry?"

"The Stark Children's Foundation picnic," Lyle explains. "And, yes," he tells Damien. "We're hoping she can juggle her work schedule and make it."

Since I know nothing about this, I just smile and try to look eager.

"Oh, good," Nikki says. "I'll keep my fingers crossed. And as for you," she adds, pointing a finger at Lyle, "I should warn you that you created a monster the last time you were at the house. Lara is all about being an airplane now."

I look between the two of them, baffled.

"Her little girl. One arm, one leg, and then we spin." He does just that, holding an imaginary kid while some of the other guests look on, amused.

"She can't get enough of it," Damien adds.

"Which is unfortunate," Lyle says, "since I end up

with an afternoon of vertigo. I'll be a dead man once Anne's old enough to join the fun."

"You have no one to blame but yourself," Nikki chides. "You're the one who started it."

"Guilty as charged."

"How old is she?" I ask.

"Very firmly in the terrible twos," Damien says, his voice full of love and affection.

I'm about to ask about the other daughter when the music starts up and the docents remove the rope.

"Next week," Nikki says, as she and Damien wave, then fall in with the moving crowd.

We do the same, and soon we're in the dim hallway, the only illumination provided by the spotlights on the life size images that line the walls.

The photos are in a progression, each one more daring than the next, as if showing the progress of a woman coming into her own. And the woman, I realize, is Kelsey. The images are meant to be anonymous, but having met her, I recognize the angles of her shadowed face. Her posture. Her hair.

And the way that Wyatt has shot her...

Well, it's like looking through his heart at the woman he loves.

Lyle's hand rests against the small of my back, and I feel the pressure increase as we move through the exhibit. As the photos become more and more sensual.

By the time we exit the hall into a small, round room, I'm having to focus on breathing, because I'm so hyperaware of his touch that nothing else seems to matter.

Photos line the walls here, too, and the center is a stage entirely surrounded by a scrim. We make the circle, but now I'm not even really seeing the images. Instead, I'm imagining me.

Stretched out naked on a bed, my wrists bound with a bright red ribbon.

My legs spread as I straddle a chair, my eyes an invitation to the man just outside the frame.

Water sluicing over me in the shower, hot and steamy, my hand between my legs as I imagine him—

"—right here," Lyle says, and I actually jump. This time, at least, I don't have to worry about the blush. It's dark enough that he can't see my face.

"What?" I say, finally processing his words.

"I said we should stay right here." We're only a few feet from the stage, and as he speaks, he moves to stand behind me. Slowly, he wraps his arms around my waist, and the brush of his hands over my dress followed by the pressure of his arms tight around me is almost more than I can stand. My pulse kicks up, my mouth goes dry, and he's pressed so close that I'm certain he can feel the way my body has tightened and my heart is skittering.

The room lights dim as the stage lights come up, illuminating the inside of the scrim, so that we see the shadow of the woman behind it, her body bending against a pole as she holds a pose while the introductory music rises.

The scrim rises as well, leaving only a gauzy curtain through which we can clearly see Kelsey in the spotlight, a mask over her eyes, her lips painted blood red.

"Are you ready?" Lyle whispers as the music builds,

and all I can do is nod, my eyes fixed on Kelsey. The way she moves in time with the music, her body performing a sensual tease as she unties the wrap dress, then lets it drop to the floor, revealing a corset, garters, and shoes that really don't seem danceable, but to Kelsey seem to be as easy to move in as slippers.

The music starts out wild and hard, then shifts into slow and sensual, and the choreography matches each mood perfectly.

But it's neither the dance nor the woman that has captured my attention. It's the man behind me. He's pressed so close that I can feel his erection against me. And he's shifted his hands, so that now he's holding me in place with one hand on my rib cage, positioned so that his thumb strokes the curve of my breast as his other hand eases lower, until his palm is at the junction of my thigh, and his thumb could be stroking me oh, so intimately if it wasn't for the layer of chiffon and La Perla.

My entire body is stiff as I fight the urge to moan, to shift. To manipulate my position just enough so that he can touch me even more intimately in the dark. So that he can take me to the places this dance is leading.

So that I can simply melt inside the circle of his arms.

Except it's not real.

I close my eyes, reminding myself of that little, frustrating fact as I unsuccessfully will my body not to respond. My skin not to tingle. My core not to tighten with need.

I'm completely and totally turned on, and I swear that if he spun me around and stripped me bare right then, I wouldn't blink at all.

I shouldn't want this. Shouldn't want his touch or the fantasy that this could lead somewhere. I should just play the role I'm supposed to play and move on.

But there's this craving inside me…

And that's really not a good thing.

His hand rises, the edge of his thumb brushing my nipple, and the wave of longing that cuts through me is so intense it's almost painful.

As Kelsey continues her dance in front of us, I step forward, breaking contact. Immediately, I breathe easier, but the sense of loss that washes over me is almost as overwhelming as the heat that lingers from his touch.

"Sugar?" His voice is low, barely audible above the music.

I turn and manage a smile, trying to seem unaffected. Even nonchalant. "I know you're supposed to be proving to the world that you have a girlfriend, but you still have to keep up the nice Iowa boy rep, right?"

A grin tugs at his mouth, and in that moment I'm certain that every one of my thoughts is completely transparent. "I think my reputation can handle it."

"Oh." I draw in a breath. "Right. It's just that we should probably go. Because it's already getting close to nine, and we have to get back to Venice, and I have to change before Blacklist, and—"

He cuts me off mid-babble by taking my hand. "You're right. Let's go."

We ease toward the exit as the music starts to build to a crescendo. And as it explodes—as I turn to see Kelsey slide into her final, sensual pose—Lyle squeezes my hand, meets my eyes, and says very simply, "Soon."

CHAPTER 12

CHRIST, HE WANTED her.

Those photos. That music. That seriously hot dance.

It all combined to work on him like an elixir. A damned potent one, too, considering he was still hard, despite the fact that they were miles away, now speeding down the 10 in his Volvo as they headed toward the beach.

But while the show may have started the fire, it was Laine who turned it into a raging inferno. Laine, who'd somehow managed to work a spell on him.

Because it had to be magic. How else could he explain why he'd been unable to get her out of his head since the moment he'd met her? Or why all he could think about was touching her, losing himself in her?

Soon.

That's what he told her, and he wished that that he'd said *now*. Because at the moment, waiting was torture.

Lyle couldn't remember the last time a woman had gotten under his skin like this. For that matter, had a woman ever gotten to him this much? He didn't think so. Not even Jenny, who'd been his best friend and his first. He'd been a walking pile of hormones back then, but even that wild and woolly teenage lust had felt tame compared with the driving, demanding need that pounded through him now.

A need so intense he couldn't even wrap his head around it.

He wanted her—that was the long and short of it, though *want* seemed uniquely inadequate. Especially since he'd wanted each of the women Marjorie sent him. But that had been an entirely different kind of craving.

With them he'd wanted—*needed*—something like a drug. A quick fix.

With Laine, it wasn't about quick. Wasn't about the explosion.

It was about the journey, and he intended to savor every minute.

The back and forth of conversation and flirting. The slow seduction of caresses and kisses. And all of it— every touch, every caress, every moment—dedicated to her pleasure, not his.

He intended to see her writhe. Beg.

His goal was to spend the entire night taking her to the absolute heights of pleasure, and then holding her close as she cried out his name.

Damn, but he wanted it. Wanted *her*.

And tonight, he intended to have.

"Just take Fourth Street," she said, pulling him from his fantasies. "Then you can cut down to Neilson Way and take that almost all the way to my house. It's not much farther." She smoothed her hands down her skirt, looking a little skittish, then glanced sideways at him. "I appreciate the ride home."

"Did you think I wouldn't come back with you?"

"I—" She cut herself off with a shake of her head. "Nothing."

He frowned as he took the exit and maneuvered the surface streets. In the gallery, he'd felt her tremble beneath his touch. Had heard her soft moans as he stroked her and felt the pounding of her pulse when he pulled her body against his. And when they'd left—when he'd all but promised that he would have her soon—he'd heard her soft intake of breath and saw the way her nipples hardened against the soft material of the that barely-there dress that he longed to rip off her.

Her arousal was like a palpable thing, and yet she'd sat prim and stiff in the car all the way from downtown to the beach. And he didn't have a goddamn clue why.

Well, screw that.

He reached over, put his hand on her bare thigh, just below where the hem of the dress grazed her leg. Slowly, he brushed his thumb back and forth, and was gratified to see her close her eyes and bite her lower lip. "Tell me," he demanded. "Tell me what you were going to say."

She hesitated, then licked her lips. "It's just that what you said—*soon*—I didn't realize—I mean, I thought tonight you were hiring me only for the show."

It was as if she'd kicked him in the gut, and he yanked his hand back to the steering wheel, his eyes straight ahead. "You're saying you want more money?" He spoke calmly, telling himself this was no big deal. But for the first time in forever, the idea of paying for sex made him vaguely ill.

"No!" She blurted out the word with such force he almost slammed on the brake out of reflex. "No," she repeated more softly. "That's not what I—oh, God. Never mind. Just turn here. And then that's my house right there," she added, after he complied. "With the stucco fence."

He pulled up in front, astounded to have found an actual parking space, and killed the engine. "Laine—"

"Please. Let's just drop it." She opened her door, and he did the same. "I appreciate the ride, but you don't have to get out," she said.

"I'm walking you to the door."

He thought for a moment that she was going to argue, but she must have sensed his determination, because she nodded once, then paused at her gate while he circled the car. She keyed in the code, and he followed her into a delightful front lawn filled with flowers and whimsy, all of which seemed to suit her perfectly, right down to the little concrete frog by the front steps.

"Your house is charming," he said as they reached the front porch.

"Thanks. I grew up here," she added, and he noted that the nervousness he'd heard in the car had disappeared. "I've done a lot of work to this place over the last few years."

She pushed open the front door, then paused on the threshold. "Anyway, thanks again. I should hurry. I still need to change, and—"

He shut her up with a kiss.

For a moment, her lips were hard as stone against

his. Then they parted just slightly, and he took advantage, his tongue sweeping in to taste her. To tease her.

She moaned, letting herself fall further into the kiss, and he held her close, one hand at the back of her head, the other at her waist. She tasted like summer. As warm as sunshine and as sweet as cotton candy.

Hell, she tasted like hope. And damn him, he couldn't get enough of her.

He broke the kiss long enough to murmur, "Inside," then steered them both into the dark room. Already he mourned the lack of contact, and he pushed the door shut, then pressed her against it before impatiently sliding his hand up to her breast as he bent to claim her mouth once more.

He didn't make it.

Instead, she twisted her head to the side, her palm pressing against his chest to hold him at bay as she said, "I have to get ready. I can't be late for my shift."

He cupped her chin in his hand, then turned her head to face him. "Skip work. Stay with me." He punctuated the words with a slow, deep kiss. "Not because I'm paying you," he said, "but because you want to."

"What if I don't?" Her words were so soft he could barely hear them.

"Not an issue. Do you think I can't tell?" He pressed his fingertip to her trembling lip, then drew it slowly lower, tracing her jaw, then stroking her neck as she arched back, whimpering a little as she offered herself to him.

He bent his head and kissed her neck, moving lower

and lower until he reached her breast. Then he closed his mouth over her, teasing her through the material of her dress.

"Please," she murmured as the hand on his chest clutched his shirt, and her other hand cupped the back of his head, forcing his mouth harder against her body.

Frenzied now, thinking only of tasting her, having her, he used his teeth to tug the bodice aside, exposing the curve of her breast. With one hand, he cupped her, his thumb teasing her nipple as his tongue tasted her heated skin. As his lips burned from the contact, and his cock hardened to steel.

"Sugar," he murmured, then immediately knew that it was the wrong thing to say because her fingers released his hair and the hand that was tugging on his shirt to pull him closer now pushed him away as she nimbly shifted sideways and free of him.

"We can't," she said, breathing hard as she stood only inches from him. Then she reached for him, and for a moment he thought that she'd changed her mind, but all she was doing was flipping a light switch, filling the room with the bright glow of incandescent light.

He swallowed, his eyes taking in the picture of her. Hair mussed, lipstick smeared, and her dress so askew that he could see the exposed brown tint of her areolae. He wanted to rip the dress off and see more of her. All of her. And at the same time, he wanted to take it slow and undress her little by little, as if he were unwrapping the most fragile of presents.

Slowly, he stepped toward her, but she held up a hand, keeping him at bay.

"We can't," she repeated. "I have to change. I have to get to Blacklist."

She turned, presumably to head toward her bedroom, but he grabbed her hand, pulling her back.

"Don't go."

"I have to. Work. Job. It's what I do."

"You're working until closing?" He asked, and when she nodded, continued with, "What is that, four hours? Five?"

"Yeah. So?"

"I'll pay you five hundred an hour," he said, then pressed a finger to her lips before she could protest. "And not for sex. But for your time. That's a hell of a lot more than your hourly wage plus tips."

"Lyle," she said when he let her speak. "I can't."

"You're facing foreclosure, Sugar. You need the money."

"I do. I really do." She drew in a breath, then exhaled noisily. "But I still can't. No," she continued, cutting off his protest. "It's not about the money. Late night on a Saturday? David's relying on me to work. I'm not going to leave him in a jam at the last minute."

"Right," he said, frustrated at being denied, but relieved that it wasn't about desire, but responsibility. "Get changed. I'll drive you." And maybe while she changed he could take a quick cold shower. Or go outside and douse himself with the garden hose.

"It's okay." She met his eyes, then looked away as if shy or uncertain. "I like to walk."

He nodded slowly. "Okay. Fine. I'll walk with you."

"You don't—"

"It's late."

"I do it all the time."

"And tonight, you'll do it with me." He flashed a mega-watt smile. "You can tell me to go to hell, but the sidewalks are open and free, and either way I'm shadowing you to Blacklist."

She quirked a brow, though he wasn't sure if she was amused or irritated. "Fine. Suit yourself. I'll be right back." She pointed toward the kitchen. "Make yourself at home. And grab me a Diet Coke for the road, please."

Since a cold shower wasn't on the agenda, he downed two glasses of ice water, then met her back in the living room with her soda. This time, there was a tabby cat sitting at her feet, looking at him with jealous green eyes.

"Skittles, meet Lyle. Lyle, this is Skittles."

He bent, extending his fingers, and the cat came over to sniff. "Hey, buddy," he said, then scratched Skittles behind the ears, eliciting a satisfied purr.

"Well," Sugar said. "I guess you pass that test."

He grinned up at her, more pleased than he should be by winning the cat's approval.

And speaking of approval, she looked great. She'd changed out of the slinky dress, of course, but he thought she looked just as sexy in skinny jeans, black Converse sneakers, and a black T-shirt embroidered with the Blacklist logo.

She'd refreshed her makeup, so she no longer looked freshly kissed, and he was tempted to kiss her again, just to mark her as his.

Except she wasn't his. Couldn't be his.

But that reality didn't erase the desire.

"Come on," he said, more gruffly than he intended, but the small house felt suddenly claustrophobic. "You don't want to be late."

"Right." She fell in step beside him, and he was impressed to see she didn't carry a purse, a rarity with women in his experience.

When he told her as much, she just shrugged. "What's the point? I have my ID and a credit card in my back pocket. And it's not like I can freshen up at work—we're always too busy—and I don't need to carry a key since I'm not driving."

"Still," he said as they left her yard and started down the sidewalk to the intersection. "You're clearly not from planet Hollywood."

She laughed. "Is that a good thing or a bad thing?"

"In my book? A good thing."

For a second, she just looked at him, as if he was a puzzle. He anticipated a question, but when it didn't come, he asked her how she liked the neighborhood.

"Are you kidding? I love it. Of course, I've never lived anywhere else, so…" She trailed off with a shrug. "But unless the 'anywhere else' has a beach, I don't think it would suit me."

"Do you surf?"

"Nope."

"Morning swims for exercise?"

"God, no. If I manage yoga twice a week, I feel like I'm overexerting myself. Besides, I'm on the two-waitressing-jobs fitness plan. Trust me when I say it's one of the best training regimens ever."

She paused in a circle of yellow light cast by one of the streetlamps and looked him slowly up and down, the approval he saw on her face pleasing him more than it should. "Your training regimen seems pretty good, too."

"I'll tell Riley you said so. And you're changing the subject. Why the beach?"

"I don't know." She started walking again. "It just suits me. I've always known it." She tilted her head, looking at him. "Haven't you ever felt that way about something? Just knew in your gut that something was right?"

God, yes.

He felt the thrust of the answer, so quick and firm, like he'd walked smack into a wall. *Her.* She felt right. She'd slammed into his life like a bolt of lightning, and the world hadn't been level since.

All true. Not to mention confusing as hell. His life was a damn mess, after all. Hell, *he* was a mess. And right now he was on the crux, his career about to explode. He didn't have time for the messiness of a relationship. He needed to keep his eye on the prize.

"Really?" She was looking at him with interest, and he was mortified to realize he'd said *yes* out loud. "So what was it? Your thing that struck you as right?"

"Acting," he said, because that was true, too. He hadn't come to Los Angeles to be an actor—that had been Jenny's dream. But when he'd landed that first job, he'd been enchanted by the process. The ability to slide out of his own life, even if only for a while. To become someone else. To see the world through their eyes. To take all of his emotional crap and filter it into something not only different, but good. Something that entertained or moved people.

"Then I guess we're both lucky," she said, and he felt a frisson of connection when she casually took his hand. "I'm by the beach, and you have your dream job."

"I guess we are," he said, ignoring the little twist in his stomach that he felt every time he thought about the upcoming years of the Blue Zenith franchise. Three more movies they wanted him to commit to, plus an option for two after that.

Now, however, wasn't the time to ponder career planning. Not when the night was as beautiful as the woman holding his hand. A woman he wanted to know thoroughly.

"How old were you when your mom and brother died?"

"Eighteen," she said. "And don't bother doing the math. That makes me twenty-three now. Twenty-four in the fall. And you're twenty-nine," she said, then grinned. "I told you I looked you up."

"Very industrious. But I'm interested in you. You were in school when they died?"

"First semester at UCLA. I was a history major, but only because I threw darts at my course selection book. So after the accident, I dropped out. Seemed smarter than racking up student loans when I couldn't even see a career path."

"How'd you manage the house? Life insurance?"

"Mom didn't have any. Honestly, she barely made ends meet."

"Your dad?"

She shrugged. "Went into the wind when I was a kid. But he paid off the house before he disappeared, which was how Mom managed to afford to live here. All she had to cover was the bills and the taxes and food."

"You, too," he said. "Once it all fell on your shoulders."

"Me, too," she agreed.

"You've had it rough." In some ways, she'd had it just as rough as he had, back in those days before Hollywood started throwing money at him, when he and Jenny were still suffering in Iowa. Before they'd run.

"I guess. I mean, it was horrible losing my mom and my brother, but I can't spend my whole life thinking how much the universe has screwed me. At least I still have my house—for now, anyway. And if I lose it, I have only myself to blame. And I have jobs I can walk to and some really good friends. All in all, I'm doing okay."

Maybe it was ridiculous, but her words, said so matter-of-factly, seemed to glow inside him, like a little beacon of hope. He lifted her hand and kissed her fingertips. "You really are an exceptional woman."

"I think your perspective might be a little off, but I'll just say thank you and leave it at that."

"Good plan," he said with a laugh. "But if the house is paid off, what's driving the foreclosure?"

"The place needed massive repairs. I managed to get a short-term loan, but it was the balloon kind. Tiny payments up front, one giant payment at the end."

"And the end, as they say, is nigh."

"You got that right." She sighed. "I probably should have found a different way to get the money back then, but I was alone and freaked and stupid and—well, doesn't matter. That's the situation I'm dealing with."

"Can't you get another loan?"

She made a face. "Apparently, it's a miracle I got the first one. Turns out my absent father is on the deed as some sort of co-owner. I went to one of those legal clinics at the law school and they explained it to me. The bottom line is that no bank's going to want to lend me money. They can, but they won't."

She exhaled loudly. "I tried, though. I figured it happened once, maybe someone would do it again. No go. I'm pretty sure every bank in the State of California has turned me down."

"I could lend you the money. Promissory note. Lien against the house. Just like a bank."

For a moment, he thought she might agree. Then she shook her head. "It's a really sweet offer. But I've had some other friends offer the same thing, and I just can't do it. Besides, you've already helped me get a lot closer. I'll make it." She turned toward him with a sweet smile. "I'm absolutely determined."

He wanted to argue with her. To tell her it was no big deal. That it actually gave him pleasure to spend the money he earned in Hollywood to help out women like her who were struggling.

But he couldn't get any of that past that one simple word—*Friends*.

"Is that what we are?" he said instead.

For a moment, she looked confused. Then her eyes went wide. "Oh. Wow. Right—that was kind of presumptuous of me, wasn't it. But it's just that—"

"Friends," he repeated, then hooked his arm around her shoulder. "And if I play my cards right, maybe even friends with benefits."

As he'd hoped, she laughed.

"Okay, friend," she said. "Your turn. Did you always want to act?"

He shook his head. "Actually, I didn't get the bug until we moved here."

"You were sixteen then, right? What did you want to do before?"

Survive.

It was the truth. But, of course, he couldn't say it. "I was a sixteen year old guy. I'm pretty sure my singular goal at that age was to get laid."

She looked at him with narrowed eyes. "Well, I'll believe that was *a* goal. But I think there's more to you than that, even back then."

"Not really. I'm basically as shallow as they come."

She rolled her eyes, and he resisted the urge to put an arm around her and pull her close for a sweet, gentle kiss laced with absolutely no agenda. Something he hadn't wanted to do with a woman in, well, pretty much forever.

"What do your parents think of your skyrocketing fame?" she asked as they turned right at the next intersection. "They must be incredibly proud."

His chest tightened, and he fought the urge to just chuck it all and tell her the truth. It was a battle he won—and why not? He had years of practice keeping his secrets.

Instead of the truth, he said, "They have an entire

shrine to me in the guest bedroom. Embarrassing, really. And lately I haven't won the good son award. I've been so focused on my career I don't visit or call nearly often enough."

"I'm sure they understand. And speaking of careers," she added, nodding at the main door to Blacklist. "Thanks for walking me. And let me know if you ever need another girlfriend stand-in, okay?"

"Actually, I thought I might hang out and walk you back. Unless you have plans after."

Her brows lifted. "I got three hours of sleep last night. My plans after involve crashing facedown on my bed."

"All the more reason for me to walk you home. It'll be late. You're tired. You'll be too exhausted to pay attention to your surroundings. And don't tell me the neighborhood's safe. Nothing's safe that late."

She crossed her arms and cocked her head. "You realize my shift is four hours."

"I'll have a drink, catch up on some emails on my phone."

"You're determined, aren't you?"

"You're very perceptive."

She sighed, but he thought she looked amused. Maybe even pleased. "Suit yourself."

He did, grabbing a seat at a table near a wall so that he'd have a view of the entire restaurant. He wasn't in her section, and his waitress—Nessie—spent the first few minutes fawning over him before Laine came over and told her to get over it.

"I couldn't believe it when I saw those pictures of

you two on Twitter," she said after he ordered a burger with fries and two shots of bourbon on the rocks. Riley would give him shit for the burger, but he'd deal with that later.

"I mean, I figured it was some sort of stunt where you pay to have your picture taken with a celebrity."

"No," he assured her. "She's my girl."

"Wow," she said, then thrust a napkin at him. "Would you sign?"

He did, fearing that would send a flood of other employees and patrons to his table, but that possibility was forestalled when David, the owner, plunked himself down in the seat opposite him.

"You're dating our girl, Laine?"

"Yes, sir."

"I don't want to hear about you pulling any Hollywood asshole crap with her, you got me?"

"Absolutely," he said, meaning every syllable. "You have my word."

David stared at him through narrowed eyes, then must have decided that Lyle wasn't tossing bullshit his way, because he grunted approval, then left the table, telling Nessie and the bartender to make sure that Lyle was left alone. "He's here to drink, not to put up with all of you."

After that, Lyle wasn't bothered. And he spent the next four hours watching Laine, and completely ignoring his emails. She was graceful and efficient. She chatted with the staff and the customers, seemed to know most everybody's name, and she did her job with superlative efficiency.

It obviously wasn't her passion. Just a job. But that didn't matter to her. She took it seriously. The way she took her life, her responsibilities.

It seemed like a lifetime ago when she'd come to his hotel room, scared and determined. He'd seen only one side of her then, and he'd liked what he saw. But he'd been seeing through the eyes of sex. Of lust.

Now, he was seeing the real Laine. A woman he admired. Who moved him in so many ways.

A woman he could truly fall for.

And, frankly, that made her pretty damn terrifying.

CHAPTER 13

"**Y**OU'RE REALLY DATING Lyle Tarpin?"

It's ten minutes to closing, and Nessie has me cornered in the back, where we've both just finished helping with prep work for tomorrow's opening shift.

"I really am," I lie. "Surreal, huh?"

"Beyond surreal," she says. "How'd you meet him?"

I tell her the story about the cookie dough ice cream, and she swoons against the walk-in fridge. "Wow. I mean, really, that is so wow. Is it serious?"

I lift a shoulder. And then I say the only true thing that I've said since this conversation began. "I honestly don't know."

I *should* know. I should be absolutely certain that whatever is between us is business as usual.

But then I think about the way he kissed me on the porch. And the frustrated, almost angry look on his face when I mentioned money for sex as part of tonight's agenda.

We're walking a very thin line, he and I. And I'm not at all sure where pretending ends and reality begins.

"Well, I would totally love to watch part of the filming of *M. Sterious*. Do you think he could arrange that? I mean, they're starting filming pretty soon, I think. And I'm like the biggest Blue Zenith fan ever."

"I'll ask," I say, and make a mental note to do that. Nessie can be a spaz, but she's sweet.

"You're the best. And go ahead and cut out. I'll finish up."

"You sure?"

Her smile practically lights up the back room. "Sure. Just tell him I did him a favor. Maybe he'll toss in a few cast autographs."

I laugh. "Right. See you next week."

"Ciao!"

I find Lyle leaning against the bar chatting with David. I don't know about what exactly, because I heard the words *Formula One racing* and just tuned right out. Not my thing, but I'm glad that Lyle gets along with my boss.

I frown, because I'm genuinely happy they get along, and that's just one more bit of evidence in the case of *Are They or Aren't They? The People v. Laine and Tarpin*.

I roll my eyes. Clearly, I'm not doing well on a measly three hours of sleep.

"Hey," Lyle says, looking up at me with the kind of smile that sends sparks of electricity skittering over my skin. "You ready?"

I nod, then tell David that Nessie is finishing up.

"Night, kids," he says, and Lyle and I both laugh.

"I haven't felt like a kid in a long time," I admit once we're outside.

"No? Well, then we need to do something about that." He takes my hand and turns toward the beach. "This way. Unless you're too tired?"

"What? Me tired? I got a whole three hours of sleep last night."

"Fair enough. I'll take you home," he says, and when he starts to turn toward the short route home, I realize that he thought I was serious.

I grab the lapel of his jacket and tug him back to me. "I'm fine," I say. "And I get to sleep in tomorrow. I have a rare day off, and since I'm better than on track toward my payoff goal, I decided not to beg anyone to let me cover their shift at Maudie's in the morning. All of which means that I'm a girl without a curfew."

"Very interesting," he says, as we head toward the beach.

"You do realize it's after two in the morning."

"And the moon is full and the breaking waves are glowing in the moonlight. And you and I are going for a walk. Take your shoes off," he says as we reach the sand.

"You're still in a suit." I run my fingers over the lapel of his jacket. "A really nice suit, actually. Also, you remember the Pacific is freezing, right?"

He takes off the jacket and puts it around my shoulders. "The wind's chillier the closer we get to the water."

We leave our shoes and socks by a signpost—at this hour, I'm not worried someone will walk off with them—and once I've shrugged into his jacket, he takes my hand.

I laugh as and we run toward the breaking waves. "What exactly are we doing?"

"Playing," he says.

And that, in fact, is exactly what we do.

We kick waves toward each other. We dig in the wet

sand with our toes. And we race down the beach and back, splashing in the surf, before I take off down the beach again, daring him to chase me.

"Wait," he calls after me. "You have to see this."

He's standing still, the waves coming in over his feet and soaking the hem of his trousers. I hurry toward him, my jeans damp around my ankles as well. "What is it?" I say, glancing at the sand that surrounds him, wondering if he's seen a crab or a starfish.

"This," he says, and draws me close.

I gasp, completely unprepared for the pressure of his mouth against mine, and when my lips part, he takes full advantage, capturing me with a kiss that is hot and open. A kiss so full of longing and need that it makes my knees go weak, and so full of sensual heat that electric sparks ricochet inside me until finally settling between my thighs, making me hot. Needy. *Wanting.*

When we break the kiss, I'm breathing hard. "Wow," I say as his thumb gently strokes the line of my jaw. "Is this when you get your explosion?"

"No," he whispers. "This is when you get your seduction."

We hurry back to the house, fingers linked, pausing only once so that he can press me against a lamp post and take my mouth in his. "I want you, Sugar," he whispers. "I want you naked beneath me. I want you wet, your legs spread for me, your fingers clinging to my back. I want to lose myself inside your heat, and I want to make you come like you never have before."

"Yes, please," I murmur, his words firing my senses and tempting me to pull him down to the sand and beg him to take me now.

I manage to hold off, but by the time we reach my house, I'm mostly non-functional. All I want is him. All I know is him. My body burns with sensual longing, and I'm so completely rattled by the force of my desire that I can barely punch in key code.

As soon as I do, we practically tumble inside, our mouths locked, our kisses frantic. I taste blood and don't care. All I need is Lyle. All I want is Lyle. The feel of him. The heat of him.

"Too hot," I murmur, then reach for the hem of his shirt and pull it free of his slacks. He's still dressed for the opening, and my fingers fumble as I try to unbutton the shirt. He, however, has no problems with mine. He pulls the Blacklist Tee over my head, then tosses it aside.

I'm still wearing my new La Perla bra, and he tugs the pretty lace down, freeing my breast. At the same time, he groans, the sound deep and passionate. "You're beautiful," he says, then holds my lower back as he bends over me, arcing my body as his mouth closes over my breast. He uses his tongue to tease my nipple, and I feel the sensation like a hot wire cutting straight through me, all the way down to my wet, needy core.

"Bedroom," I murmur, which is about as much co-herent thought as I'm capable of.

He doesn't hesitate. He scoops me up, and I curl against him, my bare skin rubbing against the cotton of his shirt.

In my bedroom, he puts me down gently, but there's nothing gently about the way I grab his shirt, fisting my hands in the material so that I can tumble him down beside me. I roll over, then attack those damn buttons until he finally takes over the task and peels off his shirt.

"Jeans," he says, his hands going for my waistband, releasing my button fly, and then finally tugging the denim down so that I have to quickly kick off my shoes or be tangled in a mess of clothing and sneakers.

"Here," he says when I'm naked except for tiny lace panties. He pulls me onto him, and I straddle his waist as his fingers stroke me through the damp panties, then slip in under the thin satin to find my core. "Christ, Sugar, you're so damn wet."

I am, and I writhe against his hand, wanting more.

He knows exactly what I want, and his fingers thrust inside me, and I ride him, grinding myself shamelessly against this man who I can't seem to get enough of.

I use my thighs to lift and lower myself, and he thrusts his fingers in time with my movements. "That's it, baby," he says. "That's so fucking hot."

I'm like a wild thing, wanting more—him. I've never in my life been this turned on, and it's been far too many years since I felt a man's cock inside me. I want it now. Hell, I need it as badly as I need oxygen.

Except.

The thought is simple and fast and unwelcome. A slight hesitation. A gentle push.

Now? Like this? After waiting so long?

I want to push the thoughts away. To scream *yes, yes, this is what I want.* Who *I want.*

But I know it's not right. It's not real.

I like Lyle, probably too much. But this isn't the promise I made myself. And at the end of the day, he's going to leave, and I'm going to have to live with my decisions.

I screwed up once and regretted it.

I'm not going to do that again.

"I'm sorry," I whisper, putting the brakes on so hard and fast he'll probably have whiplash.

"I'm sorry," I repeat, as I climb off him, completely mortified.

He's watching me, and I can see the confusion. Thankfully, I don't see anger, and for some reason that makes me feel even more wretched.

"I should never have let this get so out of control," I say. A tear rolls down my cheek and I brush it away. "It's just that I want to—I do—but at the same time, I don't. I can't."

I squeeze my eyes shut to stifle a flood of tears. "Please don't hate me. I didn't mean to be a tease."

"Hush," he says, pulling me close as I press my face against his bare chest. He strokes my back gently, so sweetly, and when he whispers, "Do I look like I hate you?" I break out into fresh sobs, unable to hold it all in any longer.

He holds me until I'm able to breathe without choking, and then a little bit longer until I feel strong enough to let go and talk to him.

Finally, I pull away, then lift my head to look into his eyes, certain I'll see frustration there. But all I see is concern and strength. "You don't have to say anything, baby. You never need an explanation for saying no."

"Maybe not. But we met because you hired me to sleep with you, so it's only fair that you'd be a little surprised if I suddenly tell you to back off."

"That was business," he says. "This isn't. Do you think I don't understand the difference?"

I lick my lips, suddenly uncertain. "It's just that I like you. A lot. Probably more than I should."

"I'm glad. I like you, too. Probably more than I should."

I meet his eyes and manage a little half-smile. "If this was for money, I could justify it. Just business, right? But like this—because of desire and attraction and all that wonderful stuff ... well, honestly, I'm having a hard time remembering why I'm fighting it. All I know is that I don't want to be angry with myself in the morning. And if we do this, then I will."

Even with the sheet pulled up to cover me, I feel naked and exposed and very, very vulnerable. And when he reaches for me, I hold my breath, certain that he's going to touch me, and all my resolve will fade away.

But he doesn't. Instead, he simply twists a lock of hair around his finger. "Can you tell me why you're fighting it?"

I lick my lips. "I've never actually told anyone," I admit.

He nods slowly, then releases my hair and takes my hand. "It's okay. Like I said, you don't ever have to give a reason——"

"But I think I can tell you," I blurt. And as soon as the words are out, I realize I want to. I don't know why—honestly, I barely know this man, but I've seen enough to know that he's broken. So why the hell am I adding to the drama of my own life by inviting him in?

I don't have an answer. Not a sound, logical one, anyway. All I know is that I like him and I trust him.

Most of all, I feel alive around in him a way I haven't felt since I lost my mom and Andy.

And, really, why should I care if it's fast, so long as it's right?

I draw a deep breath, then start talking. "The day of the accident, we were supposed to go to Disneyland. Did I tell you that before?"

He shakes his head.

"We hadn't been in forever, and I haven't been back since. It was supposed to be a treat. The last day of my first semester. And then this cop comes to my door, and a day that was supposed to be special was ripped completely apart."

He says nothing, and I'm grateful for the silence.

"Something about that irony made it worse for me. The idea of the accident—that fucking drunk driver—destroying a moment along with three lives. I don't know. It ate at me, I guess. Then I met a guy at Blacklist who said I'd been in his English Lit class. I didn't remember him at all, but he asked me to go out dancing. I said yes."

I'm clinging to Lyle's hand so tightly that my fingers are numb, but I don't let go, and he doesn't flinch.

"Anyway, we got drunk, and I was a virgin, and I slept with him." I say it all matter-of-factly, even though it doesn't feel matter-of-fact at all. "And then I hated myself, because I had always wanted that first time to be—"

"Special," he says as he cups my cheek with his free

hand. "Of course, you did."

"I was so angry with myself that I made a promise. And I haven't slept with anyone since. I've done everything but," I add with a wicked grin, "but I haven't gone all the way. And I won't until I know it'll be special."

The moment the word's out of my mouth, I wince.

"Oh, hell. Don't take that the wrong way," I say. "I'm sure being with you would be mind-blowingly special. I just mean that I want it to be real. I want there to be at least the possibility of a future. Maybe not an engagement ring, but I want it to be with someone I'm in a relationship with.

"And like I said," I continue, stumbling over my words, "I really like you. But being your fake girlfriend isn't what I had in mind."

I bite my lip as I glance up at him. "I didn't mean to lead you on tonight, truly. And I have no philosophical problems with, um, doing pretty much everything else. But I guess I want to pretend like I didn't make a huge mistake giving my virginity to some random guy."

I lean back and shrug. "So that's it. Like I said, I'm sorry."

"You don't have anything to be sorry about." He slides closer, then pulls me gently against him, letting me rest my head on his chest.

"Thanks," I whisper as he strokes my hair.

"I was right about the poem," he says. "You do have an unconquerable soul."

I close my eyes, nodding as a single tear spills out.

He holds me like that for a few minutes longer, then gently releases me as he moves toward the edge of the bed. "I should go."

I reach for him, my fingers twining with his. "You don't have to go," I say. "It's late, I mean."

He stays still for a moment, then he lifts the sheet and slides under, holding out an arm for me to join him. "Just sleep," he says, as he pulls me close. "I'll be right here."

CHAPTER 14

THE MORNING SUN filtered in through the gaps in her curtains as Lyle stood by the bed watching Sugar sleep, and in that moment, he wanted nothing more than to crawl back into bed with her and stay locked in this bungalow for the rest of the day.

Not happening.

He should never have stayed the night. That was why he had his routine, after all. That was why he'd set up his life the way he had, with Marjorie on speed dial. So that he never ran the risk of getting too close.

And yet as he watched her clutch the pillow, her breathing so soft and steady, he knew that if she opened her eyes and asked him to, he'd pull her back into his arms and stay.

Why?

Why did this woman affect him so much? Why was it so easy to be around her?

Was it the show they were putting on? The fact that he was playing a role? Or was there truly a deeper connection between them?

He didn't know. All he was certain of was that somehow Sugar had snuck in around the edges. He might not know how she managed to do it, but he couldn't deny that she had. And that simple fact scared the shit out of him.

Didn't he know better than anyone that connections meant pain and loss? Hadn't he seen that his whole life? His mother? Jenny?

Which meant that he didn't get involved. He just didn't. It was too messy. Too complicated. Trying to build a relationship at the same time he built a career was a recipe for failure on both counts.

All he wanted—all he needed—was to keep his career on track. Last night, Sugar had helped serve that purpose. But she wasn't really his girlfriend—they both knew that.

And he shouldn't feel any guilt at all for leaving this morning. The job was done, after all. Clean. Simple. Time to move on.

At least that's what he told himself.

But as he went into the kitchen to write her a note, he couldn't deny the lump in his stomach. And as he got in his car, he had to actually take a moment to hold onto the steering wheel and do nothing but breathe as a storm of emotion roiled inside him. Loss and guilt, longing and shame.

He was a goddamned asshole.

Yeah, well, maybe he was. But as he started the car and pulled out onto the street, he also knew that he had no choice. Not if he wanted to keep his life sane and his career on track.

Not if he wanted to keep his all his secrets.

USUALLY, LYLE HATED organized media events, especially when they ate into his weekend. Today, however, he was happy for anything that took his mind off of Laine. Even a series of costume screen tests to which the media had been invited.

Even if that meant that he had to wear tights.

Lyle had already had his turn in the iconic *M. Sterious* costume as well as the tux he'd wear to an action-filled party scene. Now, he was just waiting for the wrap-up so that he and the other cast members could field questions and pose for a few additional shots.

That should be soon, thank God. At the moment, Frannie was preening in front of the camera in a black skin suit with neon blue accents. A cluster of reporters and social media influencers were gathered around, snapping pics and shouting questions between shots.

Most of them he'd seen before. The tall, thin guy who ran a particularly snarky blog. The bubbly woman who worked for one of the glossy entertainment magazines. A leggy blonde who hosted one of the local morning shows. And then there was the athletic guy in jeans and a denim jacket who was sporting a goatee and a baseball cap worn low over his eyes. Lyle couldn't get a good look at him, but something about him seemed so damn familiar.

It didn't matter, of course, but the question tugged at his mind anyway.

"Time to quit daydreaming," Evelyn said, taking his elbow and steering him to a corner. "The contracts for the next installments came in. I've got the legal team looking over them, but the bottom line is what we talked about. They want you for three more Blue Zenith movies after this one, with an option for another."

"And the pay?"

"Step increases with every film, plus significant back-end. One of the best deals I've ever negotiated, if I do say so myself. And I think you'd be a fool to take it."

He exhaled, frustrated. "Dammit, Evelyn."

"Yeah, yeah. You want to make it big, I know. A huge splash in the giant cesspool that's Hollywood. Trust me, I get it. Because believe me, that's a story I've heard before. And I'm all for fame and fortune, but in your case, I don't see this making you happy, Iowa. Being a superhero isn't your jam, and we both know it."

"I'm not signing on for *Arizona Spring*. An indie film with no upfront payday and very little chance of making it on the back-end? Is that really the direction you think I should go?"

"I think if you sign on for the franchise it's going to be like wearing golden chains. And I think *Spring* is one of the best scripts I've ever read. You did amazing work in the sitcom, and you'll be great as M. But if your goal is for the world to see your acting chops, you need to do a drama. Not comedy. Not comic book. Drama."

"Fine," he said sharply, because he just wanted to end this conversation. "I'll think about it." Except there was no thinking to be done. He and Jenny had come to Hollywood so that she could explode onto the silver screen. And while he may have destroyed Jenny, he hadn't destroyed the dream. And so long as he was able, he intended to see that dream become reality. *That* was his goal.

It had to be.

He started to walk toward the reporters, because even that was better than going another round with his agent, but she called to him with a sharp, "Hang on there, Iowa. One more thing."

He paused a moment, his back to her, then forced a smile as he turned, ensuring he wiped away any trace of his melancholy thoughts. "Yeah?"

"You did good." She passed him her phone, which was open to a picture of him and Frannie and Laine.

He bit back a wince. For the last thirty minutes, he'd managed to not think of her at all, and now there she was, back in his head again. The way she laughed. The way she felt.

Most of all, the way she made him feel.

"She's a great girl."

"You should bring her to the SCF brunch. That would be another nice photo opp."

He shook his head. "I played the game. The vultures got their pictures. Frannie met her, blessed her. As of now, I officially have a girlfriend. One who doesn't like the spotlight and who works long hours."

"Lyle." His name was delivered like an order.

"No," he said, because on this he was holding his ground. He needed to cut ties. Needed to stay clear. A woman who snuck into his life as quickly and deeply as Laine had could end up spinning his entire world out of whack. "We're good right now. Just let it be."

He could tell she didn't want to, but before she could

argue, Frannie strutted over. "You should have brought Laine," she said. "She probably would have enjoyed seeing this."

He ignored the way Evelyn's eyebrows quirked up in a definite told-you-so kind of way. "She's not big on the limelight," Lyle said. "She's home having a lazy Sunday."

"Well, it's your call, obviously. I just thought it would be a nice time to announce your engagement to the press."

He froze.

He just plain, fucking froze.

"What do you think you know, Frannie?"

Her eyes went wide, her expression genuinely horrified. "Oh dear. I didn't realize it was still a secret. I mean, I figured if Rip knew, then most everyone did. Especially since you two don't talk that much anymore."

"Rip told you that Laine and I are engaged?"

"Last night at the gallery."

"He knew her name?"

"I think so." She frowned. "I mean, he asked me who you were with, and I told him. Then he nodded and said that he thought so. He hadn't met her yet, but he said that the two of you were engaged."

He clenched his fists at his side. "What else did he say?"

"That it was a whirlwind, but that you were gloriously happy and telling all your friends." She lifted a shoulder, pouting a little. "I was hurt, actually. Considering everything, I thought you would have at least mentioned it to me."

"Actually, Rip's just being an asshole," he said, working damn hard to keep his temper in check. "We're not—"

Evelyn coughed loudly beside him.

"—ready to announce yet. Not officially, anyway."

He caught Evelyn's eye, saw the subtle rise and fall of her shoulders.

"Oh," Frannie said.

"A few close friends know, and I was planning on telling you after this madness," he added, wondering just how long his nose was going to grow. "Someone must have told him without thinking."

"Well, now I feel doubly bad. I just assumed it was out there, and when I was talking to a group of media guys, Gordy asked if I knew about the woman you were with last night, so I told him."

"Gordy?" he asked, as a cold chill started to snake through him.

"The one who's so big on Instagram. You've met him, I'm sure. He's right over there. The one in the baseball cap." She turned, her arm up to point. Then she dropped it with a, "Huh. I don't see him."

She turned back to Lyle with a shrug. "I guess he left."

But Lyle barely heard her. Because now he knew why he recognized Gordy. He'd seen the bastard in the lobby of the Stark Century Hotel the night he'd first met Laine.

And when he'd followed her to the elevator, he'd passed a man in the hallway. A man in a baseball cap.

Gordy took the picture. The one that started it all.

Lyle was certain of it.

Just like he was certain that the little cockroach was

on his way to Laine's house right now, probably with a half dozen others racing there behind him.

And somehow, someway, Lyle needed to get there first.

CHAPTER 15

"OKAY, BUT YOU still haven't told me what the note actually says."

Joy's voice over the phone is far too rational. And I'm not in a rational mood. Call me unreasonable, but I tend to get cranky when a man I spend the night with skips out without even saying goodbye.

And, no, leaving a note on the kitchen table really doesn't count. Especially not one that says *I enjoyed last night more than I can say. Thank you for being such a perfect girlfriend for the night. — Lyle*

I mean, really? *"For the night?"*

That couldn't be any more of a kiss-off if he'd scrawled *fuck you and have a nice life* across the bottom.

"I should never have let you talk me into this in the first place," I continue, because I'm working myself into a truly righteous rage. "How could I have been so stupid? Easy ten grand, my ass."

"Slow down and rewind, or I swear I'm going to tell Cass I can't work today and come right over. As it is, I have fifteen minutes before my first appointment, and I want details."

"Fine." I suck in a breath, then catch her up, giving

her the quick story about how Marjorie had called and I'd agreed to be his paid date for the night.

"It's not real," I say. And then, because I'm a completely hopeless moron, tears actually prick my eyes. "But we had a really good time. I mean, sure, he was paying me to be his pretend girlfriend, but it was fun. And it was real. And then when we got back to my place—"

"Oh, sweetie, that's the job. They take you out, they show you off. Then they take you home and bang your brains out. It's pretty much a time-honored tradition."

"That's not how it was," I say, except maybe I had it all wrong. "He wasn't paying me for sex. Just for the date. But when we got back here—"

"Oh, really?" Her voice rises with interest.

"Dammit, Joy, do you want me to tell you or not."

She makes contrite noises, and I lay out what happened. "And when I told him I wanted to put the brakes on, he—"

"Went all asshole on you?"

"Joy…"

"Fine, fine, fine."

"He was great, actually. Total gentleman. Completely understanding. Except it turns out that it was all a big act, and—"

"Maybe it wasn't an act," Joy says. "Maybe he really was happy to just be there for you. I mean, you're likable. But in case you've forgotten, he doesn't go in for repeat performances, and yet he went two rounds with you. He probably figured it was time to get gone before he made you a habit."

I frown, but say nothing.

"And, honestly, it just goes to show you."

"Yeah? What exactly?"

"When you have the chance, go for the sex. Because you never know when you might end up losing it altogether."

"Thanks," I say. "I feel so much better."

And I do. Sort of.

I'm still pissed as hell, but I'm no longer a raging lunatic.

"But the opening was fun?" Joy asks. "Cass said the art was amazing and the performance was spectacular."

"I was seriously impressed," I admit.

"I went to Brighton with her," she adds, referencing a prestigious private school in LA that seems very un-Joy like.

"Who?"

"Kelsey. The dancer. We lost touch when she moved away. I didn't even realize until I saw an article about the opening in the paper this morning."

"Too bad you weren't at the show."

"I know, right?" Her voice turns muffled, and I hear her talking to someone else. Then she's back on the line. "I gotta go. You okay? I can switch stuff around and come over…"

"No, it's good. Greg's on his way to show me some pictures of the house we're going to be working on. He'll be here any min—Oh, he's here." My gate buzzer rings to my phone, and I have an app that lets me unlock it remotely. I do that now as I tell Joy goodbye and head to the front door to let him in.

I pull open the door, ready to tell him to beware because I'm in a pissy mood, when camera flashes burst like popcorn right in my face.

"What the—?"

I blink, but otherwise, I'm frozen. I should probably step back inside and slam the door shut, but I'm too baffled by the sight of at least a dozen shouting strangers, most with cameras, surrounding the steps up to my front door.

I open my mouth to try again, but this time, I don't have to ask the question. Because the reporters' shouted queries tell me everything I need to know.

"How long have you been engaged?"

"How did he pop the question?"

"Have you set a date?"

In the distance, I hear the squeal of tires.

At the same time, Greg pushes through the crowd, trying to get to me.

A car screeches to a halt in front of my house, stopping in the middle of the street. The door is flung open, and Lyle barrels out, only to freeze on the sidewalk when a booming voice calls out, "Miss Laine!"

I turn toward the source of the voice, and frown at the vaguely familiar guy with a goatee and a baseball cap. "Is it true that you and Lyle Tarpin are engaged?"

In front of me, Greg's mouth drops open.

In the street, Lyle meets my eyes. And then ever so subtly, he nods his head.

And now it's on me.

I can answer the question the way he wants, or I can express my displeasure at his kiss-off note by telling the world that I haven't got a clue what they're talking about.

I turn back to the crowd as Lyle pushes his way toward me. And then I say—very slowly and clearly—"Of course it's true. He asked me on the beach. And, no, we haven't set the date yet." I hold out my hand for him as I tell the crowd, "The truth is, I'm not crazy about public appearances. But I know I have to get used to them. So one picture, okay? And then if you could leave us alone for a while, that would be just swell."

He's already climbing the stairs as I say the last. *Swell?* he mouths, but I just broaden my already tight smile.

Behind him, Greg is climbing the steps, too, and he dodges around Lyle to get close to me. I know what he's going to say, of course. Or, rather, what he's going to ask. And I really can't risk one of the reporters overhearing him or reading his lips.

So I throw my arms around him, give him a big hug, and whisper very softly, "Go inside. Please, please don't argue or ask question. Just wait inside."

I take it on faith that he will, then I turn back to Lyle and face the crowd.

Lyle slides an arm around me, but I wriggle away. I take his hand, though; after all, I'm the one who kept this ridiculous charade going.

"Okay, people," Lyle says. "You heard her. Just one photo, and then we're going inside. As you can imagine, this isn't the announcement we had planned. Not to mention, you're trampling her lawn."

There's a general murmur of consent and apology from the crowd. More snaps and flashes, and then they start to shuffle away. Lyle pushes the process along by getting into the crowd and herding them like sheep.

Then he snaps my gate shut and turns to face me.

I meet his eyes, turn my back, and slam through the door into my house, only to find Greg right there waiting for me. "You're engaged?"

"No!" I blurt without thinking.

His eyes widen, and he shakes his head, the picture of confusion. "In that case, what the hell is going on?"

Before I can even think how I'm possibly going to answer that, Lyle bursts inside, his expression tight, as if he's holding in a burning rage. "I'm sorry," he says, then looks around, as if ready to kick something. An assumption that's borne out when he lashes out brutally and punches the air. "God, Sugar. I'm so damn sorry."

"Really?" I snap. "And what exactly are you sorry about? Sneaking out of my house this morning? Setting a horde of reporters on me? Making up a fake engagement? Because I'm a little fuzzy on the details of your apology."

"All of the above," he says. "Except I didn't make up the engagement. I came here trying to warn you and do damage control."

His voice is calm. Rational. And I don't care at all. Right now, I'm not in the mood to be soothed.

"Well, thanks for that tiny little favor. Now do you think you could quit with the hollow apologies and just tell me what the fuck is going on?"

"I'll second that," Greg says, making me jump. He's only standing a few feet away, but I'd been so focused on Lyle, that I'd completely tuned him out. "I saw your picture from last night at that art thing, and I was going to ask how you know an actual celebrity. But fake engagement? I mean, Christ, Laine. Are you in trouble?"

I shoot an angry glance toward Lyle. "Not the kind you mean."

"Then what kind do you mean?"

"Look," Lyle cuts in. "This is between Sugar and me."

"Greg was invited," I snap. "You weren't."

"Exactly," Greg says, looking smug. "And she prefers Laine," Greg says, and my stomach twists a little. Because generally, Greg is right. But when Lyle says Sugar, it sounds like an endearment. And even as furious as I am right now, I kind of like the sound of it.

Shit.

I square my shoulders, reminding myself that he is not off the hook—not by a long shot—then turn my attention back to Lyle. "So?" I demand. "Tell me what this is all about."

He cuts a glance toward Greg, and stays silent. I sigh. "However this plays out, I'm not keeping it a secret from Greg or from Joy."

"Dammit, Laine. You—"

"You don't agree? Then leave right now. Because I'm thinking that we're way, way, way outside any NDA. And you know what? Even if we weren't, you can just sue me." I put my hands on my hips and stare him down.

And the bastard actually smiles.

Okay, he's fighting it. But I can see his mouth twitching.

I cross my arms and glare.

"Fine," he says. "But right now, can we talk in private? And the two of them need to be able to keep a secret."

Greg steps forward. "Who the hell do you—"

"Please," I say, taking his arm. "You have to keep this to yourself. It's important."

"To him?"

"To me," I say. "And I really will fill you in, but later. Right now, I need you to do something for me."

It's his turn to cross his arms. "What?"

I turn to Lyle and hold out my hand. "Give me your keys."

He stares at me, clearly baffled by my out-of-context request.

I snap my fingers. "Now would be good."

To his credit, he drops them into my hand before he asks, "Why?"

"You're double-parked in front of my car, and you're going to end up getting towed. Greg's going to take your car to Totally Tattoo and leave it in the back with the keys under the mat." Cass is one of the few business owners with an actual parking area on her property. "You can tell Joy what's happened," I tell Greg. "And that Lyle will get the car soon, and I'll fill her in more later. They both know Lyle, so I don't think anyone will mind."

To his credit, Lyle doesn't balk at this plan.

"I don't like leaving you here like this," Greg says. "That mess outside? He's the one who set you up for that." He points an accusing finger at Lyle, who holds his hands up in defense.

"Please," I say, suddenly exhausted. "I really need—I

just need to talk to Lyle alone."

"Fine," he says curtly.

"Thanks," I say, then give him a hug. "I'll explain everything later, okay?"

He doesn't look happy about it, but he nods, shoots Lyle a nasty glare, then heads out the front door.

The moment it shuts behind him, I lash out. "You son-of-a-bitch. I let you into my house—I bring you into my home—and you skulk out without even saying goodbye? In case you forgot, last night wasn't a commercial transaction. So how the hell do you think that made me feel?"

"I wanted to let you sleep."

I tilt my head and give him my look of doom. "You know what? Fuck it. Just go. I put on the little show for your reporters, and now I think we're done here." I start to push past him toward the kitchen.

"Wait." He reaches for my arm, but I twist out of his grasp. "Please. I really am sorry. I didn't mean—"

"What? To leave? I'm pretty sure you meant it."

He exhales, looking completely worn out. Then he walks past me and sits on my couch.

"Make yourself at home," I mutter as Skittles jumps onto his lap, curls up, and starts to purr.

I take a seat across from him on the coffee table, mostly because I want to see his eyes while we have this conversation. Except he doesn't start talking. "Well?"

"About this engagement thing, I swear I didn't—"

"Hold on, there, pal. We're still at the part where you left me in bed, wallowing in humiliation."

His exhaustion seems to shift into frustration,

though whether it's aimed at me or at himself, I can't tell. "I apologized, Laine. Do you think I don't know I screwed up? That I hurt you? I get that. But I'm not used to this."

"Not used to what? Waking up next to a woman whose body you *didn't* pay for? Gee, I wonder why. Maybe it's because you're an emotional idiot who doesn't have a clue how to deal with a woman who's not on his goddamned payroll."

My anger propels me up and off the coffee table. I turn, lashing out to kick a wicker basket full of pillows. They tumble out soundlessly, and the whole thing is so anticlimactic, I drop to the floor and clutch one to my chest.

"Oh, crap. I'm sorry." I take a deep breath, mortified by all the vitriol that just came out of my mouth. "But you've really managed to piss me off."

"I see that," he says. "And if it's any consolation, you're right."

"Good to know. About what?"

"Pretty much everything," he says, coming to sit on his heels in front of me. "But you can lead with the emotional idiot part."

I have to force myself not to smile, but there's no denying that I feel better. This is the guy I like. The one who made me smile last night.

Who made me feel things I haven't felt in a very long time.

I twist my fingers together, my head bent now, because if I look into his eyes, he's going to be the one who sees too much. "You left," I say again, only this time I sound much calmer. "There was something between us—at least I thought there was. And you freaked, then you bolted. And you didn't even care how that would make me feel."

"Hey," he says gently, taking my hands, so that right then, his touch is the only thing I'm aware of. "Emotional idiot, remember?"

"Why did you go?" I pull my hands away. His touch is too soothing, and I'm not sure I want to be soothed.

"I had to be at a media circus at nine. But you're right. I should have said goodbye."

He brushes my cheek, then cups my chin, so that I don't have any choice but to look at him. "Last time, okay? I really am sorry."

He leans forward, and I feel my chest tighten in anticipation, my lips tingling from the memory of his kisses. I want that, damn me. That closeness I felt last night. And I lean forward, not even thinking. Just reacting.

And it's only when I feel that first tentative brush of his lips against mine that I realize what's happening, and I turn my face sharply away. "No," I whisper. "I don't think so."

For a moment, I think he's angry. But then he nods, just one quick jerk of his head, before he stands up and returns to the couch.

I stand as well, but I'm too restless to sit. "All of that was just door number one, remember? Now it's time to talk about the press invasion on my front lawn."

"Yeah," he says, pinching the bridge of his nose as if to ward off a headache. "About that…"

"Why would you tell someone we're engaged? And then not clue me into that little fact?"

"I didn't. Rip did."

It takes me a minute to process that information. "The guy you were in that sitcom with?"

He nods. "Apparently, he did a little rumor spreading during the opening last night. And then Frannie chatted up a few reporters, and it spun out of control from there."

"Why? I mean, why would Rip do that? And for that matter, why did it have to start spinning? Couldn't you have told Frannie or the reporter or whoever that Rip had his facts wrong?"

"As for the first, he probably did it to piss me off. He knows I don't date and don't like to be in the spotlight where relationships are concerned. And he's a little jealous that I'm doing movies now, and his last show was a web series.

"And as for why I didn't correct him," Lyle continues, "I honestly didn't think about it. Then again," he adds softly, "maybe it was there in the back of my mind."

"What was?"

"That if you were my pretend fiancée, I'd get to see you again."

"Oh." I draw a breath, hoping he can't tell how much I like hearing those words.

"Will you do it?" he asks. "Backing off now would draw the kind of attention I don't want. And besides, being engaged is a sure fire way to keep Frannie at bay for the filming."

"The filming? You aren't even set to begin for weeks, right?"

"Our engagement doesn't have to be that long. Two weeks, very public. Then we can break up. With any luck, Frannie will have found another man. And even if she hasn't, I can claim a broken heart and the hope of reconciliation. She'll leave me alone," he says with certainty.

"And that's it? That's all I have to do? Pretend to be engaged?"

He nods. "You in? I'm willing to pay."

"Damn right, you are," I say. "This is going to be an arms-length transaction or not at all."

He laughs. "Well, then name your price."

I think about it, then nod. What the hell, right? I might as well go for broke. "Sixteen thousand, nine-hundred seventy-four dollars."

"Well," he says with a small frown. "That's a very exact number."

"The amount I need to pay off the loan, minus the ten I already applied, and the five you paid me for our date. I'm not applying the value of the thousand-dollar bill, because I think it's cool, and I don't want to sell it. And I'm not applying the two grand I've saved because that would clean me out. Or the money I could get as a cash advance off my credit cards. Because then I'd just have more debt." I shrug. "So that's the number. Take it or leave it."

"Done."

"Really?" I grin. I was expecting more of a battle.

"Really," he acknowledges. "You're my adoring fiancée, in public and in private."

I take a step toward him. "Fair enough," I say. "As long as we're clear on one thing. I'll be your girl, and I'll put on a show for whoever's watching. As for the private part? You can sleep here, or I'll sleep at your place. And we can take day trips together and put on quite the show for the media. And if you really want me to, I'll even do your laundry."

I'm right in front of him now, and I press my finger to his lips, then trace it down, down, down, all the way to the fly of his jeans. "But that's as far as private goes. This," I add, cupping his crotch, "isn't part of our deal at all."

I back away as I feel his cock stiffen under my hand, then smile sweetly. "Those are the terms," I say. "Take them or leave them."

CHAPTER 16

LYLE CAUGHT HIMSELF smiling as he walked toward Totally Tattoo. The kind of big, goofy grin that spreads across a guy's face when the cute girl in fourth period agrees to go out with him. A happy smile, chock full of possibilities and promise for the future. Or, at the very least, one really awesome night in a parked car.

A smile that, in Lyle's case, was nine kinds of ironic considering Sugar had pretty much shut him down cold.

But he didn't care. Or, more accurately, he considered no sex a small price to pay to have her at his side for the foreseeable future.

And that was ironic, too, considering that just this morning he'd practically bolted from her house with his tail between his legs.

But that was when it had been a free-range type of situation. Without rules or parameters or expectations. Now, they both had roles to play. Which meant he was back in his comfort zone. He was a guy in love. A guy planning his wedding. A guy happy to finally have it out in the open that he'd found the girl he wanted to marry.

He could play that role. Hell, he could play that role so well they'd give him a damned Oscar even without an actual movie.

With a chuckle he rounded the corner and came up the alley behind Totally Tattoo. As he approached the low brick wall that blocked his view of the parking area, he slipped his hand into his pocket for his keys, only to remember that they weren't there.

He frowned, hoping Greg remembered to put them under the mat like Sugar had said. Surely he had—what else would he do with them, especially since it wasn't as if Greg had borrowed the Volvo to go joy riding.

But they weren't there.

Lyle checked all four mats, and there was nothing. Not even a loose coin or a cellophane wrapper from a mint. The car was completely pristine, just the way he liked it. And it was also completely absent of keys.

Well, hell.

He considered calling the guy, but he didn't have his number. And, he realized with a frown, he still didn't have Sugar's. He'd meant to get that at her house—it would have been a hell of a lot easier to warn her about the possible flood of reporters if he'd been able to make a call—but after their negotiation, he'd totally forgotten.

Most likely, Greg had left the keys inside with Cass, so Lyle headed toward the back door, surprised when it opened and Greg stepped out.

"I was just coming to look for you," Lyle said. "Well, you or my keys. Do you have—"

But he didn't get the last words out. Mostly because the rock solid punch that Greg landed in his gut knocked all the wind out of him.

He reeled, but came up fast, Riley's diligent training

coming in handy as Lyle caught Greg's arm, twisted it behind his back, and held it there, mere inches from breaking.

"Fuck, man," Greg yelled. "That hurts."

"It's supposed to. And your punch wasn't exactly a tickle, either."

The door slammed open again, and this time, Joy rushed out, her eyes wide. "What on earth is going on back here? Lyle! What the hell? Let him go."

Lyle did, releasing him and shoving him at the same time, so that Greg stumbled, lost his balance, then fell on his ass.

He got up, scowling as Lyle thrust out his hand. "Give me my damn keys."

"Hold on," Joy said, coming between the two of them, and spreading her arms like a referee in a boxing match. "What just happened?"

"This asshole just punched me in the stomach."

"And that prick set Laine up. Engagement my ass."

A fresh wave of anger boiled inside him, but before he could lash out again, Joy spoke.

"No, he didn't. I just got off the phone with Laine, and it's not his fault, okay? I told you—Lyle's a good guy."

Greg made a scoffing noise, and Joy's brow lifted.

"Fine," Greg said. "Whatever."

She lowered her hands and backed away, then pointed a finger at each of them in turn. "Play nice, you two."

"Hey," Lyle said. "All I was doing was getting my car."

Greg drew in a noisy breath. "We're cool," he said to

Joy. Then he faced Lyle. "But if you hurt her, we'll be a long way from cool. And I swear, I'll make your life a living hell."

"Not a problem," Lyle said. "I won't hurt her." That, at least, was a promise he intended to keep.

For a moment, he thought Greg was going to say something else, but all he did was toss Lyle his keys, then turn around and head back inside.

Lyle exhaled, all the tension draining from him. "Thanks, Joy," he said, then started toward his car.

"Hold up there, Cowboy."

He paused, not sure if he was exasperated or pleased that Sugar had so many good friends. "She told you what happened," he said. "I didn't set her up with the reporters."

"I know. It's cool. It's the rest we need to talk about."

He frowned. "The rest?"

She crossed her arms and cocked her head. "I know, Lyle."

"Know?" His skin felt clammy, and a heavy lump settled in his stomach. "What exactly do you know?"

"I'm Marjorie's cousin. And her assistant. I'm one of the few that has access to everything. All above board and legal," she added, her hands going up in supplication. "You read the NDA. You know her team has access."

"What do you want?" The words were harsh. Tight.

"Not a damn thing. It's what I don't want."

"What's that?"

"Christ, Lyle, what do you think? I don't know what

goes on in your head, or why you hire escorts, and I don't really want to know. I figure you have your reasons, and I'm fine with that. No judgment here—I'm not that big of a hypocrite.

"But you don't date," she continued. "You don't repeat—at least not before Laine. And all of that adds up to one big screaming red flag called *issues.*"

"Your point?"

"That I don't give a fuck what your issues are. I like you, okay, and I hope you work through them. But whether you do or don't really isn't my problem."

He stood tense and silent, hating feeling exposed, but waiting it out because he needed to know what she was getting to, since it obviously had to do with Sugar.

"There's one thing Greg and I agree on completely," Joy said. "If you hurt her, I will take you down. Slowly, painfully, and as publicly as I can. And screw the NDA. As far as I'm concerned, it's no more important than a grocery receipt if you hurt my friend."

"I meant what I said. I'm not going to hurt her."

She searched his face, holding his eyes for longer than was comfortable. Then she nodded. "All right then. We're cool." She flashed a smile as bright as the afternoon sun. "Enjoy the rest of your Sunday."

"Wait," he called as she started to turn away. "Do you know when and where she's working tomorrow?"

"No. Why?"

"Can you find out?"

She crossed her arms over her chest. "Probably. You want to tell me why I should?"

He took a step toward her. "It's just that I need a

little favor…"

LYLE WAS UP before the sun on Monday, which meant that Natasha was as well.

"Can I just turn in my resignation?" she asked, her voice sleepy over the phone. "Because it's barely past six, and I think this constitutes unreasonable work conditions."

"I need you to reschedule everything I have for today and tomorrow."

"Um, okay." There was a shuffling, and he assumed she was sitting up in bed. "Why?"

"Something's come up."

"Something named Sugar Laine?"

"Nat…"

"Hey. Fine. And no, I'm not going to ask why you're suddenly engaged to a girl who I, as your personal assistant, didn't even know you were seeing until you introduced her at Wyatt's opening."

"You heard."

"Everyone heard. Well, except people who never get on the Internet, and I'm pretty sure that breed doesn't live in Southern California."

"Good point, and yes. We have plans. So I need you to clear my schedule."

He waited for her to say more. To ask about their relationship, about how long they'd been together, about why she'd never arranged details for any other date.

But all she said was, "No problem."

And that, he thought, was why she was such a good assistant. "I need you to do a few other things as well. Some reservations I need you to make first thing, and then there's a pile of paperwork on my desk for you to go through and a few calls you need to return. You have your pad?" Natasha never went anywhere without her red portfolio, and Lyle assumed she kept it on her nightstand when she slept.

"Of course. Go ahead."

He ran her through the list, she promised to handle it all, and he hung up feeling that everything was on track.

Hopefully, it would stay that way.

His office was in his condo, and he showered and changed and was on the road well before Nat arrived. As his PA, she had access to pretty much all aspects of his life, and while he sped down Santa Monica Boulevard away from his Century City condo, he wondered just how much she'd figured out.

Did she know about the girls he'd hired over the years? Had she guessed that he was paying Laine for the pretend engagement?

It wasn't out of the realm of possibility. Nat was smart and observant—two of the reasons he'd hired her. She was also discreet, and anything she knew or suspected would stay locked in the vault. That much he was sure of.

She also wasn't judgmental, and he was certain that she genuinely liked him, despite whatever of his flaws she'd picked up on.

With all that in mind, he shouldn't care what she knew.

But he did.

The possibility that she knew he'd paid Laine for a night in his hotel, to be his date at the opening, and now to be his fiancée … well, that possibility ate at him.

Not because of what Nat might think about him, but because he didn't want her thinking less of Laine. He'd already thrust her into the spotlight. And though the public comment was congratulatory right now, he knew damn well that sentiment could turn on a dime. And Laine shouldn't have to put up with any of it.

When he reached Venice he pulled through a drive-in coffee shop and grabbed two lattes. Hopefully that was her drink, because even though they were on the verge of matrimony, he didn't have a clue as to any of those little things. He needed to find out—method acting, after all—and he had to admit he was looking forward to submersing himself in the role.

This time he had to park almost a block away, and he walked to her house carrying her coffee and sipping his. He rang the buzzer at the gate, surprised when there was no answer since it wasn't yet eight.

Maybe she was asleep. Or in the shower.

Or maybe she was pulling your chain last night, thought better of getting up close and personal, and is hiding inside, hoping you'll just go away.

Sadly, that probably wasn't an outrageous theory. Except for the fact that she loved her house, and while he might not know a lot about her, the one thing he was sure about was that she'd do anything to save her home.

He was considering climbing the fence and waiting on her front porch when a dog's deep bark sounded from the end of the block toward the beach, followed by Sugar's familiar laugh, then her gentle chide for the dog to slow down.

"Come on, Lancelot. Time to get you back home so I can shower and—*oh!* Lyle. Hi."

She came to a dead stop in front of him, the dog still tugging at the leash so that she had to work to stay in one place, the muscles in her arm straining as she held tight to keep the dog from bolting.

"Lancelot? Is he your knight in shining fur?"

"It's a good thing your work is scripted. You'd never make it in stand-up comedy." Her eyes dipped to the coffee. "Is one of those for me?"

"I hope you like lattes?"

"I guess that makes you my valiant knight. I'm seriously caffeine deprived this morning." She took a long swallow, then sighed with pleasure. "At the risk of sounding ungrateful, why are you here?"

"We have business."

"Um." Her forehead creased and she looked a little baffled. "Right. Well, okay. But I need to get him back next door and then I need to shower and then I have to get to Maudie's for the morning shift. So if there's something engagement-y that we have to do, can we do it in the afternoon?"

"Is he yours?" Lyle nodded toward the dog.

Her mouth twisted with annoyance, presumably because he'd ignored her question. "My neighbor's. He pays me to walk him most mornings so he can study. We just finished. I was taking him home."

"I'll go with you."

"Well, okay. Suit yourself."

He followed her to the garage apartment behind the two-story house beside hers. The dog trotted up the stairs, then barked at the door, which was opened by a dark-haired guy in gray sweats and a bare chest, his hair still damp from a shower.

"Hey, Sugar. Hey, Lancie boy." He crouched down and nuzzled the dog. "So I'll see you next on Wednesday, right?"

"It's Laine, Jacob," she said, and Lyle noted her exasperated tone. "And what? You don't need me to walk him tomorrow?"

"Are you kidding? I'd love for you to walk him tomorrow."

She stared at him, clearly confused, until finally Jacob said, "Duh. Joy called. Said you needed to skip?"

"Joy said?"

"She's wrong?"

"No—no, that's all good." Her brow furrowed, and Lyle could tell that she was trying to decide if she'd forgotten about some plans she'd made with Joy. "Anyway, I'll see you Wednesday, then."

"Cool." He shut the door, and she hesitated on the stairs.

"Let's get back," she said. "I need to phone Joy."

"You don't," Lyle said as they reached the bottom of the stairs. "She called him as a favor to me."

"To you?"

"I told you. We have business to take care of today."

"And so you had her call out for me? From everything?"

"Just today and tomorrow."

They'd reached her gate, and she paused, looking more than a little put out. "You do know that the loan's not the only thing I need money for. There's still the pesky matter of food, utilities, transportation, and taxes. Plus, on occasion I like to go to a movie or buy a book."

"I'll have my assistant email you an expense report," he said dryly. "Full reimbursement for all funds lost due to any activity you undertake in the capacity of my faux fiancée. Fair?"

"Pushy and controlling—and a lot annoying since you didn't run it by me first—but on the whole it's fair enough."

She was, he noted, fighting a smile. A fact that he considered a very good sign.

"So what is this business we have to deal with, anyway?"

"First off, I thought we'd go to Tiffany's."

"Why?"

"Well, you need a ring."

"Oh. Right." She glanced at her hand. "I hadn't thought of that."

"And then we need to hit your bank and take care of your loan."

She looked up at him, her eyes wide. "Really?"

"That was the deal, wasn't it?"

She swallowed. "Well, yeah. But I thought—well, I figured I had to play the part first."

He couldn't help but smile. "You planning on backing out on me?"

"Of course not."

"Then let's go. I don't like that it's hanging over your head."

She blinked, and he saw tears in her eyes.

"Thanks." Her voice quavered, and her voice was thick. And right then, he thought, she positively glowed.

The knowledge that he'd done that sent a potent rush of pleasure through him, like a jolt of electricity.

And he couldn't help but wonder, if he ever really proposed to a woman, if she'd look even half as happy as Sugar looked right now.

CHAPTER 17

EVEN SITTING AT the loan officer's desk, I can't stop looking at the ring. It's silly, I know, because it's nothing more than a prop. But still…

I hold out my hand, letting it glow under the bank's fluorescent lights as I wait for the woman to return with my paperwork. "Sparkly," I say, grinning up at Lyle, who's leaning against the wall checking his phone.

To his credit, he doesn't run screaming out of the room despite the fact that this is probably the fifteenth time I've said that between Tiffany's and the bank.

"I'm sorry," I say. "But it's so pretty, and it looks different everywhere we go. Sunlight, incandescent, fluorescent." It's a platinum-set classic round cut on a diamond studded band, and I think it's about the most beautiful thing in the world.

"It is a wonder of nature," he says, and I wrinkle my nose at him.

"Let me be girly," I say. "Besides, if anyone's paying attention they'll just see me being appropriately giddy."

I hold out my hand and wiggle my fingers so that it seems to shoot off sparks. "It's just that engagement rings mean something," I say as Lyle takes the seat next to me. "Or they should."

I force myself not to look at my hand for a moment. "When I was nine, we almost lost the house."

"Really? What happened?"

"Taxes. My mom thought my dad had paid them, but of course he hadn't. That's the year he left us. So when the bill came, she had nothing in the bank."

"She sold her engagement ring," he guesses.

"Good call. But can you guess the punch line?"

His brow furrows as he shakes his head.

"It was fake. Completely fake. Wasn't even worth two hundred dollars. I wasn't supposed to know—she was trying to be the good parent and not tell me the truth about my asshole of a dad—but I overheard her talking with a friend one night."

I frown, remembering. "Even then, she tried to cut him slack. She said that it was the sentiment, not the price tag. Because the ring was just a symbol that they were together. But as far as I was concerned, the sentiment was that he didn't value her enough to get her a real ring. It didn't have to be expensive, but it should have been something other than a craft store stone."

Once more, I hold my left hand out for him to see. "But this—well, this has real sentiment. And it's a symbol, too. The symbol of my victory over this loan," I say, tapping the desktop where Lyle's check for the full balance had been sitting just minutes before.

"So thank you," I add, then shrug, a little embarrassed that I got off on such a tear.

Lyle doesn't seem to mind. In fact he takes my hand and brushes his finger over the stone, then looks up at me. "What did she do?"

"Do?"

"About the taxes?"

"Oh." I frown. "I don't know. I guess she got help from someone. Maybe a friend."

"Like you," he says, his grip tightening slightly on my fingers.

My heart trips a little in my chest.

"Yeah," I say softly. "Like me."

The loan officer comes around the partition, and I catch a glimpse of her nametag. *Joan.*

I start to pull my hand away, but Lyle twines our fingers, then winks at me. *Engaged,* he mouths, and I roll my eyes. But I squeeze his hand, too. For Joan's benefit, of course.

"All right," Joan says. "You're all set."

I look from her to Lyle and then back again. "That's it?"

"That's it," she confirms. She hands me a receipt that shows a zero balance. "You'll be getting the rest of the paperwork in the mail, but your part is done."

"So no foreclosure. No more loan payments. Just … done."

"You two should go celebrate." She nods at the ring. "I probably shouldn't say, but I saw your pictures yesterday. You make a lovely couple."

"Thanks," I say, standing.

"I think Joan is right," Lyle says. He's standing now, too, and he slides his arm around my waist. I lean happily against him, because that's what newly engaged couples do.

"Celebrate," I say. "You know, I think that's an excellent idea."

Joan congratulates us again, and we head out into the bright California sun.

As soon as the door closes behind us, I hold out my arms and spin, laughing like a little kid. Then I spin my way over to Lyle, who catches me mid-twirl and holds me by my waist.

"Hi," I say, easing close, so that I'm pressed against him, my arms tight around his neck. I rise up on my tiptoes and kiss his cheek. "And thank you."

"You know, we're getting married," he says. "People might be watching."

"Good point," I say. "I can see why you're such a good actor."

"I like to get into the part," he says, and I'm suddenly very aware of the way he's holding me. Of the scent of his cologne.

There's a low thrum of awareness growing inside me, and before I can talk myself out of it, I capture his mouth with a kiss, then just about reel under the intensity with which he kisses me back. So thoroughly and completely that I'm not sure if I've ever really been kissed before. Like all other kisses were just practice for this one. This man.

I'm lightheaded when he breaks the kiss, and he has to hold my arm to keep me from stumbling.

"Well," I say breathlessly. "You really are a great actor. I think that kiss convinced anyone who was looking."

"Same to you," he says, his eyes never leaving mine.

"I really believed you were enjoying it."

I manage a flicker of a smile, then look away. I'm aware of every single nerve ending in my body right now, and all I really want to do is continue that kiss. Well, that and all the things the kiss might lead to.

Stop it.

I need to think non-sexual thoughts. Things like asphalt. And cars. And—I glance around the street—bank buildings.

Which reminds me of my loan.

Which reminds me of Lyle.

Which puts me right back where I started.

I grab his hand. "We should walk. We look silly just standing here."

He glances at his watch. "You're right, it's getting late."

I pull out my phone and check the time. Between the two hours it took to browse and buy at Tiffany's, drive time back to Venice, and the hour we spent waiting and then talking with Joan, it's now almost two o'clock. No wonder I'm hungry.

"Should we grab some lunch?"

"Actually, we should probably eat on the road if we want to have any time at the park today."

"Park?"

"Sugar Laine, you just paid off your loan," he says in a booming announcer-style voice. "What are you going to do now?"

I just stare at him, my eyes wide.

"Go to Disneyland?" he says, making the tagline of the familiar commercial a question.

"Lyle. I don't—" But I can't get the rest of my words out. My throat's too clogged with tears.

"Oh, shit," he says. "I'm so sorry. I thought you'd want to. You said you hadn't gone since the day of the accident, and I know how much the house means to you, and I thought that after paying it off—*fuck*. I asked Joy if you'd like it, but I should never have sprung it on you like this."

"No," I say, then throw my arms around him and sob against his chest. "These are happy tears." I hiccup a little, getting his T-shirt all wet.

He holds me, letting me dump all of that emotion on him, and when my tears finally stop and my breath isn't coming in painful heaves, I take a step back and manage a broad, watery smile.

"Thank you," I say sincerely. "That's probably the most thoughtful thing anyone's ever done for me."

"I should have asked. I'm thrilled you're happy, but that was reckless of me. I was only thinking that I wanted to do something nice for you. But those could have been sad tears."

"But they weren't," I tell him. "A little melancholy mixed in, maybe, but in a good way. Thank you," I say again. "Really."

I take another deep breath, then check the time again. "Yeah," I say. "Lunch on the road." I glance down at my jeans, T-shirt, and canvas flats. "I'm good to go now if you are."

"Then let's hit the road."

It's not as simple as that, of course. His car is parked in a lot four blocks from the bank, and then we have to navigate to In-N-Out for our mobile lunch. After that, we hit traffic getting to the freeway, and then, of course, there's construction on the 91. So by the time we actually park, get our tickets, and step onto Main Street, it's almost five o'clock.

I really don't care, though. We still have lots of hours, and I fully intend to cram in as much as possible.

To his credit, Lyle doesn't balk at my insanity, which starts out on Main Street at the theater where we watch *Steamboat Willie* and all the other vintage cartoons. Then we start working our way through the park, seeing all my favorites from my childhood, especially Pirates of the Caribbean.

We shoot aliens with Buzz Lightyear, go underwater in the submarine, and zip around the Matterhorn. And, because you're really never too old, we also hit the carousel.

We hold hands for every ride, which I enjoy more than I probably should considering our relationship is pretend. He holds my hand while we walk, too, which makes sense in case we're seen. But he's in a ball cap and sunglasses, and as far as I can tell, no one recognizes him.

Best of all, he puts up with all my detours, my squeals of delight when I see a character walking the street, and my very frequent window-shopping excursions, during one of which he buys me a vintage Mickey tank top.

I'm pretty much in heaven, and by the time the Electric Light Parade starts at eight forty-five, I'm also exhausted.

"We can stay longer," Lyle says from our primo spot on Main Street. "But if you're hungry, I have a reservation at one of the restaurants at the Disneyland Hotel."

Except for some snacks from the fruit stand in Adventureland, we haven't eaten since lunch. I hadn't felt hungry before, but now my stomach growls. Loudly.

We both laugh. "Maybe dinner would be a good idea," I say, taking his hand. "Thank you so much. Really. This was one of my best days ever."

"Mine, too," he says.

The restaurant is Steakhouse 55, and when we're seated with our wine and bread, I remember that I'd intended to apologize for Greg's punch, but got sidetracked by the stunning diamond now glowing in the dim light.

"He's just overprotective," I say now, after delivering the belated apology.

He nods thoughtfully. "Is there something between you two?"

"What? No. Well," I amend, "we're trying to start a business. But there's nothing sexual between us, if that's what you mean."

"Do you want there to be?" He asks the question casually, but there's an undercurrent of heat in his voice. And I can't deny that I like it.

"No," I say firmly.

"Good," he says, and that heat seems to settle inside me, warming my blood and making me tingle.

"Why good?" I ask, looking at my wine and not him. "Because it's convenient for you? What with me being shown off to the world as your wife-to-be."

He reaches across the table and takes my hand, and I look up into face, his blue eyes dark with an emotion I don't recognize. "Maybe I'm the jealous type."

"Oh." I swallow, tugging my hand away so that I can wipe my palms on the napkin in my lap. "Lyle, this is…"

I want to say this is starting to feel real, but I can't quite get the words out past my fear of utter mortification if he tells me it's just another acting gig for him. Which is why I finish lamely with, "…a really nice surprise. Thank you."

He says, "You're welcome," as the waiter returns with my steak, and we spend the meal on safe topics. The food, which is delicious. The wine, an entire bottle of which we finish off. The pro's and con's of Disneyland versus Disney World, a topic I'm unprepared for since I've never been to Florida.

"As far as I'm concerned, Disneyland is the sentimental favorite," he says.

"Noted. Why?"

"It's the original. And," he adds as he lifts his wine glass, now filled with the first glass from our second bottle, "I'm here with you."

"Oh." I twist my napkin in my lap, feeling ridiculously pleased.

"I had a really good time today." His voice is low and earnest, and although I know that the appropriate response is, *I did too*, my mouth has other plans. The kind of plans that are going to toss cold water all over these tingly feelings, and yet I can't stop the words from coming.

"Why don't you do this more often?" I ask.

"Well, we only just met…"

"I'm serious," I chide. "And maybe it's none of my business, but from everything I've seen, you're this really great guy. So why don't you date? Why do you, well, do what you do? With the hotel and the girls and the paying, I mean."

"I know what you mean. And I told you before. It's hard to date in LA, especially if you're a celebrity. You never know for certain why a woman's interested."

"That's what you said, but I don't buy it."

"Well, it's the truth. Take it or leave it."

The sensual tone is gone now, and I want to kick myself. Because just like I said, it really isn't any of my business. And yet I had to poke the beast, and probably mess up a pretty nice evening. And all because I'm attracted to the guy who's paying me to be with him. Really not a recipe for future bliss.

"Forget it," I say. "I should never drink wine. It makes me both nosy and stupid."

He doesn't look at me. Instead, he picks up the salt-shaker and stares at it as he slowly twists it between his fingers. "I know you must think I'm an asshole, but I do have my reasons."

"I don't think you're an asshole."

"No?" He looks up from the saltshaker. "What do you think?"

For a moment, I consider lying or dodging the question. But he deserves the truth. "I think you're lonely," I say. "And I think you're exhausted."

His forehead crinkles. "Exhausted?"

Now it's my turn to fiddle with the table setting. I

pick up a packet of sweetener and turn it over and over in my hand. "It's just that it's a lot of work pretending to be someone you're not." I shrug, as if these words are easy and casual. "Hard enough doing it in your job. But you do it in your life, too."

He says nothing, but I'm watching his face. I see the shadow in his eyes. And I see the way his throat moves as he swallows.

"Maybe I'm wrong," I go on. "But I think I'd like the Lyle Tarpin you're hiding. Just saying," I add with a tentative smile, "in case you ever want to introduce him to me."

CHAPTER 18

HER WORDS SEEMED to hang over the table in a cartoon balloon, and Lyle wanted more than anything to reach up with a pin, pop the bubble, and have everything she'd just said crumble into dust.

Across from him, she winced. "I really should have stayed quiet. Like I said, me and wine and words can go very, very wrong."

"It's okay," he lied. "Really."

"Good." She twisted the engagement ring absently. "That's good."

For a moment, an awkward silence hung between them. Then she pushed away from the table. "I'll be right back. Ladies' room," she added before moving with remarkable speed across the restaurant.

He wasn't sure if she was leaving to escape what she'd said, to give him space to ponder, or if she really needed the restroom.

He didn't care.

Right then, he was grateful to have a moment alone.

Because she was right. What she'd said was spot on. Bottom line. End of story.

The not-so-fun toy surprise in the bottom of the cereal box.

He'd been playing a role for years, and she was the first person to ever call him on it.

Which was both a delightful surprise and rather disconcerting.

With a sigh, he ran his fingers through his hair, then pulled out his phone.

He held it for a moment, his finger poised over his contacts. Then he drew in a breath and pulled up Marjorie's name.

It would be so easy, he thought. So simple to make a call and find a woman who didn't see his baggage. Who took money in exchange for sex, and that was it. Clean. Simple. Uncomplicated.

So easy to go back to the way it was before Sugar. A time that seemed years away, not just days.

Easy, he thought again, as he tapped the button.

Not to make the call, but to delete the contact entirely.

Symbolic, maybe, but important.

Because since he'd met her, something had shifted inside him. And no matter what happened with Sugar, he knew that he'd never be able to pay a woman for sex again.

"I have a plan," she said as she returned to the table.

"For world domination?"

"Not exactly." She slid into her seat and looked at him earnestly. "This day was perfect until I went and shoved my foot into my mouth. So I propose we go back to Disneyland and pretend like dinner never happened."

He leaned back in his chair and crossed his arms. "I'm listening."

"That's it. That's my entire plan. It's pretty much all about turning back the clock so that I don't feel like a bumbling ass. But if you'd rather stay and have dessert than let me off the hook, then you just go right ahead and be evil."

"I don't do evil," he said, his expression totally bland as he signaled the waiter. "Don't you read the trades? I'm that nice actor from Iowa."

"Well, then. I guess we're going back to the park."

By the time they were back on Main Street, it was eleven-fifteen, which left them only forty-five minutes inside the Magic Kingdom, but Lyle figured that would be enough. She was right, after all, just being back inside the gates felt like a second chance.

"This is what I used to think it was like," he said, surprising himself with the admission.

She turned her head, frowning slightly. "What do you mean?"

"I didn't grow up in the best of homes. It was … challenging." He remembered the cramped rooms. The leering men. The haunted women.

"When I was little, I used to hide in the cellar. I'd sneak down after I'd done my chores, and I'd sit on the dirt floor and I'd close my eyes and let myself fall asleep as I fantasized about this perfect place. Where the people were friendly, and everyone was happy, and the streets were clean. Where there weren't needles and condoms in the wastebaskets, and a kid didn't have to plan out when to talk to his mother, because without precise timing, she'd either be drunk or high."

They were walking side by side, and now she reached over and took his hand. "I'm so sorry."

He tightened his grip, taking comfort in the feel of her skin against his. "I ran away," he said before he could change his mind. "I was sixteen, and I wrangled a fake identity, and I ran away."

"Oh, Lyle…"

"Only one other living person knows that," he said. "So you were right about the hiding. The truth doesn't exactly fit my Iowa farm boy persona."

"Thank you for trusting me."

"I don't think trust is something you thank someone for. I think it just is."

Her soft smile tugged at his heart. "Then that's even sweeter," she said as they walked toward Sleeping Beauty's castle, now shining in the dark.

By the time they reached it, the park was closing up, the employees starting to herd guests toward the exits.

"I had a really nice time," she said. "Thank you so much. For everything. The house. The ring. This," she added, her arms wide to indicate the entire park.

"You're welcome," he added, not mentioning that the house was her price and the ring was a prop. He didn't want to think about the show they were putting on for the public. Tonight felt too genuine to spoil it with harsh reality.

"It's been magical," she added, then pulled him to a stop beside the circle of flowers at the center of the town square. Then she kissed him, very slow and very sweet, and his arms went tight around her, holding her close as he reveled in the taste of her. The feel of her. As he imagined so much more, and then tried to shove those fantasies aside, knowing that wasn't what she wanted.

She'd made perfectly clear that sex wasn't on the agenda, and he couldn't blame her. She deserved something real with a man who wasn't broken.

Gently, he eased back, and his heart twisted at the way she was smiling at him. Like this had been a real date and they were a real couple. But they weren't. How could they be when she still didn't know the truth?

Once she learned it—*if* she learned it—she wouldn't want him anyway.

"Hey," she said. "You okay?"

"Just a little melancholy. I like this fantasy." He indicated the park, but meant something else entirely.

"Me, too."

"No regrets? In coming with me?"

"Just one."

He frowned. Considering the way she'd kissed him, the answer surprised him.

"We got here so late, we didn't get to do everything. And we didn't have the chance to do anything twice."

He laughed, relief sweeping over him. "That kind of regret I can handle. In fact, I was kind of hoping you'd say that. How do you feel about the Disneyland Hotel?"

She squinted at him, obviously completely baffled. "What are you talking about?"

"I had Nat book us a suite. Just in case you wanted to stay."

He watched as happiness lit her face, as bright as the afternoon sun.

"Are you kidding? That would be amaz—oh. But I can't. Tomorrow. I've got work. A full schedule, actually, and I have to—"

"You don't."

Her mouth tugged into a frown. "Remember my speech about eating and taxes? Money is an unfortunate necessity."

"I mean you don't have to work tomorrow. Joy cleared you for Tuesday, too. And if I'm not mistaken, Nat's already emailed you an expense report."

"You were serious about that?"

"Reimbursement? Of course."

She nodded slowly, licking her lips. "Does that mean Natasha knows? About me, I mean."

"That our engagement is a show?" he asked, surprised by how much saying those words stung. "Yeah, she knows." He hadn't forwarded her an official memo, but she'd been in the gym when he'd discussed the fake girlfriend issue with Evelyn, and Nat was more than capable of putting all the details together.

"Oh."

"In fact, we'll probably have to make up a few details for her to share. She doesn't talk about my personal life to the press, but in this case, it might be smart to let her leak a few facts. Just to build up the backstory we've invented."

"And the rest?"

It took him a second to realize what she was asking, but when he did he rushed to reassure her. "About meeting you through Marjorie? No. Absolutely not."

"So she doesn't know about you and—"

He shook his head. "No. Or, at least, if she's figured it out, she hasn't said anything." He considered the question seriously for the first time, and the truth was that Nat just might know he'd hired call girls in the past. He relied on her to run his life, especially when he was filming and had no time. She was smart and observant and—

"Hell," he said. "The truth is I never told her. And I never let myself think about the possibility that she might figure it out. I'm careful, but she sees a lot. She might know about the women, which means she might—"

"—know about me. Right. I figured."

"Is that so horrible?" He knew the answer would be yes. Hell, just the thought that Nat might know the kind of life he'd been leading all these years was enough to make his gut twist.

She stood still for a moment, then shook her head. "No," she said, surprising him. "I had my reasons, and they were valid. I'd just rather she heard it from me than from rumors."

"If you want, you can tell her," he said.

"That you hired me to be your fiancée?"

"That," he agreed. "And how we met."

"Then she'd know the truth about you for sure."

He nodded, realizing he could live with that. A close secret among people he trusted.

It was something else that ate at him—the possibility that his past with those women would go wide. Especially now that they were permanently in the past.

"You okay?" she asked. "You look pensive."

"Just thinking about tomorrow," he lied. "We should start with California Adventure," he added, referring to the other Disney park. "And, hey, I can always clear your schedule for Wednesday, too."

She laughed, but he was half-serious. How nice would it be to stay here indefinitely, just the two of them lost in this clean, shiny world with none of the drama and pain of the real world?

"I wish I could, but Wednesday's not a day I want to miss. Greg and I have work stuff."

"Greg," he repeated, his voice flat. He had the sudden urge to punch someone—ideally Greg himself—and he realized that he was jealous.

He tamped it down. "What kind of business are you and Wonder Boy starting?"

She playfully hip bumped him as they strolled to the exit. "Flipping houses," she said, then told him about a new venture with Greg and Anderson Morton-Gray.

"I worked with his husband on *The Price of Ransom*."

"I know. Small world, right? At any rate, I can't wait to get started, and Anderson emailed that we can go walk through the property on Wednesday. Which means I can only afford one more day here."

"Fair enough," he said, and realized he was still a little jealous. Only this time, not of Greg, but of her. Of the fact that she was diving into a job she genuinely loved.

Oh, sure, *M. Sterious* was a solid script. But it was solid for a superhero movie where he'd be doing most of his work in front of a blue screen. And, sadly, the script had gone through so many revisions that it had lost a lot of its heart—a fault that the producers didn't care about so long as sequels were in the works.

No, it was only the paycheck that Lyle was looking forward to now, not the work. It had been a long time since he'd looked forward to the work.

How ironic that he was living his dream in the biggest way possible, and yet his world still fell flat.

Or, he amended as Sugar reached for his hand, it had been flat until she'd bounced into his life, all vibrant and thoughtful and genuine. She'd flipped a switch in him, and he didn't know how to turn it off.

For that matter, he didn't know if he wanted to.

CHAPTER 19

B Y THE TIME we get back to my house late Tuesday evening, I'm exhausted and sunburned.

As far as I'm concerned, we did Disney into the ground. We started the day at California Adventure, stuffing ourselves on fresh sourdough bread and tortillas inside the park even though we'd already had breakfast in the hotel.

We'd *ooh'd* and *aah'd* with the other passengers as we flew over the world on the Soarin' ride. And then we'd screamed ourselves hoarse when we were dropped from an astonishing height in the Guardian's of the Galaxy ride, where Lyle clutched my hand so tightly it still aches.

"I'm not a huge fan of being dropped from an insane height," he'd said calmly, once we were safely on the ground.

"Why did we ride it, then?"

He'd just smiled and shrugged. "We're here. We're doing Disney. And as far as I'm concerned, it's go big or go home, right?"

I agreed, and we'd followed that advice to a T.

All of which explains my exhaustion now that we're back in Venice. Not to mention my incredibly happy mood.

"This was such a great treat," I tell Lyle. "I needed a mini-vacation more than I can tell you."

"My pleasure," he says as he kills the engine in front of my house, then turns to me. "I enjoyed every single moment of it."

"Me, too," I say, then look down at my hands, unsure if the longing I hear in his voice is real or my imagination.

I want it to be real. Because the truth is, while I fully enjoyed the park, I enjoyed the company more.

I like the way he makes me laugh, the way we can talk. I like the way I feel when he touches me, even casually.

And I really like the anticipation that wells up inside of me when I'm with him—a delicious sort of craving that will be satisfied only when he touches me with intent.

Bottom line? I'm falling for him.

The problem? I'm an idiot. Because I'd intentionally and purposefully pushed him away the night of Wyatt's opening. Clearly, I'd been a shortsighted fool.

But he'd scored big points when he'd backed off with such sweet understanding. Hell, he'd been the perfect gentleman.

Now I'm thinking I'd like to see a little bit of a bad boy.

My fear is that by shutting him down once, I've shut him down forever.

Go big or go home may have applied where amusement park rides were concerned. But I'd had a different kind of ride in mind last night, and he hadn't made the slightest bit of an overture.

No big. No home. No nothing.

Nothing physical, anyway. Hand-holding, sure. And a few kisses when we were in public, because you never know who might be watching, and we were there as a happily engaged couple.

But none of that was real, as I very firmly reminded myself after each kiss. And after each time he gently wiped chocolate off my face, laughing at the way I succumbed to my love of frozen chocolate Mickey treats.

And after every time he held my hand or looked at me tenderly or even did something gentlemanly like drying my seat before I sat down in the Splash Mountain flume, even though we both knew it was just going to get wet again.

All of those moments felt real and romantic, but it was all a charade. Because when we were in the suite, all of that touching fell away.

No contact. No overture. No advances of any kind.

Which was expected, I suppose. Because I'd told him my terms. I'd pretend to be his fiancée in public, and that was as far as it went.

But now I can't help but wonder if the attraction is one-sided. If he'd only wanted an easy lay the night of the opening, and all of the heat I feel between us now is nothing more than my own desire reflected back on me.

I don't think so … but I don't know. How can I know? He's an actor, after all. A damn good one.

And now I'm afraid that the only way to find out if this attraction is one-sided is for me to make the first move. Which, considering how little experience I have in that department, is a hell of a lot scarier than the drop in the Guardians of the Galaxy ride.

Even so, I draw a deep breath and plunge into what I hope will prove to be very warm and receptive water.

"Do you want to come in?" I ask, feeling oddly shy considering how much time we've been spending together. "I can make you a cup of coffee for the road. Besides," I add, "we should sort out the souvenirs."

"I'd love coffee," he says, and I consider that a good sign. It's almost midnight, after all, and I know he's tired, too.

There's a pile of mail in the box that attaches to the inside of my gate, and I grab it on the way in, noticing that one large brown envelope came by courier and not regular mail. But I'm not interested in any of it right now, and I toss the whole batch on the kitchen table as I start to brew us both some coffee.

Lyle's leaning against the counter, telling me something about the farewell party we're attending tomorrow night for his friend Noah, but I'm not listening. I'm gathering courage. And when the Keurig is finished brewing the first cup, I put it down on the counter beside him, then take his hand when he starts to reach for it.

He stills, then looks down at my hand on his. When he looks back up, there's a question in his eyes. And, I think, an invitation.

"I don't want this night to be over," I admit, barely able to hear my own words over the pounding of my heart.

"Sugar…"

I don't know where he's going with that thought, but I'm not letting him get there. I rise up on my tiptoes and kiss him, and—thank God—he kisses me back. Gentle at first, but with enough heat that it sets off a riot of sensations inside me.

I moan, my fingers twining in his hair as he draws me close, taking the kiss deeper. Wilder. Until he's claiming me with such intensity that I'm certain that this isn't one-sided at all. On the contrary, it's very, very two-sided. And, as my body clenches and my pulse quickens, I can't help but hope that it will be horizontal soon, too.

His hands grip my shoulders, and he breaks the kiss long enough to look at my face. I know what he sees. My flushed skin. My swollen lips. My eyes wild with desire.

"Please," I beg, and it's as if I've flipped a switch. I gasp as he presses me back against the refrigerator in one swift motion. He gives me no time to recover, instead taking full advantage of my surprise. His mouth closes brutally over mine. Teeth and tongue and heat and passion—a heady potion that's making me drunk. Making me wild. Eager.

I'm craving him like a drug, my hands roaming his body. Seeking. Claiming. And when I slide my hand roughly down to stroke his erection, he practically growls as his teeth tug at my earlobe and his hands roughly cup my breasts.

I stroke him, feeling him grow harder under my hand. All coherent thought has left me, replaced by basic, primitive emotions—*want, need, have, take.*

His hand slides down to cup me through my jeans,

and I whimper, shamelessly stroking myself against his fingers, wishing he'd just open my fly and slide his hand inside my pants and touch me.

Oh, God, how I want him to touch me…

And he wants it, too. I'm certain of it.

Which is why I'm so damn surprised when he gently pushes me away, looking at me with heated eyes, his desire held tightly at bay.

"What?" I demand. "What's wrong?"

"You don't want this," he says, and I curse myself for having stupidly shut this down that first time.

"I do," I say. "Lyle, dammit, please."

"Sugar, baby—"

The frustration in his voice is palpable, and I know how hard he's working to hold back. And, dammit, I don't want him holding back.

"Please," I say, as I peel off my T-shirt and toss it aside. I stand there in my simple cotton bra. "Please," I repeat, then reach back to unfasten the bra as well, then drop it to the floor. "No may mean no, but this is one of those times when yes really does mean yes."

"Christ, Sugar…"

I can hear the battle in his voice. Raw. Hard. As if it's taking all his strength to keep his hands off me.

I'm going to break him.

I take his hands and put them on my breasts, then tilt my head back and sigh as his fingers tighten around my nipples. "Yes," I whisper. And then, because I can't bear the thought that he'll stop again, I take one of his hands and slide it ever so slowly down my bare torso, teasing myself with this light touch until I reach the waistband of my jeans.

I release his hand, and as his fingers brush my abdomen, I slowly unbutton my jeans. "Touch me," I demand, and since he still may not comply, I guide his hand all the way down, then moan when he finds me wet and aroused and so very ready.

"Fuck, Sugar," he murmurs, then scoops me up and carries me to the bedroom.

"Strip," he orders, but he doesn't wait for me to comply. Instead, he tugs down my jeans and underwear as I start to toe off my shoes. We're a tangle of arms and legs and desperation, and when he's managed to get me naked, he slides between my legs and closes his mouth over my pussy.

I arch up, completely unprepared. I'd expected a trail of kisses up my thigh, but this—oh, God—this is incredible, and I writhe shamelessly against him. Wanting his mouth. His tongue.

Small tremors cut through my body, precursors to the orgasm to come, and I grasp his hair in my fists, and shamelessly beg him to please, please fuck me.

He shifts, and I whimper when he takes his mouth off me, his hands now on my hips as he holds me steady. He lifts his head, then meets my eyes.

I'm breathing hard and so is he. And I want this so much. The feel of his body against mine, his cock deep inside me.

"Lyle," I beg. "Please, now."

But he doesn't move. And I watch, confused, as his eyes cloud and he sits up, then stands and grabs my robe. He tosses it to me, and I grab it automatically, pulling it up like a sheet to cover me as he shakes his head and says, "I'm so sorry, but we can't. Not like this. Not until you know everything."

CHAPTER 20

"EVERYTHING," LAINE REPEATED as she sat up beside him, her forehead creasing with worry as he got out of bed.

He started pacing, trying to decide where to begin.

"Lyle?"

"I told you I ran away," he said, stopping only inches from her. "I didn't tell you from what. Or, at least, I didn't tell you all of it."

She nodded, apparently realizing that it would be easier for him to keep going without interruptions. Although, really, none of it was easy.

"I grew up in a whorehouse," he finally said. "A run-down old farmhouse just outside of town. Everyone knew what went on out there, but no one ever tried to shut it down."

"Your mom?"

He nodded. "Worked there. Lived there. And God only knows which one of her customers was my dad."

She scooted back on the bed until she was leaning against the headboard, then drew her knees up and hugged them. "I didn't even know places like that still existed," she said, and he was grateful she didn't offer empty condolences.

"When she worked, I'd have to go to the basement. Those were the best times, actually, because usually Jenny was down there, too. And we used to act out stories. Mostly made up, but sometimes we'd read lines from plays we stole from the school library."

"She was another kid?"

"It was just the two of us. The only children in the house. We grew up together on that packed dirt floor. We were best friends. Hell, for a long time we were each other's only friend. We went to school, but the kids all knew where we lived and what went on in that house. We weren't exactly running in the cool crowd."

"You loved her."

He nodded. "Very much, but not like you mean. She was my first, but that was out of curiosity more than desire. Maybe even boredom. But it was sweet and I don't think either one of us regretted it. I think it made sense to both of us that we'd be each other's first."

He closed his eyes, swallowing as he tried to gather up his emotions. He'd never loved Jenny romantically, but she'd been his best friend. Hell, his only friend until they met Riley when he was ten and Riley was thirteen.

She knew him as well as he knew himself, and vice-versa. And even after all these years, the pain of losing her was palpable.

"Did she die in a car wreck? Is that why you drive the Volvo?"

He almost smiled. Instead, he got back on the bed, then sat facing her, his back to the footboard. "You're getting ahead of the story. That's act three. In act two, the bitch who owned the house decided that Jenny needed to either leave or work."

"What about her mother?"

"Her mom was a junkie. She would have flat out sold Jenny if she thought she'd score some crack."

"Oh." She licked her lips. "And your mom?"

"She was a wreck," he said, "but I loved her. And she thought she was doing her best by me. Thought that by working in that house she was feeding me and clothing me. Keeping me off the street. *Shit.*"

He winced as sharp-edged memories sliced through him.

"Lyle—" Hearing his name with her sweet voice was like a balm, and when she scooted down the bed and took his hand, it just about shattered him.

He closed his eyes, trying to block the memories. Of all the times he'd tried to convince his mother to leave that life. To tell her that they'd survive somehow.

He knew they could; he'd met folks in the house who could help. It wasn't high class, and most of the johns had records as long as their arms. Even when Lyle was barely twelve, he knew who to go to if he needed a gun or a fake ID or drugs. Not that he did drugs—he saw too clearly what they did to Jenny's mom. But information was the only currency he had, and so he watched, and he soaked it all in.

He drew a breath, then continued his story. "And then one of my mom's johns beat the shit out of her. I was fifteen, and I'd snuck up from the cellar to the kitchen. I heard her scream, and I ran to her room, but he knocked me back, and I hit my head. I didn't pass out, but I couldn't get up. All I could do was watch as he—"

"He killed her?"

He clenched his fists, willing words to return. "That would have been kind. Instead, he beat the shit out of her while I slumped there, totally useless."

"You were hurt." Her words were a whisper, meant to soothe.

It didn't work. He'd heard those words before, and they were always hollow.

"She died three days later, and even though she was in a hospital, I saw the pain on her face. Even with a goddamn morphine drip, I know she suffered."

He'd been looking at his hands, but now he lifted his head and saw the tears streaming down Laine's lovely face.

"What did you do?" she whispered.

"I stayed. I was so fucking pathetic that I earned my keep cleaning the damn house and doing minor repairs. Three long months, and then everything changed. Because that's when the bitch who owned the house said that it was time for Jenny to start working."

"You ran. You both ran."

He nodded. "Jenny dreamed of Hollywood, and I knew she could make it here. She wanted to be huge. Top billing. Tons of money. The world at her fingertips. And so, yeah, we ran. I stole some crack from her mom and traded it for fake ID's and records from one of the johns. And Riley helped us steal a car from the impound yard."

"The impound yard?"

"His dad was the sheriff. Riley's three years older than me, but he came around the house with his dad enough that we became friends. He's seen a lot, and he knew the score."

"His dad came to arrest the women?"

Lyle scoffed. "No one bothered enforcing prostitution laws. Hell, there would have been a riot. No one admitted going there, but for a place no one acknowledged, it was always full."

He pinched the bridge of his nose. "No, his dad—well, his dad was a good guy. He knew what Riley did for us, and he turned a blind eye."

"Lucky break."

"Maybe too lucky," Lyle said. "I was the one with the plan. I had the idea to steal the car. To get new identities. And when we finally took off down the highway in the dead of night, I hadn't slept in days, I'd been so hyped up on plans and fear and adrenaline."

He sighed, remembering those few hours when he and Jenny had been free. When it had been good. Those few precious hours before he drove straight into hell.

"It was my fault," he said, so low that he wasn't sure Laine could even hear him. "I drifted off. Just for a second, but that was enough. An eighteen-wheeler had crossed into our lane, and it was too late. I swerved, he hit the side of the car, and we went off the road and into a ravine."

He could still hear the twisting metal. Smell the rubber burning on the asphalt.

"Jenny?"

"She died instantly." The words tasted bitter. "I

didn't even get a scratch."

"Lyle, I'm so—"

But he just held up a hand. He had to get it out. Had to push past this one horrible memory.

"The police came. I gave them my real name—it's John, by the way. My mother had an odd sense of humor. John Rivers. And the police decided it wasn't my fault. No charges, but they shoved me into foster care. I stayed for about a month—I was too numb to do much else—and then I ran away to LA, used my papers, and became Lyle Tarpin."

"You wanted to come here for Jenny," she said, and he nodded, pleased she understood. "You wanted to make it in Hollywood for her."

"Not at first. At first, it didn't even occur to me that acting was an option. But then it all started to fall into place. Almost like it was destiny."

The corners of her mouth curved down. "And I was right—about the escorts, I mean. You are railing against something. That's where you go when the memories get too bad. Like the night we met. That was the anniversary of Jenny's death, wasn't it? You pretty much told me so at Wyatt's opening."

"Yeah," he said. "It was."

She nodded thoughtfully. "At Disneyland, when I asked you about why you went to the women, you never really answered me."

"That was because I'd already told you—it's just sex. Because a relationship's hard when you live in a spotlight."

"Right. You did tell me that."

There was an emotion he couldn't place in her voice, but before he could ask, she continued.

"Is that why you pay so well? Tip so well? Because of how you grew up? Because the women around you struggled so much?"

He nodded. "It's not the same, I know. And I don't sleep with streetwalkers, although I do donate to a half-dozen organizations that help with rehabilitation. But, yeah, I like to feel like maybe I'm helping them, even if just a little."

He drew in a deep breath, surprised that he felt re-markable good, like he'd just gone a few rounds in the ring, but had quit before all his energy left him.

"So that's who I am. That's the man you invited into your bed. A guy who ran away from home in search of some perfect pretty fantasy of a life, and in the process managed to get his best friend killed."

"No, you didn't," she said gently. "But I can under-stand why it feels that way."

She paused, her head tilted as she thought. "Did Jen-ny like Invictus? Because I was wondering why you had it with you that night. Why you gave it to me."

"It was one of the books we kept in the basement. She used to read it aloud. She said it was our theme. That we were unconquerable."

He ran his hand over his hair, as if combing away the memories. "I had it with me because I reread it every year on that day. And I gave it to you because it fit. I already told you that. You needed the money. You did something scary. You didn't let life defeat you."

"So you didn't just pass out those thin little poetry

books to every woman you hired."

For the first time since they'd begun the conversation, he laughed. "No, not hardly. I have some of those thousand dollar bills that I use as tips, but not the book. Never that. In fact, until I actually put it in your hand, I wouldn't have believed that I had it in me to give it away. That little book's been with me a long time."

"And yet you did."

He eased toward her on the bed, then reached out to stroke her silky hair. "Yes," he said, hoping she understood what that meant. That he'd seen something special in her—in *them*—from the first moment he'd met her.

"Thank you for telling me this. It means a lot that you trust me with the truth."

"I trust you," he said, moving his hand from her hair to her temple. "It's late. I should go so you can sleep."

"No." She grabbed his hand and tugged him closer. "Stay here? We can just sleep. That's fine. But it's too late for you to drive home."

"Is that what you want?" he asked. "To just sleep?"

She licked her lips. "I don't know. I thought—what with the heavy conversation—"

"Do you know what I want?"

She shook her head, her eyes wide.

"This," he said, and then kissed her, tentatively at first, but then wilder as she opened to him, her desire for him so real and intense it humbled him.

She still had the sheet over her chest, but now she let it drop, then moved onto his lap, so that she was naked and straddling him over his jeans. "Touch me," she demanded. "Take me."

He moaned, so hard now it was painful. And it wasn't even her body that was affecting him—though Christ knew he wanted to lose himself in her soft curves. It was the fact that she wanted him. That she so clearly desired him.

And that the truth about who he was hadn't extinguished the fire between them. If anything, it had strengthened it, because he knew that she wanted *him*. That it was him. The man, not the actor, not the prostitute's son. *Just him.*

He let his hands roam over her back, her soft skin. Then he cupped her head and pulled her close, kissing her wildly, making her moan.

She whimpered, and he couldn't get enough of her. And when her hips moved and she rubbed herself against his jeans, he thought he'd come right then.

"That's it, Sugar. Baby, that's so hot."

"You're teasing me."

"I like watching you want me. Your skin flushed. Your lips swollen. I want to tease you. To draw it out. To make you beg so that there's no doubt that you want me."

"I've wanted you since the first moment I met you," she said, and he felt the truth of her words cut through him. "But that was only physical. Now I want *you*, Lyle," she said, and his head spun with the satisfaction of hearing his own thoughts reflected back at him.

"Please," she murmured. "Please."

"What do you want, baby?"

"Everything." She climbed off him, then stretched out on the bed. "Everything, but mostly you." She licked her lips as she met his eyes. "Touch me," she demanded. "Touch me, please. Touch me, and then make love to me. I want to explode, Lyle. I want you to make me explode."

That was an offer he couldn't ignore, and as she watched him, her eyes heavy with lust, he stripped, then got back on the bed.

Roughly, he spread her legs, then just sat there on his knees as he let his eyes roam over every inch of her. Her polished toenails. Her smooth legs. Her sweet, wet pussy, open and ready for him. She was completely smooth, and he could see the flower of her core. The heat of her need. And when he lifted his gaze to her face, he also saw that she was biting her lip, her head turned as if embarrassed.

"You're beautiful," he said. "Do you have any idea how turned on it makes me seeing you like this? Wet and open and ready for me?"

She didn't say anything, but she met his eyes, and didn't turn away again as he continued his lazy inspection, this time punctuating his examination with kisses. Her belly button, her abdomen, her breasts. And then finally her sweet mouth.

"Please," she begged when they broke a heated kiss. Her arms went around him, her fingers clutching her back. "Please don't make me wait."

"Your wish," he said. "My command."

He trailed kisses back down to heaven, wanting to taste her first. To take her to the edge and push her over, making her come before he thrust himself inside of her.

When his mouth closed over her pussy and she

trembled under the torment of his tongue, he knew that it wouldn't take long. She was so aroused, so damn close. And when he flicked his tongue over her clit, then sucked gently, she arched up, crying out even as she reached for his head, holding him in place as he ate her out, as she cried his name, as she shattered all around him, letting herself go completely in his arms.

He didn't let up, not even when she begged, and he used his tongue to squeeze the last bit of the orgasm from her until she was begging him to fuck her, to be inside her.

"Please," she demanded. "Now, Lyle, I want you now."

He didn't hesitate. How could he when he was so close he was about to explode? When he was so desperate he thought he might go insane if he couldn't feel her tight around his cock. He couldn't go slow—he tried, damn him—but she was so wet and so ready that when he thrust into her, he went hard and deep.

She moaned, her soft whispers of *yes* driving him as he pistoned inside her, chasing a rising passion until, finally, he couldn't hold everything inside him any longer. She was tight around him, milking him, her hands on his ass as she worked with him, forcing him harder and deeper so that when he finally exploded, it felt as if they were one person.

And when the world fell away and he collapsed beside her, he knew that he had never felt like that before. Because it wasn't about sex, but about the woman beside him. A woman who'd gotten under his skin and into his heart. A woman who murmured his name and curled sleepily against him.

A woman who'd seen all of him, and wanted him still.

He breathed deeply, pulling her closer, not wanting to lose the connection even as exhaustion overtook him and he drifted into the dark.

HE DIDN'T KNOW how long he slept, but he came awake with a start when Skittles jumped on his chest and began sniffing his face. "Hold up there, tuna breath," he said. "This is a little too much intimacy considering we don't know each other that well."

"Speaking of intimacy," he murmured as he rolled over, disappointed to find only rumpled sheets. He considered asking the cat where Laine was, but the question was unnecessary. Even if the smell of frying bacon didn't give her away, the house was small. It wouldn't take too much effort to find her.

He slid out of bed and pulled on underwear and his Tee, then headed toward the bedroom door, patting his leg so the cat would follow him.

Skittles, however, was turning circles on his pillow, apparently ready to settle down for his mid-morning nap.

"Suit yourself," Lyle said. "But don't expect me to save you any bacon."

"Sorry, what?" Laine asked as he stepped into the kitchen.

He waved the question away. "Just talking to your cat."

"Yeah?" She slid into his arms for a good morning kiss. "And just when I thought you couldn't be any more perfect, you go and impress me with your feline-human relations."

"Oh, is he a feline? 'Cause I'm not sure he realizes that."

"Good point. I know you like bacon since you ate your weight in it at the hotel, but the eggs at the buffet were scrambled, so I don't know if you like fried."

"Fried is perfect. You're perfect," he added, standing behind her with his arms around her waist as she flipped the bacon. "I had no idea you could cook."

She turned in his arms. "If by *cook* you mean bacon, eggs, slice-and-bake cookies, tuna salad, and anything with Stouffers on the label, then I'm a righteous chef. As for all other categories? I'm pretty much a disaster."

"Peanut butter sandwiches?"

She wrinkled her nose as she shook her head. "I always rip the bread."

"Pasta?"

"I can never remember how long to boil it."

"Canned soup?"

"Okay. You caught me. I guess I really do have mad cooking skills. Now let me focus or you'll have raw eggs and burnt bacon."

In the end, he had to applaud her bacon and egg skills, and he dug in as she stood beside the coffee maker waiting for her cup to finish brewing.

"There is a serious amount of junk mail in this world," she said, tossing flyers aside. "Not one real— oh."

"What is it?"

"I saw it last night and forgot about it—I wonder what could have distracted me," she added with a sexy little smile.

She held up a brown envelope, then sliced it open with a steak knife. "Someone sent a letter by courier."

"What is it?" he said, noting her frown as she glanced at the thin sheath of papers she'd pulled out.

When she didn't answer, he stood up, worry running through him like ice water. "Laine?"

"It's about my house," she said, her voice flat and dull. "It's from a lawyer. My father's filed papers with the court as a co-owner."

"Asking the court to do what?"

She met his eyes, hers full of hurt and confusion. "It's called a partition," she said. "And it means he's going to force a sale."

CHAPTER 21

A PAINFUL COLDNESS sweeps through me, leaving my skin prickly and everything just a little bit painful.

Numb. I've gone completely numb.

I force myself to swallow, then look at Lyle, who's looking right back at me, his face lined with such horror and confusion he could almost be a mirror.

"I can't lose my house," I say. "Not now. Not right after you paid it off."

"Not ever," he says firmly. He's right beside me now and he takes my shoulder, turning me so that I have no choice but to face him. "He's your father. Can't you call him? Ask him to put the brakes on? Figure out a way to stop this?"

I try to think. "I don't have his number. Hell, I don't even know where he lives."

"But this lawyer might. Call him. Tell him you want to meet with your dad. Ask why he's doing it."

"Okay." My voice sounds horribly small in my kitchen, and when Lyle holds out his arms, I'm ridiculously grateful for him to just hold me.

"What time are you supposed to meet Greg and Anderson?"

"Nine-thirty," I say, forcing myself to think like a businessperson.

Which, I realize with a sudden start, is what this is all about. I step back so that I can pace as I think. "He must have gotten some sort of notification that the equity loan was paid off. And maybe that gave him the idea."

"To partition?"

"To sell," I say. "After so many years and with property values so high in this neighborhood right now, this house is worth so much more than my parents paid for it. Real estate agents chat me up all the time. The last time I asked, the woman said she could get close to two million. And that was before I finished the renovation."

"And he'd get half," Lyle says. "That's how a partition works. Unless you two can work it out, the court orders the property sold and you split the proceeds."

"Unless we can work it out," I repeat, thinking that those really aren't pretty words.

"He's your dad," Lyle says. "It's worth a shot."

"I'll call, but it won't matter. He left when I was nine, and never wrote or called. Not even a birthday card. Not even after his son died. No," I add when he steps toward me, obviously intending to draw me into a hug. "I appreciate the thought, but I'm over being hurt by my dad. It was a long time ago. My point is that a man like that isn't going to care if he's hurting me or if he's stealing the memory of Mom and Andy right out from under me. He just wants his million.

"And that," I say, "is about a million more than I have."

"THANKS FOR THE last-minute meet," I say to Joy forty minutes later, when we meet at the Java B's a few blocks from my house. "Especially since I can't even stay that long."

Lyle's been great, but this is a situation that calls for the kind of mass quantities of caffeine and sympathy that only a best friend can provide.

"Are you kidding? Anytime your asshole father comes out of the woodwork I am *totally* there for you."

I actually crack a smile, which feels really good.

I'd explained the whole thing earlier on the phone, and now she asks, "What are you going to do?"

That's the question that's been haunting me all morning, and the answer is that I don't know. An answer that Joy marks with a very definitive thumbs-down.

"You have to be proactive. Find out where he lives. Rat him out on social media."

"That only works on people who care about social media in the first place. I'm thinking that's not my dad. And besides, it would feel really icky."

"You can get over icky," she says.

"Noted. Next idea?"

"You could just kill him, but since it's not the kind of deed where you get the whole house if he dies, then it wouldn't do you any good unless you're in his will. And you're probably not." She sips her latte. "Probably wouldn't work, then."

"I'll pass on the murder plot," I say dryly. "Another suggestion?"

"Pay him."

"Yeah, right."

"I'm serious," she says. "He's just interested in the equity. So buy his interest for what he would make when the court forces the sale."

"I know what you meant," I say. "But where am I supposed to get that kind of money? I doubt Marjorie has a client who'll pay a cool million. And honestly, I wouldn't do it even if she did. Not now."

Joy's brows lift. "Interesting. And relevant. Because I was going to suggest you ask Lyle for the money."

I've just taken a sip of coffee, and when I gasp it goes down the wrong way, making me cough and choke as I try to suck in a coffee-free breath of air.

"You okay?"

"Lyle?" I say. "You want me to ask Lyle for a million dollars?"

"Well, sure. I mean, he pretty much paid off your loan, so he probably already feels invested in the house. And we know he likes you."

She frowns. "He does like you, right? Because I have to admit, I'm still a little confused. Are things between you real-serious or pretend-serious? Because honestly, I'm not sure if I should apologize for getting you into this in the first place, or say you're welcome."

It's like she's flipped a switch, and all sorts of gooey thoughts and feelings fill me up. "Things are great," I say, unable to fight my brilliant smile. "And thank you," I add, then wink.

"*O.M.G.,*" she squeals. "That's so fab. I'm really happy for you. And see? I bet he'd totally give you a million to save the house."

"Joy, that's—"

"Perfect. I know. I'm a genius"

"No," I say. "Not even close to perfect. I can't ask him for a million dollars. There's no way I could earn that much working for him—and don't you dare say sex. And I couldn't pay off a loan. Not in this lifetime, anyway."

"But he'd probably do it for you, anyway."

"Even assuming he has a million lying around, I can't ask him for it. I'd be putting him in a horrible spot. And what if things don't work out between us?" I ask, the thought of losing him making me vaguely queasy. "It would be beyond uncomfortable."

"Maybe, but at least you'd have the house."

"At that price? I'd rather just have my memories."

The words come without thinking, but as soon as they're out of my mouth, I know they're true. I love my house, and I'm still going to call the lawyer and I'm still going to fight this stupid partition action. But if it gets down to the wire, I'm not going to destroy myself or a relationship trying to save it.

Because at the end of the day, I'll still have my memories.

And maybe, if things keep on the way I hope they will, I'll have Lyle, too.

CHAPTER 22

"—KNOCK DOWN THIS wall and open the kitchen up to the dining and living areas, don't you think?" Greg asks.

I snap back to attention, frustrated that my mind has once again wandered to my house. But as soon as I arrived, I'd asked Anderson to explain exactly how partitions work, and based on what he told me, I'm even more sure I'm screwed.

Mentally, I rewind Greg's words. "I like it," I say. "But I think that we should have the sink on an island with bar seating. That way someone can be working at the sink and talking to someone either sitting at the bar or in the living room."

Anderson and Greg look at each other and nod. "All right," Greg says. "That sounds good." He glances around the area, then back at me. "I think we're done. Pretty cool, huh?"

"It's going to be amazing. Do you want me to write up what we talked about?" I ask Greg. "I can do a quick sketch too, if you want."

"Perfect."

I flash a smile at the two of them. "I can't believe

we're really starting. Anderson, seriously. Without you—"

"Believe me, I'm equally indebted to you two."

"Should we go celebrate?" Greg asks. "Drinks? Fried food?"

I check my watch. "I'd love to, but I have plans with Lyle. A going away party for one of his friends."

"Congratulations, by the way," Anderson says. "You must be very excited."

"I am," I say, playing the role perfectly and flashing my ring.

But underneath the shiny smile is a layer of melancholy. For the house I will probably lose. And for the man I'm falling in love with. Because I'm wearing his ring without having the slightest clue if this is really going anywhere.

Wait.

Whoa.

Back-up.

Love?

I reach out, steadying myself against the kitchen cabinet, the word making my knees go weak.

Had I really thought that?

More, had I really meant it?

"You okay?" Greg asks, and I nod automatically.

"I'm a little light-headed. Too much sun the last couple of days." I glance toward the door. "I'm going to head home and see if I can't draw up that sketch before I have to leave. Here tomorrow? Nine?"

They both agree, and I hurry out the front door toward my seriously under-used Toyota. I'm eager to get inside, close the door, crank up some tunes, and drive, letting these feelings and revelations settle inside me.

Greg, however, gets to me before I have the chance.

"Hey, wait up," he calls, bounding down the front steps.

I slide my hands in my pockets as he approaches. "Did we forget something?"

"No. But I—I wanted to say I'm sorry about the other night. I didn't like the way he threw you to the wolves."

"He didn't," I promise, then wince. "I'm sorry. I told you I'd explain everything, and I've been so busy…"

"It's okay. I got it from Joy. So I know the score. But I still worry. And I swear this isn't coming from jealousy. We're friends, right?"

"Absolutely."

"I'm just afraid this is going to blow up on you. A fake engagement? That's a recipe for disaster."

"It'll be okay," I say. But the truth is, I'm worried now, too.

Because I really do love him.

And for better or for worse, love makes you vulnerable.

"FASTER! FASTER!" LARA cries as Lyle swings her in a circle, airplane-style, then finally slows down and plunks Nikki and Damien's little girl onto the lush lawn. "Again," she calls, clapping her little hands.

"Maybe later, kiddo," he says, sprawled on the grass beside her. "You've worn me out."

From the seat beside me, Riley chuckles. "Wimp. Clearly, we're going to have to up your training regimen."

Lyle lifts his head and scowls at his friend. "I'd say something rude, but there are children present. Hey, beautiful," he adds, turning his attention to me.

"Hey, yourself."

We're in Malibu at what has to be the most amazing house—and view—I've ever seen. I tell Nikki the same when she comes over to the large stone table and offers me a mimosa.

"It really is spectacular," she agrees. "And I can say that with absolutely no ego. It was mostly finished when Damien and I got together, although I did have a hand in decorating the interior."

We've been here for a few hours now, and I'm surprised at how comfortable I am. Before Lyle, I'd never really brushed up against money, but the Starks and their friends and family are all down-to-earth, and everyone has put me completely at ease.

"My turn!" A dark-haired little girl rushes up to Lyle the moment he stands.

"Ronnie Steele, you're getting too big for that."

"Mom-*my*," she complains.

"You and Lara go play on the swings and let the grownups talk."

She pouts, but obeys, and I turn around to see Sylvia behind me, holding her little boy on her hip. Cass is her best friend, so I've met her a few times before at Totally Tattoo, but I hadn't met her husband Jackson until tonight. He'd been at Wyatt's opening, so I'd seen him from afar, but I hadn't asked Lyle to introduce us.

Just as well. He's a world famous architect, and when I met him today, I'd pretty much embarrassed myself by fawning all over him. Thankfully, he was incredibly gracious about my groupie behavior.

Syl tells me that Cass and Siobhan were invited but already had plans with Siobhan's parents. "And I won't be one of those annoying women who asks about your plans for a family," she says, glancing at my ring as she takes a seat, putting Jeffery on her lap. "But I will say that if you do want kids, it's worth it. Work," she adds with an exaggerated eye roll, "but worth it."

"Thanks for the tip," I say. "I think that starting out we're going to have our hands full with my cat."

"You two look cozy," Lyle says, joining us. "Should I be worried?"

"Very," Syl says. "We're talking girl stuff."

"Speaking of girls," Lyle says, "do you know where Jane went? She disappeared before I could introduce her to Laine."

"She went with Dallas and Noah into the garage," Nikki says, as she and Damien come up. "They wanted to see Damien's cars." She aims a quick grin at her husband. "I figure we'll see them again in a week or two."

"My wife is a comedian."

"My husband likes cars."

"But the garage is like the bat cave," Sylvia says. "So that makes the car collecting cooler."

"True," Nikki says. To me she adds, "It really is a pretty impressive collection. But I just stick with Coop."

I raise a brow in question.

"Her Mini-Cooper," Damien explains. "My wife is a one man and a one car woman."

She narrows her eyes at him. "Did you miss the part about how many cars you own? Should I be worried?"

He pulls her into his arms. "Never," he says firmly, then kisses her.

I swoon a little—and then a little more when Lyle takes my hand and squeezes it.

"I would like to meet Jane," I say. "We can walk to the garage if you want."

"You should probably wait," Damien says. "They might be talking cars. But other topics could come up."

Riley's been sitting quietly. Now he lifts his head. "Like what?"

"Dallas and Noah have their hands in a lot of pots," Damien says vaguely. "And they've been friends for a long time."

I don't have a clue what Damien could be talking about, and I don't think Riley does either. Not specifically, anyway. But it all sounds very mysterious.

I do know who Dallas Sykes is. Before he and his wife, Jane West Sykes, got married, they were at the heart of a torrid scandal. And before that his name was all over the tabloids. They called him the King of Fuck, and he had a playboy reputation that has faded since his marriage.

Honestly, these people are a bit like a puzzle, their lives crossing and overlapping and all of it woven together in a tapestry of friendship and family.

"I like your friends," I tell Lyle later, as we're walking

along a stone path toward the tennis court.

"I'm glad. I know Jane best since we worked together on *The Price of Ransom*, but I've gotten to know Nikki and Damien through the Stark Children's Foundation, too. They're all good people.

"Tarpin!"

I look around for the voice, then see a man step off the courts and onto the path. He's tall, with rugged good looks and a charming smile. But it's his red hair that ensures he's unforgettable.

"Noah," Lyle calls, hurrying to pull the redhead into one of those manly guy hugs. "I've been looking for you."

"Yeah? Well, I haven't been looking for you." His smile is teasing. "But I have heard rumors about your engagement."

He turns to me and flashes a smile that seems so sweet and genuine I automatically return it. "This is who I've been wanting to meet."

"Sugar Laine, meet my friend Noah Carter."

"Very happy to finally catch up with you," I say.

"Sorry I disappeared from my own going away party. But since I'm about to be landlocked, I wanted to take a walk on the beach. I guess I lost track of time."

"Easy to do," I say, and though I don't know him well enough to be sure, I think I see sadness in his dark green eyes.

"And you looked at the cars," Lyle says, "thus losing more time."

"The problem wasn't time," Noah says. "Have you seen how far into the hills Damien's garage goes? I was just plain lost. If Dallas and Jane aren't on the patio when we get back, we should probably send a search party."

"Actually, we should all probably get back." Lyle says. "I think I heard something about heating up a grill."

"Congrats on the engagement," Noah says as we're heading up the path.

"Thanks," Lyle and I both say at the same time. "Are you seeing anyone?" I ask, then wince as Lyle squeezes my hand. Hard.

"No," Noah says, the word polite but clipped. He turns to me, and when he speaks, his voice is softer, as if he realizes how harsh he sounded. "I'm not currently looking to date. I'm much more focused on my career."

I think of Lyle, and the way he tossed that same platitude at me. Words that were hiding a deeper pain.

"What exactly do you do?" I ask, figuring that now's a good time to change the topic.

"Tech," he says. "I'm moving to Austin to be head up one of Stark International's tech subsidiaries. R and D mostly."

"That sounds great." I don't know a thing about Texas, but I think he'd look cute in a cowboy hat. "You used to work for Dallas?"

"Security at his department store chain," Noah says. "Then Damien recruited me and I made the jump from the east coast to the west. Now I'm going to the middle."

Since I'm starting to feel like I'm interrogating him, I back off, and he and Lyle start talking about a regular poker game that Noah's no longer going to be part of, and another friend named Ryan, who's in security, but isn't at the party because he and his wife are on a cruise.

As we make our way back to the patio, we bump into Jane, who calls out to Lyle, then wraps me in such a friendly hug that it's as if we've know each other for years. "You're so lucky to have him," she whispers to me. "I swear he brought emotion to my script I didn't even think possible."

We continue on toward the patio together, where we're greeted by laughter and the smell of sizzling burgers. Damien Stark is behind the grill, which makes me laugh considering he could probably buy every burger joint in the country. Dallas Sykes is standing by him, though I don't realize who it is until Jane introduces us. I've seen his picture before, of course, but he's way more attractive in person. Which, frankly, is saying a lot because he's pretty hot in those photos.

We all settle in with burgers and beer and wine and chips, and it's all so normal and not the least bit ritzy. And when Lyle puts his arm around me, I lean against him and sigh, feeling right at home.

When I'm completely stuffed and lightheaded from wine, Lyle leads me to the hot tub, and we sit on the edge—his arm around me as I lean against him—our feet dangling in the water. "This is nice," I say, and as I turn to smile at him, he takes my chin and and kisses me sweetly, and I think that it's just gotten nicer.

We stay another hour, chatting and generally having a good time, and I feel like I'm one of the group. And for someone who's been self-reliant for so long, that feeling is both surprising and wonderful.

When it's time to leave, I'm standing in the entrance hall waiting for Lyle to finish discussing something about the SCF brunch with Damien, when Riley comes up.

"Hey," he says.

"Hi. Lyle's up there if you're looking for him." I point toward the open-style staircase that leads to the third floor.

"Nope. I was looking for you."

"Oh." I twist my engagement ring, wondering what he knows. Turns out, he knows a lot. Like everything about our fake engagement. And how we met. And the fact that there was money paid.

"We've been friends for a long time," he says, and I nod.

"He told me," I say. "About you and Iowa and Jenny." I flash a tentative smile. "I think he's really lucky to have you for a friend."

Riley studies me, nodding. "Yeah, well that goes both ways." He shoves his hands into the front pockets of his jeans. "Listen, I was going to say that I hope you understand that what he told you—well, he's not one for over sharing."

"I'm not going to give away his secrets, if that's what you're worried about."

"I was. After meeting you, I'm not. But be careful with him, okay? I don't want to see him getting hurt."

"I'm not going to hurt him."

"Not intentionally," Riley says. "But he loves you. He hasn't officially told me that, but I can tell. And that means hurt might be inevitable."

"Oh." I don't know what to say to that, but my heart

seems to swell in my chest, and I'm having a hell of a time fighting my smile.

Riley looks me up and down critically, but when he meets my eyes, he's the one who smiles. "Yeah," he finally says. "I think you just might do."

CHAPTER 23

"I DON'T REALLY know him, but I thought Noah seemed sad about leaving," I say to Lyle as we ride the elevator up to his condo. I haven't been here before, and when he mentioned his view from the thirtieth floor, I begged him to detour.

It's a shiny, modern building, and Lyle told me he bought his unit when his sitcom was topping the charts every week.

Now, he leans against the interior wall of the elevator car, the corners of his mouth curved down. "You're not wrong," he says about Noah. "Bet he'd be disappointed to realize he's so transparent."

"Is he okay? Is the move about something other than work?"

"A little of both, although he hasn't actually told me as much." The elevator slows to a stop and the doors slide open. There are four elevators in the building, one for each corner. On most floors, Lyle told me, the elevator opens onto a hallway with two or three units. His unit, however, takes up a quarter of the top floor, and the elevator opens onto a private foyer with his entry door on one side, a flower arrangement immediately opposite the elevator doors, and what he tells me is extra storage to the right.

"Noah really is taking over the Austin operation," he continues. "Apparently Stark International acquired a business, and current management just isn't cutting it. But he also asked Damien for the gig once it came up. I think he wants to get away from LA. There are some bad memories for him in Southern California."

"What happened?" I ask, then say, "Oh, wow," when I follow Lyle into his sparsely decorated condo.

He was right about the view. The main area of the condo is basically a box, with a kitchen, two seating areas, and a hall that presumably leads to bedrooms.

Two sides of that box are entirely made of glass.

And now, at night, the city lights sparkle beyond one virtually invisible wall, while the hills twinkle beyond the other. It's like floating above a fairy world, and I turn to him, grinning. "It really is stunning."

He gestures for the kitchen, and I sit on one of the bar stools while he opens a bottle of wine.

"What happened with Noah?" I prompt, since I'd been distracted earlier by the view. "I struck a nerve asking him about dating. My hand's still aching from that faux pas," I add wryly.

He pours two glasses, then takes them with him to the couch, gesturing for me to follow. "He was married before. He had a wife, a baby girl." Lyle draws a breath. "They were kidnapped. Taken in broad daylight."

"Oh, God." My stomach feels queasy, and I put my wine down. "What happened?"

I watch Lyle's face. The way his skin pales. The motion of his throat as he swallows. "They found the baby," he says, his voice hollow. "She'd been suffocated. They never found his wife."

"That's horrible." The word is so inadequate that I feel foolish even having said it. "How long has it been?"

"When *The Price of Ransom* premiered, that was right at seven years. She was declared legally dead that week."

"I can't even imagine," I say, my own problems seeming so small now by comparison.

I stand, needing to move and get those terrible images out of my head. There's a bookcase on the far side of the room, and I head there, then start perusing the titles. "I'm pretty sure you have every book ever written about Hollywood."

"I didn't come here with the bug, but I got infected soon enough." He joins me at the shelves, pointing out a stack of scripts that he says he read to study roles when he was first starting. I notice that they're all classics and well-known recent dramas.

As for the books, they cover all aspects of Hollywood. "Hey," I say, pulling one off the shelf. "A biography of Anika Segel. Isn't she—"

"Wyatt's grandmother. You remembered."

I frown. "Why weren't Wyatt and Kelsey at the party? Aren't they in your circle?"

"I talked to him this morning. He said they had Noah over for dinner last week, and they sent their regrets to Nikki and Damien. But they needed some alone time. Apparently putting that show together was exhausting."

That makes sense, and I smile at Lyle, then brush my fingertips over the back of his hand. "Alone time can be a very good thing."

"I'm very glad you think so. I was hoping you could stay the night."

"I think I can swing that. I'll have to placate Skittles in the morning with tuna, but he'll only love you the more for being the reason he's getting a treat."

I'm still looking at the shelves, and I run my finger over the stage plays. Chekov. Stoppard. Shakespeare. Coward. And so many more.

"Were these Jenny's?"

He shakes his head. "No, Jenny was all about the blockbuster. Go big or go home," he says, with a melancholy smile.

"Then they're yours?"

He nods. "I was one of those guys who was discovered for his looks. A true Hollywood story. But what they don't mention is that looks don't mean shit if you can't act. So I started taking lessons, and realized I loved it.

"Jenny had the drive and the ambition—talent, too, of course," he continues. "But mostly she was the epitome of a star. Bright and vibrant and living large."

"You wanted to live smaller?"

"I wanted to act. To do something transformative. To get lost in a role. To really analyze it and find that deep character. I did a lot of theater when I was younger."

"I'd love to see you on stage."

"I don't do much of that anymore."

"Why not?"

"Because I'm one of the lucky ones. I made it."

I frown, trailing my finger over the stacks of plays. "Shouldn't that give you more freedom?"

"The concept of *making it* is relative, I guess. I'm in the top tier, that's true. But there's still a mountain to climb."

I try to process everything he's saying but something feels off. There's a dog-eared, coffee-stained screenplay on the coffee table, and I pick it up, just to have something to idly hold. *Arizona Spring.*

I clutch it, then I walk to the windows, trying to figure out what's bugging me. But it's not until I sit in the chair by the window and start flipping through the screenplay that my thoughts start to coalesce.

"Is this a movie they're trying to get you to do?"

He nods, coming closer, but staying a few feet away from me, just on the other side of the coffee table.

"Are you going to do it?"

"No," he says, as I continue to turn pages, noticing his markings throughout.

"Because the script needs so much work?"

"Actually, the script is excellent. There's so much room to develop the character, and I've been making notes and—"

He cuts himself off sharply. "It doesn't matter. It's going into production soon, and I have three more Blue Zenith movies in the pipe."

"And you said those are good scripts, too."

"They are," he says, and I know him well enough now to know that he means it. But I also can tell from his voice that the scripts aren't as good as *Arizona Spring.*

This whole conversation isn't ringing right for me,

but it's not worth worrying about now. Not when the city lights are glowing with romance beyond the window and the man I've fallen in love with has asked me to stay the night.

"Hey," I say, holding out my hand for him. "I like this chair. It's got a spectacular view and room enough for two. I'm thinking you should join me."

"Why don't you come over here with me on the couch." He takes a step backward. "More room to stretch out," he adds, with an enticing edge to his voice.

I have to admit it's tempting. But still…

"I don't know…" I go to the window, pressing my hands and forehead to the glass as I look out at the city lights, twinkling like stars in the darkness below, as if we're looking down from the heavens.

"You're the one who enticed me here with this view," I tease. "I'm thinking maybe you should come over here right now." I shift my focus so that I can see his reflection. "You can't make me believe you've never made love in front of a high-rise window."

"Believe it," he says, and there's such an edge to his voice that I turn around, confused and a little worried.

"Lyle?"

"I'm really not crazy about heights. I told you at Disney."

"Oh." I process that. "I thought it was the drop that got to you. Not the altitude. But then … well … why did you do go on the ride? For that matter," I add, "why have a chair near these windows? Why have this condo at all? Why get your pilot's license?"

He looks surprised, and I shrug. "I told you. I

Googled you. Why didn't you tell me?"

"No point. I only take her up to keep my license."

I shake my head, confused. "I don't get any of this. Why?"

"I like to face my fears."

And that's when I get it.

That's the moment I see the piece of the puzzle that's been eluding me. When I understand the whole big picture in all it's scary, horrible mess.

When I know that this might very well be the night that destroys us. Because I've known since the night I met him that Lyle was broken, but I went and fell in love with him anyway.

And now...

Well, now I have to find out if he loves me too.

And if he does, is he going to stick and heal, or is he going to push me away? Just one more desire he avoids? One more hair shirt to assuage his guilt?

Tentatively, I take a step toward him, then another and another until I'm so close I can almost hear his heart beat.

"You like to face your fears?" I repeat, then continue before he has time to answer. "The easy ones, maybe. Like tall buildings and thrill rides and private planes. But you're still a slave to the hard ones, Lyle. You're still afraid of letting go of Jenny."

At first there's only surprise on his face, but it's pushed out quickly by anger.

Clearly, I've touched a nerve.

I lick my lips, gathering courage, because I intend to keep on touching it.

"I was right that first night, Lyle. You needed a wall to rail against. The women you hired weren't for sex. They were for punishment. To punish yourself for what happened to Jenny."

"You have no idea," he says harshly. "No *fucking* idea what you're talking about."

"The hell I don't. It's all here in this condo. You're punishing yourself for Jenny's death. Punishing yourself by not living your own life. You're living her career, Lyle, not yours. Her dream condo. Her ideal career."

"No," he says, but I ignore him. I know I'm right, and I press on, forcing myself to speak, because otherwise I'm going to cry.

"That's why you don't do relationships. It's not because you've been focusing on your career or because you don't know if your date wants you or is only chasing a celebrity. That's not even an issue. It's all about punishment."

He's standing still, his expression stoic.

I have no idea what he's thinking. All I can do is continue.

"And not just punishment, Lyle, but fear. You lost your mom. You lost Jenny. What else are you going to lose, right? And it's scary—I get that."

Tears stream down my face, and I brush them away with my palms. "Losing my mom and Andy about destroyed me, but I'm also so grateful for the time I had with them."

"Sugar," he says, his voice hoarse. He reaches for me, but I'm not ready for him to touch me yet. I must get this out. He has to hear all of it.

"Do you want to know the really scary, ironic part? I'm in love with you. Completely. And I'm certain that you're in love with me, too. Maybe it was fast. Maybe that makes it scarier. But it's real.

"And I'm terrified you're going to push me away because it scares you." I put my hands on his shoulders, then press my body against his. "And you know what? If you do, I'll survive. I'll be pissed as hell and hurt and all sorts of nasty emotions. But I'll survive. And I won't regret this feeling. Not ever. Because it's real," I say, pressing my hand over his heart. "Even if it's terrifying."

I draw a shaky breath. My adrenalin rush has worn off, and now I feel a little mortified that I went off on him like that. But the fear is real. This is a man who didn't go looking for love. We snuck up on each other, creeping backwards and with blinders.

He wasn't ready, and I get that.

I just hope he's ready now.

I take a step back, certain he needs space, but he yanks me to him, then kisses me so hard I'm sure my lips are bruised.

"Was that a goodbye kiss?" I ask when my heart stops pounding.

"That was an *I don't like what you were saying* kiss."

I nod, disappointed.

But then he draws me closer and gently closes his mouth over mine. He kisses me softly. Tenderly. And when he pulls away, my entire body is buzzing with anticipation.

"And that one?"

"That kiss," he says, "means you were right."

"Oh." I let myself bask for just a moment. "Right about what exactly?"

"Everything," he says. "But mostly, that I love you, too."

CHAPTER 24

"SAY IT AGAIN," I demand, feeling as though I could melt into his arms right there.

"I love you," he says. "You, Sugar Laine." He cups my face. "I love you."

I sigh deeply. "I like the sound of that."

"I'm glad," he says. "I like it, too."

"Have I mentioned that I love you, too?"

"You might have said something about it. But maybe you could tell me again."

I flash a wicked grin. "I might. Or I might make you earn the words."

"Oh, really?" I hear the amusement and interest in his voice. "And how am I supposed to do that?"

"I was thinking that stripping me naked and fucking me senseless would be a good start," I admit. "But I'm open to suggestions."

He doesn't answer, but I see the mischief in his eyes, and when he walks toward me and hauls me over his shoulder, I'm completely unprepared.

"Lyle!" I squeal.

"Hush," he says, lightly smacking my rear and he carries me to the bedroom. "I'm a man on a mission, remember? I believe the assignment is to fuck you senseless?"

He tosses me onto the bed, and I lean back on my elbows, looking at him. "Nice to know you follow orders," I say.

"I'm feeling remarkably amenable right now. You could ask me for anything."

His words flow over me, soft and comfortable, and I hold out my hand. "But what could I possibly ask for? As I have you, there's nothing else I want."

"Sugar…"

I've never heard my name with such longing and heat, and as he starts to undress, I keep my eyes on him, letting that heat slide into me, filling me up.

He peels off his shirt first, and I sigh with prurient desire as I take in those strong, familiar arms, his muscled abs. I know he's been working hard, and it shows. But as gorgeous as the view is, what I want is the feel of him against me.

"Hurry," I say. "I like the preview, but I'm desperate for the main attraction."

His eyes lock with mine, and I see my desire reflected back at me, so potent and powerful it feels almost like a blow.

"Get naked," he orders, and I don't hesitate. I strip and toss my clothes aside as he finishes doing the same. Then he pounces onto the bed, making me laugh as he rolls us over so that I'm on top of him, my hands on his hard body.

"Kiss me," he demands, and I raise an eyebrow.

"I thought I was calling the shots."

"How about we do it together?" he asks, and since that sounds wonderful, I don't bother to answer. I just bend forward, my breasts rubbing his chest as my mouth closes over his.

As soon as my lips meet his, it's as if lightning has struck. The kiss is wild. Hot. Electrical.

It's deep and naughty and so fucking hot.

It's the kind of kiss that's a stand-in for sex—but right now, even that kind of kiss isn't good enough. I want the real thing. Hell, I'm demanding it.

I'm straddling his waist, and as we kiss, I slide down, feeling his cock brushing me. Teasing me.

"Lyle," I murmur, because I can't wait any longer. I know it's fast. I know there's been no foreplay. But I want this. I need it. To be connected to him. To be *us*.

"Yes," he says. "God, Sugar, yes."

He holds my hips steady as I lift myself, then tease us both as I slowly position his cock at my core. I lower myself just a smidge, taking in only the tip, then watching as Lyle arches up, groaning with a sound that could be pleasure or pain, or maybe a little of both.

"Want more?" I ask, my thighs burning as I slowly lift and lower myself, tormenting us both until I don't think I can stand it any longer.

Neither can he, because he grabs my hips and forces me down even as he thrusts up, so that he penetrates me so hard and so deep that I cry out, unsure where he ends and I begin.

"*Yes*." The word is torn from me, and as it echoes in the room, I ride him, my muscles straining as I lift and lower myself on his cock, as he holds my hips to steady me as he matches me, thrust for thrust.

I watch his face, our eyes locked in a shared gaze as passionate as the meeting of our bodies. I see the explosion building him, and I feel it building in me. "Close," I say, and it's the only word I can manage.

He understands, and he releases one of my hips, then slides that hand between my legs, stroking my clit as we continue this frenzied ride.

"Come with me, Sugar," he demands as his body tightens beneath mine. As he grows tense. As that same explosion builds inside me, too. A wild electrical storm that seems to coalescence in my core, growing smaller and tighter and more intense until finally—when Lyle cries, *"now,"* it all explodes outward in a universe of stars and colors and vibrant light.

I'm completely shattered, and Lyle along with me, the pieces of us mingling as we slowly—slowly—come back together, then hold each other tight, bodies quivering, arms twined, as the world starts to rotate again.

"Wow," I say when I can breathe again. I'm beside him, my head on his chest. "That was—"

"I know," he says. "Incredible."

"I'm completely wiped."

"Me, too," he says, then kisses my shoulder. "Want to do it again?"

I laugh, then roll over in his arms. "Absolutely."

I DON'T REMEMBER falling asleep, but I wake up with my body curled up beside his, my back to his chest, and his arm resting on my waist, holding me in place.

His body is warm, like a furnace, and I want to stay like this forever, curled up in a limbo filled with streams of sunlight, safe in the arms of the man I love.

Forever, however, is going to have to take a backseat to mundane reality.

I slide out of bed, then slip on the T-shirt he'd been wearing last night. It hits me mid-thigh and smells of Lyle, and right then my idea of heaven is to spend the entire day in this shirt, wrapped up in the scent of him and the memories of last night.

In the bathroom, I check my face in the mirror, wondering if I look different. I've never been in love before, and I've certainly never been in love with a man who loves me back.

I bend close, my nose almost to the glass. My eyes are bright, my cheeks just a little pink, my lips still slightly swollen, a look that a lot of women pay big bucks for.

All in all, I look like a woman who's not only in love, but who spent the night making love.

And I have to say, that whole scenario is damn good for my complexion.

My thoughts amuse me, and I'm smiling as I head down the hallway toward the kitchen for a bottle of water.

But that smile freezes and then fades the moment I round the corner.

I'm not alone.

Both Evelyn and Natasha are on the couch right in front of me, and at my gasp, they both turn their heads in my direction. Their eyes go wide, and Natasha jumps to her feet and says, "Oh, shit, Laine. I had no idea he wasn't alone."

"And I had no idea there was any meat to our manufactured engagement," Evelyn adds with amusement in her voice. She looks me up and down. "Or am I misreading the signs?"

I have no idea what to say, so I stand there like a dolt, certain my entire body has turned lobster-red, and wondering if they'd notice if I bolted back to the bedroom and hid under the covers.

It's one split-second of embarrassment, but it feels like hours. And then all the embarrassment fades as I hear a voice behind me in the hall. "Fake engagement," Lyle says as he reaches me and puts a hand on my shoulder. He squeezes lightly. "Real relationship."

"That's great!" Natasha aims her broad grin right at me.

Evelyn's smiling as well, her attention entirely on Lyle. "There might be hope for you yet, Iowa."

"Might be," he agrees, then bends to kiss my head. He lingers for a moment, then steps beside me, taking my hand as he leads me into the living room. He's wearing a pair of gray sweatpants I'd noticed hanging on his closet door, no shirt, and an air of absolute cool and confidence despite the truly awkward circumstances.

"Sorry about this Nat," he says. "Didn't occur to me to call and tell you to work from home or come in late. My office is in the back of the condo," he adds for my benefit. "A converted third bedroom."

"No worries," she says, rising. "At least not from my

end." She looks at me and shrugs. "Sorry, again."

"I'm fine. I was just surprised."

"And I'm here because we need to talk about these contracts before I go chat with Charlie. I bumped into Nat in the elevator and we rode up together," she adds, which explains how she arrived without ringing ahead, since Lyle explained to me the elevator doesn't open on his floor without a code once he's locked it down.

"Fine," Lyle says, his voice clipped. "Let's talk."

"Why don't I make coffee?" I'm not desperate for pants anymore—the T-shirt is big enough to be a dress—but I also don't need to be in the thick of it. Not when there's obviously some undercurrent of business tension that I don't understand.

"I'll help," Natasha says, hurrying toward the kitchen with me.

The kitchen is on the far side of the open area, set off by a bar that forms a ninety-degree angle to mark the kitchen's edge. "Who's Charlie?" I ask as she starts to run water for his coffee maker.

"Attorney. He's reviewing the next three Blue Zenith contracts."

At the same time, I hear Evelyn chide, "Wait too long and you'll miss the chance. *Arizona Spring* needs to lock in the cast soon."

"What's going on?" I ask quietly.

Nat takes the pot to the far corner where the coffee maker is tucked in by a mug tree, then starts to pour it into the machine as she explains that the next three movies were specifically written for the *M. Sterious* character. "Once Lyle signed on, they wanted to lock him in to multiple movies." She lifts a shoulder, as if that's all just business-as-usual, then starts to scoop coffee into the filter.

"But that's good, right? So why does Evelyn sound irritated?" Except for the fact that I've come to know Lyle enough to understand that his dream isn't to make it big in blockbusters, it seems to me that big movie roles written for an actor are something an agent should be jumping up and down about. But Evelyn's tone definitely isn't jumpy.

"Noticed that, did you?"

She glances toward the living area where Evelyn and Lyle are deep in conversation. "So, the script for the first movie was awesome when it first came in. Really great character stuff. Lots of meat for an actor to sink his teeth into. He completely covered those pages with notes, he was so into it. I mean, so many notes I had to ask the studio to email a clean copy just so he could read the actual lines."

"What do you mean by 'when it first came in'?"

She makes a face. "After *The Price of Ransom* started really kicking ass, they wanted to lock Lyle in. So they changed M's character. He went from being a trans-formed villain who sacrifices himself to save the world to a guy who saves one of the secondary characters, has an epiphany, and joins the happy Blue Zenith family."

She shrugs. "It doesn't suck, but it sure as hell doesn't pop like it used to. But the other three are sure to make a shit-ton of money, and if he signs those contracts, Lyle will be locked in to all three with a significant backend. Percentage of the profits, I mean," she adds when I look blank.

"And to do the three he has to turn down *Arizona Spring*."

"Pretty much."

"So that's it," she says as she pours the now-brewed coffee into four mugs. "By the way," she adds, taking two mugs as I grab the others, "I'm glad we've connected again. And I'm especially happy you're with Lyle. I've always thought that he—" She cuts herself off with a shake of her head, then starts over. "I've always thought that he needed someone."

"Someone real," I say, and when she meets my eyes with perfect understanding, I know that she knows about the call girls. "That's how we met," I say, because I like her and want her to understand. "I was desperate for cash and—"

"Doesn't matter how you met," Nat says. "I can see that it's real now. It's there in the way he looks at you." Her smile is genuine. "He's a great boss and a great guy, and I'm really happy for him. For you both."

"There was never anything between you?" I ask, the question surprising me because I'm not the jealous type. Then again, I've never been with a guy I cared enough about to rouse those feelings.

"I respect the hell out of him, but no. He's hot, don't get me wrong, but he's not a guy I have sparks with."

"What about Riley?"

"Mmm," she says. "That's a longer conversation for a later time, like three weeks from never."

"Fair enough," I say, laughing. "At any rate, I'm glad you're happy for us." I mean it, and I'm surprised by how much someone's blessing pleases me. "I guess we should go before the coffee gets cold."

"True that," she says and leads the way to Evelyn and Lyle.

"—that I'm going to call him today about a real estate question," Lyle is saying as we approach.

"Will do," Evelyn says, standing. "I'll get out of your hair."

She looks at me, her mouth curving down thoughtfully. "You know, Lyle, you're getting hot and heavy into rehearsals next week. Maybe you should clear your schedule until then. You've got the SCF brunch on Sunday, of course, but other than that, I think maybe you should just chill. Recharge a bit before you dive in."

He glances at me with a smile full of possibility. "I think that sounds like a damn good idea."

CHAPTER 25

"WHAT DO YOU think?" Lyle asks, once Evelyn has gone and Nat's disappeared into the back office. "Clear our schedules for the three evenings until the brunch, and—"

"I can't," I say, thinking of Greg and Anderson and the flip house. Then I frown, mentally rewinding. "Wait. Evenings?"

"Didn't you already clear your other schedule so that you could work on the flip?"

"You remembered that?" The realization is like a gentle squeeze around my heart.

"Of course. In fact, why don't I help?"

"Really?"

"Well, I don't know how much help I'll be, but I can clean paint brushes or take a mallet to anything you need knocked down."

I'm literally about to melt on the spot. "You'd really do all that?"

He cups my face, then gently kisses me. "Of course. And did I mention that I'm an expert at ordering pizza?"

❧

AS IT TURNS out, he really is a pizza expert. Usually Greg and I just order from whatever delivery place has left a flyer on the door, but Lyle orders from a place I've never heard of, but should be in the dictionary under Best Pizza Ever.

Of course, by the time it arrives, we've been working for almost four straight hours, and I'm ravenous. So my standards might be slightly skewed.

It's not just pizza that Lyle helps with. As promised, he's down for doing pretty much anything we ask, and since we're in the very first stages of fixing up the house, we're asking him to do a lot of demolition.

"Gotta love Riley and all his training," I say, when Lyle swings a sledge hammer to knock through a wall, and I get a nice glimpse of the muscles rippling in his arms and back.

"So?" I demand of Greg as Lyle is running a load of debris to the rented trash bin that fills the driveway.

"You win," Greg says grudgingly. "He's a nice guy. And there's more going on than a fake engagement, isn't there?"

I frown. "Why do you say that?"

"Oh, come on. One, I know you. And two, he'd have to be the best actor in the world to look at you the way he does and not really mean it."

"He is a pretty amazing actor," I quip. "But, yeah, the feeling is real. On both sides."

Greg nods, taking it all in.

I bite my lip as I look at him. "I love him," I say. "I really do. And he loves me, too." I draw a nervous breath. "The thing is, I really want you guys to be cool. I mean, you're one of my best friends. Not to mention my business partner. So are we...?"

He nods slowly, obviously considering his words. "We're cool, yes. And I like him. I really do. But I do think you're moving pretty fast. And I know that's not my business. *You* are, though, because you're my friend. And I'm still worried that this fake engagement thing is going to blow up on you."

"It's weird," I admit. "But there were reasons. And if it blows up, we'll deal."

"You will," he says, "because somehow you always manage to deal with everything that gets tossed at you. But will he?"

As soon as he asks the question, he holds up his hands in self-defense. "It's not a jibe. It's an honest question. I don't know him well enough. But I just wonder if a guy who makes up a fake engagement is the kind of guy who'll survive if the facade is suddenly ripped away."

I don't answer. How can I when Greg has just voiced my own deep fear?

When Lyle returns, I push the conversation and the worry aside, and by the time our workday is done and Lyle and I are off to my house to spend some quality time with Skittles and a rented movie, I'm feeling safe and happy again.

We're at my house not only because I need to feed and love on Skittles, but because I want to imbue the place with good karma in the hopes that the House Gods will smile upon me and tell my father his stupid lawsuit has no punch at all.

I know that's ridiculous, though. The odds are good that I'm going to lose this place. So my other reason for wanting to spend time at home is that I want memories in this house with Lyle. It's the place I love most in the world, and I want to be here with him.

"You're sure you don't want to go out to some restaurant or to a nightclub or something?" I ask Friday night after we return from a sunset walk on the beach. I don't want to, but he seems antsy tonight, and I'm afraid I'm cramping his Hollywood celebrity style.

"God no," he says with such conviction it erases most of my worries. "I'm exactly where I want to be."

"You sure? You seem off tonight."

"I'm not," he says, contradicting himself by standing up and putting his hands in his pockets, a habit I've noticed when he's uncomfortable or unsure.

"Spill," I demand.

He hesitates, but then admits that he talked to Charles that afternoon.

"Charles," I repeat, trying to remember why I know that name. "Oh, the attorney about your movies. Have you decided what you're going to do about those contracts?"

"Do?" His forehead creases. "It's not a question of *do*. Charles is just reviewing them to make sure the details are right."

"Oh." I thought maybe he'd decided to turn them down and go with *Arizona Spring*. "Then what's wrong?"

"I asked him about your house. About whether there was anything that could be done to stop the partition."

For a second, I'm actually excited. Then I realize that

this isn't good news. "It's bad," I say, and he nods.

"You could fight, but all that would happen is you'd incur attorneys' fees. And then you'd have to pay that bill out of the money you'll get from the forced sale."

I move into his outstretched arms and sigh as he holds me tight. "I'm sorry," Lyle says. "I was hoping he could work some magic. He's one of the most influential lawyers in town. But your father is dug in. Even the plea that he was tossing his daughter out of the only home she's ever known didn't make a dent. And he flat turned down the suggestion that you two meet face to face."

I nod. I've always thought my dad was a son-of-a-bitch, and if he wasn't then he could track me down and prove that he was a good guy.

It never occurred to me that he'd track me down and prove that he was the asshole I always believed, but I guess it's nice to know I haven't been wrongfully maligning him my whole life.

"So that's it," I say. "In a few weeks, I'm really losing this place."

"Sugar, I'm so sorry." He leads me to the couch, and I curl up against him, letting him stroke my hair as reality settles over me. It's not a hard transition, really. I've known since the first moment I opened the envelope with the court documents that this was a fight I probably couldn't win. But that doesn't make the losing less painful.

"What can I do?" he asks.

"This is good," I admit. "You holding me like this." I tilt my head so that I can see his face. "I can let it go—I can. I just need to be sad for a bit."

"You *can* let it go," he agrees. "It'll be hard, but you'll get past it."

"Yeah," I say, then sigh as I sit up, something in his words pushing me upright. "The same is true for you," I whisper. "You can let Jenny go, too."

His eyes narrow as he looks at me, his face an odd mixture of confusion and, I think, trepidation.

"We've talked about this," he says. "You were right—I told you so. And I'm putting the past in the past."

I lick my lips, hesitating. The last few days have been bliss, and I don't want to toss a firecracker into the middle of this sweet serenity. But time is running out, even if I'm the only one who realizes it.

"You're not," I finally say. "If you walk away from *Arizona Spring* to do those three movies, you're—"

"*No.*" The word is harsh. Sharp. And as it lashes out, he pulls me to him, the force of contact at least as harsh as the word. "Dammit, Laine, this is my career. Not Jenny's. You need to trust me that I'm doing what I want. What's right for me."

I nod, surrendering. Because the truth is, I know he believes it.

But I'm equally certain that he's holding on to Jenny and his past too damn tight. They're like an elastic band tying him back. And though he can move forward with me, inch by inch, mile by mile, he's still always got that cord behind him.

And unless he cuts himself free, one day when we least expect it, the elastic will pull too tight, and he'll be snapped back away from me, so hard and so fast, that I won't have the strength to keep him by my side.

THE SCF BRUNCH is nothing like what I expected. It's held outdoors on a beautiful flagstone patio and lawn that opens up behind the massive corporate building that houses the foundation's business office. The grounds are huge and there are cabins for kids to live in while they attend SCF-sponsored camps.

There's a camp this weekend, actually, and the entire area is overrun with kids, running and playing and laughing. Kids who, Lyle tells me, have very little else in their lives to smile about.

According to Lyle, this isn't the only facility like this operated by Stark. "Damien founded an education-based organization, too, that's been around much longer. And there's a similar camp area for kids in that program."

"That's impressive," I say, and he agrees enthusiastically, telling me about both organizations, but mostly about the SCF, which is specifically for abused and neglected children, and other kids who need outside help.

"How did you get involved?"

"I asked Damien," he says as we stroll the grounds, stopping occasionally to talk with the kids or throw a ball or watch one of their magic tricks, learned during this week's camping session.

"I thought about what a shit time Jenny and I had, and I wanted to be part of something that helped kids like that." He flashes an ironic smile. "The celebrity sponsor job came later. All I really wanted to do was work one-on-one with the kids, and support the foundation financially. But the sponsorship helps, too," he says philosophically. "It's just working away from the kids in front of the media instead of with them."

"Ly! Ly!"

I turn to see Lara running toward us, her short legs making good time. "Play airplane with me?"

"Okay, but why don't we go see if any other kids want to play, too?"

As I fall in step with Nikki, who's carrying her infant daughter Anne, Lyle heads toward the toddler playscape, where he proceeds to fly a dozen or so kids like an airplane.

"This is a really amazing organization," I tell Nikki.

"It is. Damien didn't have the greatest childhood. He wanted to make it better for as many kids as he could."

I think about Damien—the famous tennis player and billionaire—and I remember all the dark secrets that came out in the press a few years ago. I look at Lyle, thinking that's something he and Damien have in common. Dark secrets and broken childhoods.

"Lyle's a great asset," Nikki says, following my gaze.

"He really believes in what the SCF is doing," I say as a voice over a loudspeaker asks Mr. Tarpin and the media representatives to report to the main lobby. "Although I think he'd much rather keep doing that," I add, pointing to Lyle and the kids, "than front the press conference."

"Who wouldn't?" she asks as Lyle and Lara head back toward us and we all go into the lobby together.

Nikki and I stand off to the side in front of the podium as Damien and Lyle take the stage. Since this is a media event, the audience is entirely made of reporters, and I recognize a few from the night they descended on my house, including the one who'd dropped the engagement bomb—the one with the goatee who Lyle later told me was named Gordy.

Damien starts the conference, giving the press an overview of the foundation and a bit about the work they do. Then he introduces Lyle, who also gives a brief presentation as he runs through a slide show of images of various kids the SCF has helped.

Both men keep it short, presumably because the real point is to open it up for press questions. And as soon as Lyle does that, Gordy's voice booms out, filling the lobby.

"Mr. Tarpin," he says, "it's come to my attention that your engagement to Sugar Laine is a sham, orchestrated to hide the fact that Ms. Laine was only one in a long string of women with whom you paid to have sex. Can you comment on how, with a background like that, you're even remotely qualified to act as a sponsor for a children's organization?"

CHAPTER 26

M Y HAND ACHES, and I realize that I've reached out and am clutching Nikki's hand so hard I've probably cut off her circulation.

I turn to her, about to tell her I'm sorry, but all she does is shake her head. I see the pain in her eyes, and I realize that it's not because of what Lyle and I have done, but because of the way it was revealed.

"You'll survive this," she says, as I struggle to breathe. "Just tell yourself that you'll survive, and I promise you will."

I nod, feeling raw and violated. As if the fabric of the world has been ripped out from under me. My private choices—my personal secrets—tossed out to the media like so much birdseed, and now my whole body goes cold as the feeding frenzy begins.

People turn my direction to gawk. To pull out camera phones. To yell comments and questions.

They care nothing of my pain. Of my reasons. Of the *why* behind my choices.

And they damn sure don't care where those choices led—to a love so deep that the pain I now see on Lyle's face cuts me even more deeply that the thrust of that reporter's verbal knife.

I need to get to him. To touch him.

I need to feel our connection.

But I can't reach him through the writhing sea of bodies, and he can't break free of the security team that has taken him by the arms and is leading him off the platform, even while his eyes search the crowd looking, I'm sure, for me.

Nikki takes charge, pushing me around the podium toward another man in one of the black T-shirts that indicates he's part of the Stark security team. He flanks us, his companion closing the gap behind us and clearing the way until we reach a hallway and then, finally, a private office in the back.

I burst through the door, and Lyle pulls me against him. "I'm sorry," he says, looking as shattered as I feel. "I'm so damn sorry."

"It's worse," Damien says, from where he's leaning against the desk, looking at his phone. "He timed the question with photos going live on his site."

"Shit," Lyle says, as Damien passes him the phone. There are pictures of four women, including me, going into different hotel rooms. Innocuous enough until you read the copy, which makes clear that an anonymous tip told Gordy that the clean-cut Lyle Tarpin hired call girls, and Gordy decided to make it his mission to expose that dastardly deed.

"I don't understand," I say, as Lyle stiffens beside me. "How could he know about us? For that matter, how could he know about the others?"

"*Rip.*"

He says the name like a curse, underscored by a blood red rage.

"How?" I ask.

"We used to be close," he says, running his fingers through his hair. "And when he started having problems with drugs, I tried to talk to him. To help him through it. I told him things I shouldn't have—I never thought he'd turn on me."

"Jealousy can mess a man up," Damien says, and Lyle looks at him, then nods slowly, his face awash with rage.

"Can you find him? Your security people? Can they track down his address?"

"Lyle," I say. "No."

"He had no right—the bastard just shredded both of our lives in front of the whole goddamned world. You damn well better believe I'm confronting him."

"For what?" I press. "For being an asshole? He told the truth, Lyle. I knew from the first day when I agreed to go to your hotel that this could happen. I wish it hadn't, but it did. And you can't beat him up or arrest him or sue him for spilling the truth. It's not worth it."

He turns away, pushing out of our embrace so he can pace the office. "Guess he's the golden boy now, huh? He sure as hell messed me up, didn't he? I'm going to need to resign, aren't I?" he asks Damien.

"If it were up to me, no," Damien says. "I'd want you to tell the world the full truth about why you make such an excellent advocate for these kids, but with that caveat, I'd want you to stay.

"But it's not up to me," he continues. "The foundation's board of directors makes that decision. I have a say, but not control. So if you want to keep the position, at the very least you need to get in front of this."

"I can't deny it," Lyle says, looking toward me.

"You shouldn't," Damien says. "You should tell the world the rest of it. The whole truth, Lyle. All the reasons you wanted to be part of this organization in the first place. Trust me," he adds. "It's painful, but you'll come through the other side. I've been there. I know."

I listen with awed understanding. *Damien knows.* When Lyle went to Damien about being part of the SCF, he must have filled Damien in on everything, knowing that Stark would understand, having suffered so much himself.

I hope that Damien's heartfelt words will be enough to convince Lyle, but when he shoves his hands into his pockets instead of answering, I know that may be a long road.

But the fact that he's told both me and Damien gives me hope.

"I need to go make a statement and get on top of this," Damien says.

"Christ," Lyle says. "The SCF doesn't need this. I'm so sorry."

"Don't worry," Damien says firmly. "I've got a long track record of surviving scandal. The foundation's going to come through." He looks between me and Lyle. "We'll leave you two alone to talk."

I nod, my stomach feeling hollow. Lyle had reached for me when I first came into the room, but after that, he pushed away. And he hasn't reached for me since.

Nikki and Damien leave, flanked by the security team, and as soon as the door clicks shut, I move to Lyle's side. I reach for him, but he shrugs away, the brush-off filling that hollow place in me with heavy lead weights.

"I'm so sorry," he says, looking at me with torment in his eyes. "I did this to you. Christ, Sugar, you must fucking hate me."

"The only way I'd hate you is if I found out you hired those women after we got together."

"*God no.* Never again. Since you, there's only been you." The response is fast and vehement. I had no doubts, of course, but if I had, the force of his denial would have erased them.

"Then what do you have to be sorry for?"

"Are you kidding? Those assholes turned their cameras on you, too. You're not any happier that this is out than I am."

"Happy? No, of course I'm not. But that doesn't make you guilty. I mean, come on. I knew what I was walking into. Bottom line, I accepted a job to exchange sex for money. To fake an engagement so that my house would get paid off. *I* did that, Lyle. Nobody forced me to."

I draw in a breath, feeling remarkably better as I get this off my chest. "And, yeah, it was a secret, but so what? It's out in the world because of a decision I made. And even if the leak was because of your asshole co-star, that doesn't change the bottom line—it's out there because it's true. Because somewhere along the way, I did all those things that the reporters are saying."

"This foundation is important to me," he snaps. "And Rip and that fucking reporter just yanked it out from under me. You know I'm going to have to resign, right? There's no way the board will keep me on. They can't afford to have every event be about my behavior instead of their kids. *Fuck*."

He starts to pace. "This was one of the few things in my life that truly felt real, and they're ripping it away from me."

"I'm sorry," I say. "I am. But your talent is real. Your passion."

"I've been living a lie and it's come back to haunt me." His voice is hoarse. Tortured.

I feel the tears well in my eyes, and I try to hold them back. He's so torn apart right now, and all I want is to put him back together. But I don't know how. I'm afraid that the only one who can is Lyle himself.

"I'm not a lie," I whisper. "You and I aren't a lie."

I watch his face, but he doesn't answer, and my heart bleeds a little.

I have to swallow twice before I can speak. My throat is too thick with unshed tears. "Don't you get it?" I demand. "You're freaking out because someone shined a light on the truth. *The truth*," I repeat.

Then I draw a deep breath. "I'm sorry. I love you, but I can't live that way."

He looks up at me, his eyes as wary as a caged animal.

"Damien's right. It's time you stopped living lies. And until you do, the couple that you and I could be will stay as fake as this engagement."

I'm crying in earnest now, and I tug off the beautiful ring and press it into his palm.

"Sugar, no—"

"You need time, Lyle," I say. "I can't help—I don't know how to help. You have to get past this."

"How?"

I shake my head. "Deal with it. Own it. Jump over it, swim under it. I don't know. I wish I did."

I brutally wipe the tears from my cheeks. "All I know is that I love you," I whisper. "But your fight is inside you, Lyle, not with the world. And right now, I really have to go."

CHAPTER 27

THE PHONE KEPT ringing, and Lyle didn't give a shit.

He wasn't interested in talking to the reporters who were intent on hounding him any more than he wanted to talk to his friends.

All he wanted to do was get lost in his misery. And, frankly, he was doing a damn fine job of it.

He'd been sitting in the condo for two days, drinking Scotch, eating Bugles, and listening to country music with the blinds closed, the only light coming from the small fixtures underneath his kitchen cabinets.

He had the script for *M. Sterious* on the table in front of him, and right beside him was the script for *Arizona Spring*. And the only reason he had his phone at all was because Sugar's picture was on the lock screen, and every time someone called or messaged him, the screen flashed and her picture popped up.

And he had the ring. Hell, he was wearing the damn thing, although it only fit the tip of his pinkie finger. He had to keep it close. Had to keep *her* close.

Because he wanted her.

That was the bottom line.

He just plain wanted her, and he wasn't sure if it was

too late. Wasn't sure if he had the strength to do what it took to get her back.

A key rattled in the lock, and he scowled. "Dammit, Nat, I told you to stay the fuck away this week."

"She follows instructions," Riley said. "I don't."

Lyle closed his eyes, then rubbed his temples. He really didn't need this shit right now.

Then again, maybe he did.

"I'm a fucking mess, man."

"You got that right," Riley said as he took in the scene. "You look like some alien spawn settled in to nest."

Since Lyle couldn't really argue with that, he just flipped his friend the bird.

"Seriously, man, Laine's worried."

"Did she tell you that?" A flicker of hope sparked in his chest.

"I take the Fifth. I don't think she wants you to know that she called me."

"Right." *Fuck.*

"You want to tell me why I'm playing go-between? You had a good thing with her. How'd this bullshit with the press screw that up?"

"It didn't," Lyle said. "The screwing up was all done by yours truly. Every good thing in my life, and I drove a skewer right through it."

Except even as he spoke, he knew that wasn't actually true. He screwed up his reputation—which was his own damn fault—and he screwed up his *lucrative* thing. His *popular* thing.

But Laine had been right—neither of those things were really his passion.

And so the question was, had he screwed up so badly he'd be shut out of acting?

And, more important, had he fucked up so royally that he couldn't get her back?

"You want to know the God's honest truth," he told his friend. "I don't know what to do. I don't know how to get her back or how to get my life on track or how to climb out of this damn hole I've dug."

"Fuck that bullshit," Riley said. "You? The guy who orchestrated his own rescue when he was barely sixteen, not to mention Jenny's, too. And no—" He thrust up a hand, keeping Lyle silent. "Don't you dare tell me that your plan failed because of the accident. That's wasn't anybody's fault. Which is, in fact, why we call it an accident."

"Riley—"

"I'm serious, Lyle. You've been running your career as if you were Jenny and her manager rolled into one. But it's *your* career, yours. For once push the guilt aside and thank Jenny for introducing you to work that you love."

"Can I talk now?"

"What?" Riley's voice was harsh.

"You're right."

"Goddammit, that's what—oh. Fuck yeah, I'm right."

Lyle pushed himself up off the couch, then pressed the button on the remote to open the blinds, flooding the condo with light.

"You're right," he repeated. "I've survived worse shit than this. My whole childhood's worse than this."

"Hell, yeah. What are you going to do now?"

Lyle held up a finger, then dialed his phone. "Hey," he said when she answered. "I need to see you. I'm on my way right now."

"You're going over to Laine's?" Riley asked.

Lyle shook his head. "I've got a few things I need to take care of first."

"I don't doubt it," Riley said. "But seriously, man. The very first thing you need to do is take a goddamned shower."

CHAPTER 28

"THANKS FOR WALKING Lancelot with me," I say to Greg as we head from Jacob's apartment to my house.

"Anything you need," he says. "I'd go over to Lyle's condo and smack some sense into him, too. Except I don't actually know where he lives."

We spent the entire day and the early evening working on the flip—the long hours driven by me and my need to keep my mind fully occupied so that there's absolutely no room to think about Lyle. And then later, when Greg dropped me at my house, I saw that Jacob was about to walk Lancelot. Since the idea of a sunset walk seemed like another stellar way to keep my thoughts Lyle-free, I'd offered to take dog duty, and then I roped Greg into coming with me.

"I'm surprised he hasn't called you," Greg says. "I know I wasn't a fan at first, but I do like the guy. And I never doubted that he was crazy about you."

"I never doubted that either," I say. "I don't doubt it now." I pause at my gate. "You want to come in and watch a movie."

"Sure," he says. "Is this because you're dying for

company or because you want to keep your mind off Lyle."

"Will you be offended if I say the latter?" I ask as I punch in the gate code and we walk toward the porch.

"Neither offended nor surprised," he assures me.

"You know," I say, picking up the earlier thread of our conversation, "everything was always great between Lyle and me. And I guess that's what makes this especially hard."

"Because it's not something you did that you can apologize for or fix," he says. "I get it."

"All I can do is wait. And try not to obsess. And think about other things." I make a face. "At least all of this drama is keeping my mind off my house. And at least the press has quit hanging around."

For the first couple of days, I'd been hounded by reporters, but after a while they got bored with my repeated, "No comment."

"Do you want me to come over this weekend and help you pack? I was talking with Joy and Nessie at Blacklist the other night, and they're both down for a packing marathon."

"Not really, but you probably should." I sigh heavily. "I have two weeks before the court rules, and then I'll probably have a few weeks after that before I have to actually vacate."

"It'll suck worse if you wait and do it all at the last minute."

"I know. I just hate believing it's real, even though I know it is." I flash an ironic smile his way. "I guess I have one thing to thank Lyle for. Everything with him has totally kept my mind off my impending homeless-ness."

I punch in the code for the front door. "I just miss him," I say as I open the door—

—*and see that he's standing right there.*

Right in the middle of my living room, looking at me and holding a rose.

"Hey," he says with a small smile. "I brought a peace offering."

I take it, my pulse fluttering, and raise the petals to my nose.

"Hi, Greg," he says. "Do you think you could—"

"I'll go," Greg says, then turns to me. "You do want me to go, right?"

I nod.

"Then I will, but before I go, I just want to say that I hope you're here to try to work this out. Because I swear, if you hurt her, I'm going to string you up by the balls and then drywall over you. It'll be a century before they find your body."

"Noted," Lyle says, without cracking a smile. "As far as I'm concerned that's completely fair."

"Well, all right then."

I give Greg a hug and promise to call in the morning. Then I shut the door behind him and turn back to Lyle.

"Thanks again," I say, lifting my rose. "I should go put it in water."

"Wait." He grabs my wrist as I try to walk by him, and I have to close my eyes in defense against my reaction. It's been days since I've seen him, and the feel of his skin on mine has fired my senses. It's hard enough to think standing this close to him. With physical contact, it's damn near impossible.

"Please." I gently tug free. "I can't do this if you're touching me. I need to be able to think."

"What do you need to think about?"

I shake my head. "I don't know. And I guess it doesn't matter if you touch me or not. The truth is that you're all I think about, anyway."

He reaches for me, and I flinch back. But he holds me steady, then gently brushes my hair behind my ear. "I'm so sorry. I'm so goddamned sorry."

I close my eyes fighting tears as darkness seems to settle over me. Because I know what that means.

That means it's all over.

"It should never have taken me so long."

The words sink slowly into my mind, and I open my eyes to see him smiling.

"You're the one who pulled me back from the dark. Who made me see what's important."

"Did I?"

"Your family. Your memories. Your integrity. You held up a mirror for me, even if it took me a long time to see it clearly. I love you, Sugar," he says, his voice full of conviction. "You're the only woman I've ever loved, and you're the best thing to ever happen to me. I love you."

His words wash over and through me. Filling me with joy.

"I love you, too," I say. "But—"

He presses a fingertip over my lip, then shakes his head. "I know what you're going to say. Love isn't our problem. I know. I've been living a shadow life. But that stops now. No more living someone else's dream. No more lying about who I really am."

I stand frozen with anticipation, my chest so full of hope I can't even breathe.

"I talked with Evelyn this morning."

"Is everything okay with those movie offers? I mean, they're not going to pull the offers because of the scandal?"

He shakes his head. "Not going to be an issue," he says. "Partly because this town thrives on scandal, but primarily because I'm not doing the movies."

My eyes go wide. "What?"

"I turned down the three sequels. But we told them I'd stay attached to *M. Sterious* so long as they go back to the original script. They agreed."

"Seriously?"

He nods. "They haggled. Said how they should reduce my profit participation because of the scandal, all sorts of nonsense. But in the end, when they saw there weren't three more coming in the wings, they agreed. They're not complete idiots. They know the original script was better."

"Lyle, that's great. You genuinely liked that script."

"Yeah," he says with a smile. "Honestly, now I can't wait to start filming. Plus, without the others filling my schedule, I was able to accept the offer for *Arizona Spring*."

I shake my head, then throw my arms around him and hug him. "I'm proud of you."

"Hell, I'm proud of me, too. You were right." He tilts my chin up so I'm facing him. "Jenny wanted fame and fortune. I want to act. You saw that from the beginning, even when I couldn't see my own life clearly."

"You just needed a mirror," I say.

"And you gave me one." He brushes a gentle kiss over my lips.

"Lyle," I murmur, a familiar need coursing through me.

"I know," he says. "Me, too. But there's something else I need to tell you."

I nod, then take a step back so that I can see him better.

"I resigned from my position at the SCF," he says.

"Oh." I swallow. It's great that he's accepted that he was living Jenny's dream, but I was hoping he'd follow Damien's advice and claw his way out from under the secrets of his past.

"What did Damien say?"

"It was his idea, actually. I talked to him after I met with Evelyn."

"His idea? But I thought he wanted you to tell the board about your past. To explain how much of a connection you had with the kids."

"Which would be great if I liked the position more. I mean, I'm happy to support the organization however they need me. But I had another idea. Fortunately, Damien loved it. And when he called a few board members to see how it would fly with them, they loved it, too."

"And…?"

"I'm going to be an SCF Youth Advocate," he says. "Hopefully the first of many."

I shake my head. "Should I know what that is?"

"Nope." His grin is so wide I'm certain that I'm missing something. "I invented it. The idea is to find celebrities with fucked up childhoods and, basically, to make their pasts public. To the world, but mostly to the kids. So that they realize they're not alone."

"Lyle…" Tears spill down my cheeks. "That's such an incredible idea."

"I hoped you'd think so. I'm not doing it for you—or for us—but I can't deny that I hoped you'd understand just how much it means for me to do this."

"I do," I say, rising as he bends forward, capturing me in the kind of kiss that has my toes curling and my senses firing.

When we break the kiss, I'm breathing hard, and as Skittles starts to rub against my ankles, I take Lyle's hand, fully intending to lead him to my bedroom and have my way with him.

"Wait," he says. "There's one more thing. These last few days have been hell without you. I don't want to do that again. One day, I fully intend to give you back that ring. But right now, I'm asking if you want to live together. Because I don't want to be without you for another minute."

"Yes." I feel like I'm going to burst. "Absolutely, yes." My smile is so wide it hurts. Then I think about the logistics, and my smile fades. "It will have to be your condo, though. I'll be losing this place soon." I sigh. "I'm going to miss it so much. The house. The neighborhood. The beach."

"Actually, I think we'd rather live in my house. I can

keep the condo as an office."

"You have a house?" How did I not know that?

"I just bought it, actually."

"I don't suppose it has an ocean view," I say wryly.

"Only from the roof, but it's walking distance."

"Really? Where is it?"

"Close," he says. "You want to see it?" He takes my hand, then leads me to the door.

"We can walk there?"

"Easily."

"Um, okay." I know the neighborhood pretty well, and I don't remember a house being for sale. But then again, I've been a little distracted lately.

We walk to the gate, and as soon as we reach the sidewalk, he says, "Here we are."

I look at him, confused, then see that he's staring back at my house.

Now I'm even more confused.

"I don't understand," I admit.

"Your father wanted the equity. So I bought his share. I was hoping you wouldn't mind being co-owners. What with me being in love with you and all."

"No," I say, trying desperately not to cry as I fling myself into his arms and hold him tight, this man who loves me. Who takes care of me. And who I love with all my heart. "I really don't mind at all."

EPILOGUE

FOR IMMEDIATE RELEASE:

The Stark Children's Foundation and SCF Youth Advocate Lyle Tarpin are pleased to announce that yesterday marked the final day of shooting for *M. Sterious*, next summer's installment in the Blue Zenith universe of films.

The day, however, was about more than just the wrapping of the film. It was also about the children whose lives have been touched by the SCF, as well as by the volunteers and donors who have given so generously of their time and money.

As a special treat, over fifty past and present recipients of SCF services and grants were present during the final day's shoot and at the wrap party that followed on the studio back lot.

The entire cast attended the party, and each child was presented with a package of signed memorabilia.

The celebration didn't end there, however, as the wrap party turned into an engagement celebration when Tarpin took to the stage to formally announce his engagement to Sugar Laine.

The wedding will take place in the summer, and the SCF extends congratulations to the happy couple.

WANT MORE?

Don't miss Noah's story, *Wicked Torture,* the third novel in this scorching new series of fast-paced, provocative novels centering around the ambitious, wealthy, and powerful men who work in and around the glamorous and exciting world of the Stark International conglomerate … and the sexy and passionate women who bring them to their knees.

Coming November 2017

Only his passion

could set her free...

Meet Damien Stark in the series that started it all...

The Stark Series
by J. Kenner

Available Now

Happily ever after is just the beginning.

The passion between Damien & Nikki continues.

Stark Ever After novellas
By J. Kenner

Available Now

Jackson Steele.
He was the only man who made her feel alive.

Lose yourself in passion . . .

Stark International
By J. Kenner

Available Now

Three powerful, dangerous men ...

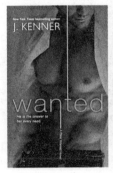

Three sensual, seductive women ...

Three passionate romances.

Most Wanted
By J. Kenner

Available Now

It was wrong for them to be together…

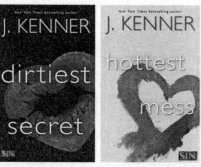

But harder for them to be apart.

The Dirtiest Trilogy
By J. Kenner

Available Now

Sometimes it feels so damn good to be bad ...

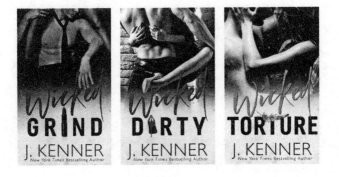

The Wicked Books
By J. Kenner

J. Kenner (aka Julie Kenner) is the *New York Times, USA Today, Publishers Weekly, Wall Street Journal,* and #1 International bestselling author of over eighty novels, novellas and short stories in a variety of genres.

Though known primarily for her award-winning and international bestselling erotic romances, JK has been writing full time for over a decade in a variety of genres including paranormal and contemporary romance, "chicklit" suspense, urban fantasy, and paranormal mommy lit.

JK has been praised by *Publishers Weekly* as an author with a "flair for dialogue and eccentric characterizations" and by RT Bookclub for having "cornered the market on sinfully attractive, dominant antiheroes and the women who swoon for them." JK has been a finalist for Romance Writers of America's prestigious RITA award five times, and a winner once, taking home the first RITA trophy awarded in the category of erotic romance in 2014 for her novel, *Claim Me.*

Before diving into writing full time, JK worked as an attorney in Texas and California where she practiced primarily civil, entertainment, and First Amendment law. She currently lives in Central Texas, with her husband, two daughters, and two rather spastic cats.

Visit her website at www.jkenner.com to learn more and to connect with JK through social media!